Photo Finish

Books by John McEvoy

Photo Finish

A Jack Doyle Mystery

John McEvoy

Poisoned Pen Press

Copyright © 2012 by John McEvoy

First Edition 2012

10 9 8 7 6 5 4 3 2 1

Library of Congress Catalog Card Number: 2011944897

ISBN: 9781464200137   Hardcover
      9781464200151   Trade Paperback

Poisoned Pen Press
6962 E. First Ave., Ste. 103
Scottsdale, AZ 85251
www.poisonedpenpress.com
info@poisonedpenpress.com

Printed in the United States of America

Inscriptions

I am convinced that horses have a sixth sense, and I know from experience that communication can take place between horse and rider in a language without words. When I am really in tune with a horse, I feel I know what he is thinking and he seems to know what I am thinking, too.

—Hall of Fame Jockey Gary Steven.

Sell the cow, buy the sheep, never be without the horse.

—Irish proverb

Chapter One

Summer 2011

"Ralph, put your horse on the phone."

It was a soft but insistent voice coming over the speaker phone in the Heartland Downs Racetrack office of veteran trainer Ralph Tenuta. He quickly answered "okay" and leapt to his feet and started for the door. "I'll be right there. I'll have my cell phone."

Jack Doyle leaned forward from his seat on the battered leather couch in Tenuta's office. "Did I hear what I just heard, Ralph? 'Put your horse on the phone'? Who said that? What horse? A phone?"

"Jack, I'll explain later," Tenuta said over his shoulder.

The screen door slammed behind the trainer. Doyle, one-time amateur boxer and former advertising account executive, now deep in the world of horse racing, sat back on the couch. Tuxedo, the black and white resident cat, gave him a typically baleful look. On Tenuta's desk an ancient electric fan swiveled, so weak Doyle estimated that it wouldn't blow out a match. The glistening new speaker phone, a recent gift from one of the trainer's grateful clients, formed an anomaly in this otherwise outmoded enclave.

Doyle picked up his copy of *Racing Daily*, the newspaper often referred to as the bible of thoroughbred horse racing. Once again, he went over the three races his new, and first, and only jockey client would ride in that afternoon.

After being "right-sized" by his ad agency, Doyle began what he recognized as a most unlikely, but necessary, career on the race-track. First, fixing a horse race. A caper he'd never stop regretting, especially since his profits from it had been stolen. Then being co-opted by the FBI to catch two sets of criminals while working as a groom. Then stints as a publicity director and a stable agent, leading to his current job as a jockey's agent. "Present a moving target" had come to define Doyle's vocational philosophy.

Doyle tossed the newspaper onto Tenuta's desk. "'Put your horse on the phone,'" he repeated. "I've got to see what the hell this is all about." He headed out the office door.

He found Tenuta in the fifth stall on the west side of the large barn. The trainer was holding his cell phone up next to the twitching left ear of a nervous gray filly named Madame Golden, a "real nut case," according to Tenuta.

"There's something wrong with Madame Golden and I can't figure what the hell it is. That's why I called the vet, Ingrid McGuire. She's over on the other side of the backstretch and can't come here now. That's why we're doing this phone business," Tenuta said.

As the soft voice poured out of the phone into Madame Golden's ear, the filly relaxed, stopped anxiously swishing her tail, got a pensive look on her long brown face.

After a couple of minutes, the voice on the phone told Tenuta to move away from the filly. Tenuta patted Madame Golden on her neck as he listened to Ingrid McGuire say, "Ralph, check this horse's left rear foot. She says there's a twisted nail in the shoe that's killing her. That's why she was so out of sorts the past couple of mornings when you sent her to the track to jog."

Tenuta said, "Thanks, Ingrid." He handed the phone to Doyle and examined the foot in question. "I'll be damned," the trainer said. Madame Golden whinnied as Tenuta held her foot. He said. "Jack, call Travis Hawkins. You got his cell?"

The powerfully built African American blacksmith was in the cab of his white Ford pickup, eating a breakfast burrito from the Heartland Downs track kitchen and going over his written schedule for the day.

"Travis, it's Jack. Can you come over to the Tenuta barn? Ralph has a little job for you. Won't take long."

Hawkins said, "What's a 'little job'?" Doyle described Madame Golden's problem.

"Who noticed that?"

"The horse told them."

"*What?*"

"This will all become clear once you get over here," Doyle said. "I think."

◇◇◇

Twenty-five minutes later, after Hawkins had carefully removed the offending nail and put a new shoe on the appreciative Madame Golden, the three men drank coffee in Tenuta's office. The blacksmith said, "Are you going to explain?"

Tenuta said, "I met this young woman, Ingrid McGuire, a few months ago. She's a veterinarian. Used to work with another vet, Eric Allgauer, that I used for quite awhile."

Tenuta refilled his coffee cup and sat down again behind his desk. "Here's the deal. Ingrid is what they call a horse communicator. She used to do mainly straight veterinary work when she was with Allgauer, but now she pretty much concentrates on this other practice. Communicating. A lot of guys back here didn't take her or her ideas seriously when she started. Me included. But I've seen the good results Ingrid gets. I'm a believer."

Hawkins leaned forward. A man who had been around horses most of his adult life, he was obviously intrigued. "Ralph, what does she do? I don't understand."

"Now," Tenuta said, "don't laugh, but what Ingrid does is like that ESP stuff I've seen on TV. Extrasensory perception I think it's called. She closes her eyes and concentrates and lets the horse come into her mind. The horse tells her things. Horses can't talk, but somehow Ingrid can pick up what they are thinking—if they want her to know what they're thinking. Some don't. Or can't. This doesn't work with all horses, she tells me. I know it sounds crazy. But it isn't.

"Ingrid said she got started with this method after she read a book by a veterinarian in England, a guy named Henry Blake. The book convinced her that this kind of horse communication was possible. So, she went ahead with it. And it worked. And it left her former partner and boyfriend, Eric Allgauer, behind."

Doyle and Hawkins exchanged eyebrow-raised looks. Tenuta said, "Here, I want to show you this. Ingrid gave me Blake's book." He thumbed through the book to a dog-eared page. "Henry Blake talks about 'the transfer of an emotional state from horse to horse or horse to human.' He says the 'telepathy involved is the transfer of specific mental pictures.' Ingrid says that's exactly what goes on when conditions are right." He put the book down and removed his reading glasses.

"Ingrid has got several clients here now," Tenuta continued. "She says her methods of dealing with horses vary. After she's first met them, some of them send messages to her when she's not with them. Others need her to be with them there in person. Others, I guess like Madame Golden, can be prompted by hearing her voice on the phone. ESP."

Tenuta became slightly agitated by the looks on the faces of his listeners, especially Doyle's.

He said, "Skeptical bastard that you are, Jack, I'm sure you think this is some kind of hustle. Well, hear this. The first time I used Ingrid I had her deal with an old gelding, Frank's Fantasy. He'd all of a sudden soured on me. He wouldn't break from the gate, and he loped around to finish dead last in three straight races. With his head cocked so he could look over the fence at the crowd. Like he was mocking me.

"I changed his feed. His exercise schedule Tried three different jocks on him. None of them could do anything with Frank's Fantasy except get hot and dirty at the back of the pack. The horse just wouldn't try. I had his regular vet, Allgaur, go over him from head to tail. Nothing physically wrong with Frank's Fantasy, so Allgauer said.

"A few days later, Ingrid McGuire came by the barn one morning and asked if I would let her work with Frank's Fantasy. I'd seen her assist Allgauer before and been impressed with her. Real nice young woman. Her mother's Swedish, her dad's a Mick. Hey, I thought, "Why not? I'm not getting anywhere with this animal. You guys want more coffee?"

Doyle said, "Go on with it, Ralph."

"Ingrid made a couple of visits to Frank's Fantasy's stall. Ingrid said Frank's Fantasy told her he was sad. Depressed. Because a buddy of his, another old gelding named Mister Twaggs, who'd been in the stall next to him for about two years, was gone. Mister Twaggs got claimed away from me.

"Ingrid asked Frank's Fantasy what could be done to make him not feel resentful, get him to try in his races? He told her he needed a new friend."

Tenuta heard Doyle's snort of disbelief. He glared at Jack. "Ingrid said Frank's Fantasy was very 'adamant' or something, whatever that means.

"I figure, 'What have I got to lose?' So I move this new two-year-old colt I just got from the farm into Mister Twaggs' old stall next to Frank's Fantasy. Colt named Plotkin. Pretty ugly name. But a very promising colt.

"These two horses get along great, old Frank and the kid. Frank's Fantasy picks up his head. He's acting better. I call Ingrid to see how it's coming. She tells me, 'Great, Ralph. Frank says he's very happy with his new pal next door.'

"I enter Frank in a race the next week. He goes to the gate prancing, like his old self, not hanging his head like he'd been doing. The son of a gun came out of the gate like a quarter horse. Won by a pole. He was bouncing around the winner's circle like he wanted to go around the track again."

Tenuta leaned back in his creaky chair, spreading his arms. "Ingrid came by the barn that evening. Had a communication with Frank's Fantasy. She said he told her, 'I am a happy horse'. And that's how he has been acting, and running. What can I tell you? I believe in Ingrid."

Chapter Two

Spring 2008

Ingrid McGuire put in her four miles of running every other day, regardless of the Champaign-Urbana weather, which ranged from blistering summer heat to winter mornings when sweat threatened to freeze on her forehead.

She had begun this regimen two years earlier shortly after enrolling in the University of Illinois and its famous veterinary school.

Moving smoothly south from University Avenue over the long blocks on Lincoln Street, past the Ag buildings and the herds of penned-up cows whose odor permeated the air no matter what the time of year, she almost always gained a sense of exhilaration, solid well-being. The release of energy somehow transferred into stamina when she attacked her studies later in the day.

This April morning, as she ran past a blooming lilac tree, she stopped and reversed herself in order to pluck a sprig. Lilac scent had always been one of her favorite things in spring. Then she heard a voice from behind her. "Is that legal?"

The speaker was a tall good-looking man astride an expensive bicycle. She could see he was kidding from the smile on his handsome face. Cut-off shorts revealed his muscular legs. He removed his riding helmet, smoothed his blond hair, and smiled at her. "Do you know me?" he said. "Eric Allgauer. We're in Professor

Ronstead's lecture class Tuesday mornings. You sit down front where you can raise a questioning hand."

He paused to drink from a water bottle. "I lurk up high in one of the rear rows. These will be my final credits before graduation. I can afford to coast." He stopped to erase the sheen of sweat on his broad forehead. "I've started riding this route every day. Ever since I happened to see you running last week when we were going in opposite directions. I stopped riding to watch you run. I've been looking for you ever since."

"Why?"

"Oh," he smiled, "you have a lovely way of moving. A tall, fair girl with great legs and buns and a long pony tail waving is a tonic for the heart." They both laughed.

Ingrid said, "Fifth year, eh? Congrats. You're almost out of here. I've got another year to go." She squinted at him through the morning sun. "I'm surprised I haven't run into you before. It's a big vet school. But not that big."

Eric put his helmet back on. "Go on with your run. But, if you like, maybe we could have coffee, or lunch, after next Tuesday's class?"

Ingrid backed away a few steps and turned to resume running. Looking back over her shoulder, she said, "That might work."

He watched admiringly as her long strides carried her on her way.

That's where it all began for them. Two months later, Eric informed his angry father that he had decided to "take a year of graduate work."

"You can pay for that yourself," Dr. Herman Allgauer shouted over the phone.

"I plan to." Eric slammed down his phone.

Ingrid and Eric moved in together the next week.

◇◇◇

The following year, Ingrid thought, went by in kind of a blur. She studied long and hard and made the dean's list again. Eric sashayed through his grad school courses. After registering at the start of that fall semester, Eric told her, "I've signed up for a creative writing course. This will drive my old man nuts." They were sitting on the small balcony outside their third floor grad school apartment. A late September breeze rustled through the leaves of the aged elm trees lining the yard in front of them.

"Why do you want to do that, Eric?"

Allgauer reached for the shaker of martinis on the small table between them. In recent weeks, he had begun preparing the drinks before each of their evening dinners.

"My old man wanted me to follow him into veterinary medicine. Fine with me, because I like it. He also wanted me to graduate from this vet school, which he had come out of forty years ago, and join him in his practice back in Naperville. The idea was that I would eventually take it over. No way."

"Why is that?" Ingrid said.

"Because I can't stand the man. Neither can my brother Rudy. The famous vet Dr. Herman Allgauer is an egomaniac with a mean streak two yards wide. And he is what I've learned is called a 'high-functioning alcoholic.'"

"Meaning what?"

"It means he drinks a lot, but can still operate his practice. Fixing damaged animals. Charming their grateful owners. Then going home at night and going from Dr. Allgauer to Mister Hyde and hide the wife and children when he's on another tear.

"When my old man went to school here, the vet school was about ninety-five percent men. Today, as I'm sure you know, it's split about fifty-fifty between women and men. For which I am very grateful. But this irritates the hell out of Dr. Herman, a misogynist of the first order." He laughed as he pulled Ingrid close to him.

Ingrid shifted on the couch. She'd never heard Eric so serious about anything, much less his family. He got up abruptly. "I want to show you something I wrote about Dr. Herman. It's a poem I wrote. I did it for freshman English. Got me an 'A' and some inquiring looks from the prof."

Eric reached into the bottom drawer of their desk. He took out a tattered manila folder and found what he wanted. He handed it to Ingrid. She read:

MY OLD MAN
A pre-noon nip to
Get the morning running?
Or a slosh at dusk to
Lay out evening's path?
He faced such vital
Choices, drinker of
The wee tot now and
Then, the vat then
Again. The measure
Of a person's not
Their measure, he
Maintained. No,
The key's just in the timing,
Of that he was convinced. Until
He and his bottle hit full throttle.

Ingrid read the poem once, then again. She said, "That's a pretty sorry picture of a man. You must have given a lot of thought to this. Your father has caused you a lot of pain." She leaned over and put her hand on his shoulder. He looked straight ahead as he answered.

"Yes, he did. That's why I'd never consider going into practice with him. I'm going up to Chicago, get my track vet's license, and set up a practice at Heartland Downs. That's my plan."

He turned and smiled at her. "And I hope you'll come with me." He refilled his martini glass. Ingrid waved off his offer to freshen up her drink. She noticed, not for the first time, how Eric at about 6:30 each evening began to slightly slur his words. She wondered how many "martoonies," as he called them, he had downed before she arrived. However many there were, they seemed to make him more caring and affectionate, especially in bed. She was in love and loving it.

Chapter Three

Summer 2011

Doyle hadn't made too many trips to O'Hare Airport's International Terminal, but he enjoyed every one. As he once said to his friend Moe Kellman, "You can't go anywhere else in Chicago and see more happy and relieved people. It's a kick."

It took him several minutes to find a parking place in the crowded International Terminal lot. He hurried across the street to the entrance, observing reunited family members and friends embracing and talking in various languages. Hurried down the stairs to check the monitor on the first floor. The Aer Lingus flight he was meeting had landed. He shouldered his way through the crowd into the reception area facing Gate B.

Doyle's route to this destination had been laid out a week before. He had just returned to his Chicago condo from his morning run and was finishing his daily exercise regimen on the living room floor when the phone rang. He did his one-hundredth push up before picking it up on its third ring.

"Hello there, Jack." Doyle smiled.

"Well, if it isn't the prince and future king of Ireland's bookmakers. Hello yourself, Niall Hanratty."

There was a short silence. "Och, how did you know it was me? Caller ID doesn't figure into these international calls, does it now?"

"Who needs caller ID with that County Cork accent of yours? Give me a minute to get settled here." Doyle placed the receiver on the coffee table in front of his couch, walked into the kitchen, pulled a carton of orange juice out of his sparsely stocked refrigerator. He smiled as he recalled Niall and his muscle man helping Doyle survive a life-threatening situation at Monee Park Racetrack a year ago. Niall had been there to try to take control of the track owned by his cousin Celia McCann. These two heirs of financier and track owner Jim Joyce finally came to an agreement that satisfied both. Doyle counted himself fortunate to have escaped with his life.

"What's going on, Niall?"

"Have you ever thought, Jack, of being a jockey's agent? I know you own a great store of racetrack knowledge, having been involved in several interesting capacities. Are you looking for something to do now? You, a young man with such energy as you have? If so, I've got something for you."

Doyle swigged his orange juice. Toweled the sweat off his face. "Actually, Niall, I'm 'between assignments' as we say over here when we're not working. What jockey are you talking about?"

"Mickey Sheehan. Just a bit over the age of seventeen, but greatly talented, believe me. And a good kid."

Doyle said, "Why would an Irish kid rider want to come here? And why would you entrust the kid to me?"

"Answering your second question first, because I trust you, Jack Doyle. As to the first question, well, I've known the Sheehan family for years. You've probably heard of Kieran Sheehan? One of our country's leading jockeys for the past five or six years?"

"I've read about him," Doyle said. "He rides a lot for the leading stables in Ireland, England, France. Right?"

"That he does indeed, the devious little bastard. Kieran wins races when he wants to, and loses them when he doesn't. Myself, and most of the rest of Ireland's bookmakers, have had to keep a keen eye on this lad for years. Much to our dismay, I must say."

"What do you mean, Niall?"

"What I mean, Jack, is that Clever Kieran, as he is known here, sets up betting scores. He's probably held, or stopped, as many horses as your man Warren Beatty held women during a month or two in his vibrant youth. But Kieran is so good at it, nothing has ever been proved against him. Even though he's been called in for questioning by the racing authorities many times."

Doyle began doing leg stretches, phone still at his ear. "So, Kieran, he's a bad apple?"

"He's a feckin' orchard," Hanratty barked.

"Then why do the top trainers keep using him, Niall? I know he's won all kinds of Group One races all over Europe."

Hanratty said, "They use Kieran because he's so damn talented. When the man rides on the up-and-up, which is most of the time, nobody matches him."

"Are there other riders over there doing the same thing as Sheehan?"

"Absolutely not. Most of them hate Kieran's guts. Not just because of jealousy, envying his talent, but his sleek way of getting his own way. He looks down his long County Monaghan nose at the other riders. And at the racing establishment, for that matter. And he's a regular irritant to bookmakers such as myself."

Doyle stood up. Drained the last of his orange juice. "What does all this have to do with the young jock you want to send over to me?"

"I have a great deal of respect for the Sheehan parents. I grew up near the mother, Blathnaid, in Dun Laoghaire. Went to school with her husband Eoin at University College Dublin. These two good people are, well, they're pretty horrified at Kieran's life and lifestyle which, I am told, involves girls gone bad and cocaine flowing through. He won't have anything to do with his parents anymore. And they want young Mickey to be as far away as possible from Kieran's possible influence. I can't blame them."

Doyle said, "Well, tell me about this youngster you want to send me. Any good?"

"Brilliant prospect, Jack. Won a couple of dozen races so far out of maybe a hundred or so tries. Twenty-five percent winning rate. Should do great over there with you because Mickey has powerful potential, talent, brains, determination. Plus a great personality. And a great gift for getting horses to do what should be done. I'm talking the whole package here, Jack. And, of course, it would be you, now, steering all that ability in the right direction as I know you could."

Doyle laughed. "You are such a blarney machine, Niall. I have to give you credit for a superior brand of flattery."

"I'll take all the credit I can get."

Doyle tossed his empty juice carton into the wastebasket. "Niall, let me think this over. I'll call you in a day or two."

But he didn't. Doyle called Hanratty in Ireland three hours later to say, "Niall, give me Mickey's arrival date and flight number."

Hanratty let out a whoop. "The arrival date is this coming Friday, Aer Lingus, flight 125 at O'Hare. Thank you, Jack. There'll be good come of this. Count on it. I thank you, my friend."

As passengers began to emerge from the US Customs area and walk toward the exit, they were waved at and called out to, and returned the waves and calls. Hugs soon followed. Doyle checked his watch. Nearly twenty-five minutes had passed since Mickey Sheehan's flight landed. The Aer Lingus flight attendant crew, six attractive lasses in green uniforms, bustled through the arrival doors and rolled their baggage past him, chatting happily. He started to wonder if Mickey had missed the flight back in Dublin. Then he heard, "Mr. Doyle! Oh, Mr. Doyle!"

Behind the voice came a small, blond, curly-headed person tugging a giant suitcase. A jockey's whip was attached to its handle. Its diminutive owner had a face sprinkled with freckles. The face wore a worried look.

Doyle took a step back. "Jesus Christ," he said, "the jockey is a girl!"

"Mr. Doyle," said the attractive young woman standing next to the jockey, "I'm Mickey's older sister Nora." She extended her hand. Mickey reached out with one of hers. Doyle, still stunned, shook both. Nora was about five inches taller and twenty well-distributed pounds heavier than her sister. Nora's green eyes shone as she enjoyed the look of shock on Doyle's face.

Regaining his composure, he said, "Ladies, this way." He gripped the pull handle on Mickey's suitcase and hefted Nora's large black bag and led them to the escalator leading to the parking lot. By the time Doyle had the women and their luggage packed into his Accord, he had his questions ready. He waited to offer them until he'd paid the two dollar parking fee to the smiling African-American attendant and started out of the airport.

"Well," Doyle said, "I've got to admit I'm a bit surprised. Niall Hanratty led me to believe that Kieran Sheehan's younger sibling was male. Not in so many words, but he did. And he made no mention of you, Nora, accompanying your sister. Or of you, period."

He turned off Manheim Road to a short cut he knew leading through Des Plaines.

"Mickey," he said. "How did you know it was me back there in the airport when you called out my name?"

"Oh, Mr. Hanratty gave us a proper description of yourself. Said you were a nice looking fella in his forties, with sandy hair and a kind of rearranged nose from your boxing days. It was easy enough to spot you."

Doyle smiled as he turned right onto Tuohy Avenue.

"Niall goes about his own ways in his own way. Aren't you going to ask us how our flight was?" Nora said sweetly.

"Hey, you're both here safe and sound. That's as much as I need to know about your travel. I would like to know, however, why Niall chose to deceive me."

"Mr. Doyle," Mickey began before Jack cut her off. "No more Mr. Doyle, please. Jack to you, always."

She smiled, relieved. "Mr. Hanratty thought that you might not be disposed to taking on a woman rider. I suppose that's why he didn't make clear to you that I am one."

Mickey looked out at the traffic congestion at the intersection of Tuohy and River Road. "Jaysus, that's a mess of autos."

They rode in silence for a couple of miles. Mickey said softly, "Jack, if it doesn't work out for you, that'll be all right." In the rear view mirror he could see the worried look on this small person's face. "I just want to show you what I can do in the saddle."

Flashing through Doyle's mind was the question of what beautiful sister Nora might "do in the saddle." He erased that licentious thought as soon as he could. "Fine, Mickey," he said. "We'll find out soon enough. I'm going to introduce you to a good trainer and a good friend of mine named Ralph Tenuta. He'll watch you horseback and give us all an idea of how we'll get on."

Mickey grinned. "Thanks, Mr. Doyle."

He put a fake frown on that she could see in the mirror. "Och," Mickey said quickly, "I meant Jack."

On the southbound Edens Highway ramp, Doyle said, "Nora, what hotel are you two staying at in the city?" He heard giggles from the back seat emanating from the sisters.

"Hotel?" Nora said. "I guess Niall did not make clear to you that we're supposed to stay at your digs until we get settled." Nora struggled not to laugh at the look of astonishment on Doyle's face. He narrowly avoided being sideswiped by a wide-load house trailer whose driver had drifted out of his lane. The trailer being transported loomed large enough to house dozens. Finally, Doyle said, "Well, that Niall. What a card."

After parking the Accord in his underground garage, unpacking their luggage, and escorting the Sheehan sisters into his condo, Doyle said, "You two can take the bedroom. I'll sleep on the couch. First comes dinner. Let me show you my vast collection of carry-out and delivery menus."

Chapter Four

Doyle had never before attempted to sleep on his couch. He tossed and turned for an hour, listening to the muffled sounds of the visiting Sheehans preparing to slumber in his bed. At 12:41 he conceded to insomnia, sat up, turned on his television, the sound muted. Found the TCM channel. Smiled to see it was showing one of his favorite movies, *Hombre,* a classic Western with Paul Newman, Richard Boone, Frederic March, Diane Cilento, and a further cast of all-stars. Doyle had seen it so many times, he could pronounce the dialogue before the actors spoke.

Nora Sheehan came out of his bedroom wearing a short green night shirt the color of her eyes. She was wide awake. "Can I join you?"

"Only if you stay quiet for a bit." He sat up on the couch. "Pull up a cushion. This movie is almost over." She sat down beside him, putting her long legs up on the coffee table next to his.

"Can't sleep?" Doyle said. "How about my jockey?"

"That girl could sleep through an apocalypse. Me, I guess I'm a bit jet-lagged."

Doyle held up his hand to shush her and took the mute off the remote just in time to hear the villainous Richard Boone say to the stoic hero, Newman, "Mister, you've got a lot of hard bark on you…"

The film ended in a flurry of deadly violence. Doyle switched it off before the conclusion, with which he was very familiar.

"Nora, would you like some tea? Maybe a drink?"

"No thanks, Jack." She shifted on the couch to face him. "It's very nice of you to be doing what you're doing for my sister and me. We really appreciate it."

"Hey, it's just another manifestation of my benevolent nature." He got up and took a Harp from the refrigerator, then sat back down next to her.

"I haven't had a chance to ask you something I'm curious about. Why did you come here with your sister?"

"I had some time on my hands, Jack. I'm a free-lance journalist working in a country where the so-called Celtic Tiger has retreated into the forest. I talked one editor into selling him a report on Mickey's progress in the U. S. for his website. Mickey is quite popular back home. Kieran's little sister, talented rider, etc. Plus I want to look out for her. Our parents were not keen about her coming over here. But they were relieved when I volunteered to accompany her. Mickey's a terrific little athlete, but she's very naïve in the ways of the world. I'm sure Neil Hanratty filled you in on Kieran's character and career."

"He told me a lot. But he never said why the famous or notorious Kieran is estranged from his sisters."

Nora sighed. "That's because Kieran, from the time he was a child, has been almost exclusively interested in himself. He doesn't give a damn about family."

She yawned, stretched, and stood up, smiling down at Doyle. "Thank you again, Jack, for picking us up, and putting us up."

Doyle couldn't hold back. As she moved to the doorway, he blurted, "You have beautiful legs."

"Thank you, Jack. You have excellent eyesight," she laughed. "See you in the morning."

Nora glanced at her watch, then back over her shoulder. "You already have, Jack. Sleep well now."

Restless and wide awake, Doyle turned his radio on to an all-night blues station in Gary, Indiana. He heard the announcer say, "And now a rarely heard example of the great actress Ethel Waters' considerable vocal talent. Take a listen to this."

Doyle sat back and listened as Waters explained why she preferred her "handy man" to all other male suitors.

"He shakes my ashes, greases my griddle,
Churns my butter, strokes my fiddle…"

He went to sleep with a smile on his face.

Chapter Five

Doyle got up at six o'clock after managing four fairly restful hours on his couch. After quickly dressing, he trotted down to the nearby 7-Eleven and bought sweet rolls and coffee and tea. When he walked back into his condo, he found the Sheehan sisters up, dressed, bright-eyed and expectant.

"A little breakfast for you first, ladies. I'll shower and then we'll get going to the track." The girls dug into the pastries and drank the tea.

He drove to the northwest suburb where Heartland Downs was located. The night before, Doyle had called Aguirre Realty and made an appointment with that company's rental agent specialist, Sandra Sucsy, a recommendation from Moe Kellman, who had an impressive gift for finding effective people.

Ms. Sucsy greeted them enthusiastically and ushered them into her SUV for a tour of rental properties. Ninety minutes later, the Realtor had Mickey and Nora placed in a furnished flat some ten minutes away from Heartland Downs.

It was in a large complex that overlooked a man-made lake. The Irish girls were delighted. Doyle wrote Ms. Sucsy a check for the deposit and the first month's rent, telling Nora, "You can reimburse me when you set up a bank account here." Then added, "Do you drive?"

"No, not on the wrong side of the road like you do. And Mickey has no license."

Doyle sighed. Nora caught it and bristled, "We can make our way, Jack. They have buses here, do they not?"

"Oh, yes, they do. Running on a fairly dependable schedule. But you can depend on me for transport to and from the track. After all, I've got to make sure my client gets to work."

Mickey said, "Thanks, Jack."

Next morning, Doyle picked up Mickey just after 5:30. She was bright as the early sun, dressed in jeans and riding boots and tee-shirt under a light jacket with the famed Irish band U-2's name emblazoned on the back. Mickey's driver/agent was not in the same perky shape.

Doyle had been somewhat over-served the previous night while playing poker with Moe Kellman and several of Kellman's Outfit-connected buddies from Chicago's Taylor Street neighborhood. The game was held at the lavish River Forest mansion of reputed Outfit chief Fifi Bonadio, who had been friends with Kellman since first grade. Doyle once before had played poker with this group and emerged an encouraged winner. Not this time. Maybe, he thought cynically, that's why he'd been "encouraged" the first time.

Kellman's friends from childhood looked they had come from the casting office for the movie *Goodfellas*. But, as Doyle well knew, they were not actors. They made a jovial group at the green felt table in Bonadio's rec room, being attended by two polite and efficient young male servers of drinks and food, the hands being dealt by another friendly, engaging young man named Tony DiCastri.

Driving the excited Mickey Sheehan to Heartland Downs, Doyle tried to repress the memory of that poker night's disastrous final hand of seven-card stud. Ahead by some $800, he had check raised, driving all the players out except his host. Bonadio raised another $400. Doyle, face flushed and heart beating, re-raised $600, thus risking his bankroll.

Jack had gone for the gold with a queens-over-nines full house, the strongest hand he'd drawn all night. He ran smack into Bonadio's four treys. Jack glowered as Bonadio pounded the table in triumph. Moe, sitting next to Jack's right, whispered, "Take it easy, Jack." Even early this morning, that defeat still rankled. But he'd shake it off. Doyle was practiced at that.

Mickey and Jack arrived at Ralph Tenuta's barn just before six o'clock. Haze still hung from the track's huge willow trees bordering the barn area as the sun warmed its way forward. Doyle had called Tenuta the night before to inform the trainer that Doyle's client had arrived. He described Mickey. Still, Tenuta's surprise at Mickey's size and youth was evident when he shook her small, strong hand. But he was gracious. "Welcome to Heartland Downs. You feel like getting on a couple of horses this morning?"

Mickey's face lit up. "Any morning, Mr. Tenuta."

"Let's just make it Ralph from now on."

Doyle and Tenuta stood at the rail observing horses going past, some jogging, some galloping, some churning their legs as fast as they could. The air filled with the sound of percussive hooves, equine exhalations of breath, comments being shouted back and forth by their workout riders.

Tenuta had turned Mickey over to his head groom, Paul Albano, instructing him to "Put her on two. Have her jog that black filly Marva's Dream a mile, then tell her to open up Plotkin for three furlongs in about thirty-six seconds for the three furlongs. We'll see how she does."

The black filly ambled past smoothly, Mickey standing up in the irons in the circus rider stance used by many exercise riders, looking very relaxed. "She's got good balance," Tenuta said. "Looks like she knows what she's doing."

"Well, of course she does. Do you think I'd be the agent for some goofus?" Tenuta ignored that crack.

Doyle shaded his eyes trying to see exactly how his jockey looked as she went by on Marva's Dream. Her short blond curls stuck out from the fringes of her riding helmet. Her short-sleeved white tee-shirt flattened against the protective flak jacket underneath it that Paul Albano had insisted she wear. "Look at the muscles in that little girl's arms," Doyle said.

Twenty-four minutes later, Mickey returned to the track aboard the stocky bay two-year-old named Plotkin. Tenuta trained his binoculars across the infield to assess this workout carefully. Mickey sat low in the saddle this time, motionless, as Plotkin sped his way toward the far turn. "He cut the corner like a quarter horse," Tenuta said excitedly. "The kid let him run down the stretch." The trainer was smiling as horse and rider flashed past the finish line.

"Hey, that looked pretty good," Doyle said.

Tenuta looked at his stopwatch. "Better than pretty good, Jack. Your little girl brought Plotkin in with their three furlongs right at thirty-six seconds as I asked. On the button. Like a pro. That's hard to do, her on this horse for the first time. She must have the proverbial 'clock in her head.' Plus, she looks great on these horses."

The two men walked into the Heartland Downs grandstand to a breakfast bar. They bought cups of carry-out coffee, Ralph adding a Krispie Kreme doughnut to his order.

As they headed back to Tenuta's barn, Doyle tried to assess what Mickey had showed them this early morning. If anyone had asked him, he would have pronounced himself "Surprised and delighted." He felt a surge of positive possibility regarding his little Irish client.

Tenuta said, "What are you smiling about, Jack?"

"Not life in general, Ralph. Life in particular. 'Tiz a great morning, surely,' as my rider might say."

"There's a race for Plotkin next week. I think I'd like to use Mickey on him. The race is just five furlongs for two-year-olds. It'll be Plotkin's first start. What do you think?"

"I've got to take Mickey over to the Racing Board office to get her a jockey's license this morning. Damn, Ralph," Doyle said, putting his arm around his friend's shoulders, "this could be fun."

On the walking path leading to the stables, trainer Buck Norman approached them slowly on his palomino pony. "Mornin', men. Ralph, I heard that two-year-old you've got worked pretty sharp this morning."

"Sharp enough. See you, Buck."

Tenuta said, "Buck has been kind of nosing around about Plotkin for the last week. He's mighty interested in that young-ster. By the way, Jack, did I tell you that Plotkin is for sale? You might want to take that into consideration. I think the price would be right."

"Consider it for who? I've got my jockey's agent license, I can't own a horse. How much do you think Plotkin would go for?"

Tenuta said, "I'm pretty sure he could be had for $50,000."

"Whew. That's too steep for me, my friend."

"What about your pal Moe Kellman? You could maybe go partners with him. I'd train this horse not for my usual $65 per day rate, but just for a percentage of what he wins. That's how strong I feel about Plotkin as a money-maker. If I don't sell him to somebody I know," Tenuta said, "his current owners are going to sell him right out from under me. Hate to see that happen."

"Who owns Plotkin?" Doyle said.

"The widow of the deceased owner, nice lady, knows noth-ing about racing and doesn't care about it. Problem is, she's got a son, Stewart, some kind of a half-assed lawyer, who has put himself in the middle of this."

They entered Tenuta's office. Ralph turned on the coffee maker. Doyle said, "Let me talk to Moe. But I know he's never going to try to get licensed. His ties to his Outfit buddies would prevent that. Mind you, Ralph, Moe has never been arrested. He came out of the Korean War with honors. But these lunkheads on the city crime commission have linked him over and over with the mob, and his old friend Fifi Bonadio."

Tenuta grinned. "Are you telling me these 'links' are, what, unreal?"

"No. What I'm telling you is that neither Moe Kellman nor I could get an owner's license. So, why would you suggest we buy Plotkin?"

Tenuta said, "There's a way to solve get around this. It's not quite legal, but it's not real bad *ill*-legal if you know what I mean. Just a way to get things done." He refilled his coffee cup. "Want any?"

Jack declined. "I'm caffeinated enough to gallop ten furlongs. What's your idea?"

"You and Moe put up the money to buy Plotkin. Then we'll officially transfer ownership to somebody we trust. My wife, Rosa."

Doyle said, "You think we could get this past the racing commission? And the Jockey Club?"

"Why not? This won't be the first or last time horse ownership has been hidden. I've never done it before. It our case, it's harmless. I'm sure you trust me and Rosa. We trust you. As I said, I'll train Plotkin without charging a day rate. I'll take twenty percent of his earnings."

"You're that confident about Plotkin?"

"Jack, I've been in this game more than thirty years. I can recognize talent when I see it. Am I confident? You bet I am."

Doyle laughed. "I'll probably bet on him, too. I'm game to try this, Ralph. Do you think the widow's son Stewart will take fifty grand for Plotkin?"

"In a minute."

Doyle got up off the battered couch, eliciting a look of disapproval from the always crabby cat Tuxedo. "You talk to Rosa," Doyle said. "I'll talk to Moe about this set-up. This might work out."

Chapter Six

The morning sun seeped through the drawn blinds covering his basement apartment windows. He heard the loud groan of a garbage truck as it reversed its way down the adjacent alley. "Aw, shit," Lenny Ruffalo said. He sat up, threw off his bed covers. "I'll never get back to sleep."

Lenny had been up late the night before, flipping television channels back and forth between the final races at California's Fairplex Park and the late night show he knew his mother was watching in her living room upstairs. Every morning, she liked to talk about whatever her favorite TV host had done the night before. Lenny tried to be responsive, although he couldn't care less about what starlet had recently emerged from recovery, what politician was attempting to show the common man just how common he supposedly was. Lenny was residing rent—if not guilt—free in his mother's basement. He figured he owed her at least that much attention.

He hadn't bet anything on his computer at Fairplex. But he had carefully watched the races. Always trying to spot a horse who experienced trouble, or a jockey who made the wrong decision on perhaps the best horse. He'd thought about getting into this TiVo stuff with the TV so he wouldn't have to stay up late so many nights. But that cost money. He didn't have much. He sure as hell couldn't impose on his mother, Elvira, for help along those lines. At least not now. As deftly as Lenny had played his adoring mother from his position as the cherished only child, he did recognize some limits.

Walking to his small bathroom, Lenny glanced appreciatively at the *Sports Illustrated* calendar model for this month. His twenty-sixth birthday was approaching. He circled the date with a ballpoint pen and drew a line from that date up into the tall, golden model's barely concealed crotch.

Lenny brushed his teeth, then washed his face with its incipient dark beard. He considered it to be his very hip five o'clock shadow. Ever since he'd been discharged from the US Army, he told people that he favored modified facial hair as kind of a personal statement. Like so many of those young actors on TV and movies who looked a lot like him, he thought.

His mother had greeted him at the downtown Chicago bus terminal when he'd arrived three months earlier after a thirty-four hour ride from Fort Hood in Texas. They embraced amid the large collection of arrivals and departures, some welcome, some not. Elvira did not inquire what had brought him home earlier than expected. But he volunteered to her that it was a cruel combination of physical ineptitude and mental deficiencies that he'd been born with. This after he had volunteered for the new, lenient Army, an organization desperate for members, in which people such as himself, with minor criminal records and IQ's hovering around the century mark, had been accepted and signed up to serve their country.

At "the Hood," Lenny could barely keep up in the dawn running drills. Could hardly sleep at night in a barracks replete with loud snorers and young men who barked out remnants of their dreams. He never connected with a buddy. Never was able to pull himself up the rope and over the twenty-foot-high training wall.

What Lenny did best was discover a young enlistee from Brooklyn who had access to a steady supply of crystal meth. Lenny eagerly embraced that connection. The meth worked to ease out his days. But one morning, on the rifle range, on a meth overload, he fired a volley of shots fifteen feet above the intended target. He was hauled in for drug testing. Then psychological evaluation. Ten days later, he was given his walking papers, actually being "all that he could be," but not in the way the Army wanted.

This Tuesday morning, Lenny pulled on his Chicago Bears sweat shirt and pants, and black Nikes and walked up the basement stairs to the backyard of his mother's home. He did some lazy stretches on the grass next to the large tomato patch. Smoked a Kool menthol light, glancing over his shoulder to be sure Elvira wasn't looking out the kitchen window at him. She had made it clear on the first day he was back that she didn't want him smoking in her house, or at all.

Lenny took a last drag. Tossed the butt into the alley. Went around the side yard to the front and picked up that morning's *Chicago Tribune*. When he returned to the back yard, Elvira was watering her large bed of flourishing tomato plants. She smiled warmly at her only child.

"Are you ready for some breakfast, Lenny?"

"Always ready for breakfast, Ma. I'm gonna take a quick shower."

Elvira said, "Lenny. You want eggs or pancakes?"

"How about both?"

Elvira watched him fondly as he went down the stairs to his apartment. When he'd lost his most recent job, as a pizza delivery man, she welcomed him back, understanding that he could no longer afford the Berwyn apartment he shared with two old high-school buddies after returning from the Army.

Elvira's next door neighbor, Pat Sena, waved across the fence. Elvira momentarily lowered the bell-shaped spray of hose to wave, say good morning. She turned back to concentrate on her tomato plants and think about her son.

Lenny's recent job loss was part of a pattern that began to unfold from the time he was expelled from high school early in his senior year, for smoking pot. He'd been trying to sell some, too, and was fortunate in not being nabbed for that. But she persuaded herself that maybe, now, out of the Army and back home, he might find his right track in life.

Elvira walked to the faucet on the side of the house and turned it off. Looked back proudly at her impressive tomato patch and neatly kept back yard behind the bungalow she'd paid for with proceeds from the Berwyn florist shop she'd owned for the last sixteen years.

She had no outstanding debts. And she was lonely. Had always felt she had not done enough for or right by Lenny. He'd been a challenge from the start. A difficult birth. Three years of infant Lenny awakening off and on throughout one exhausting night after another. Elvira had taken him to five different doctors. None could pinpoint what was wrong with this troubled child.

Dr. Gerald Greenberg, the last of the five, told her, "It's not physical. It's not neurological, Mrs. Ruffalo. It's just, well, not explainable."

Rolling up the hose on its circular rack, she thought again what Lenny might have been like had he had a father in his life. Elvira and Bruno Ruffalo had been married seven years before they managed to produce her lone pregnancy.

Jubilation spread in Bruno's large family. His two older sisters finally warmed to Elvira. Then, a week before Lenny was born, Bruno Ruffalo toppled over one brutally hot July afternoon on a Berwyn bocce court, dead of a heart attack.

"Enough memories for today," Elvira said. She walked into the kitchen and gave Lenny an affectionate pat on the head. *The Racing Daily* was laid out in front of him on the table. He was intently scribbling notes and figures on the margins of the paper.

As he polished off his breakfast, Lenny kept his eye on the Weather Channel showing on the small TV set on the kitchen counter. "Heavy rains over much of the East Coast" came the prediction.

Lenny smiled. "That'll make an off track at Belmont." His most rewarding betting involved horses running in the mud.

He kissed his mother. "Great breakfast. Thanks." Skipped down the basement stairs to get his jacket, his money, and his concealable stash of meth.

"I'll be home for supper, Ma," he hollered back up the stairs.

Lenny hurried to the El station for his familiar trip to downtown Chicago and the off-track betting shop on State Street. He'd been going there for almost a month now, getting to know the regulars. Some of the guys were there every day, including a few he knew from high school. Also present were Pakistani taxi drivers double-parked outside, harried traders from the nearby exchanges rushing in to wager, and then the tables of regulars. Retirees, most of them

African-American, some elderly Italians, one old Jewish man who sat by himself in the room Lenny favored. Lenny's presence reduced the average age to sixty-five plus. The lone females on hand were the bartender, Kitty, and Juanita, who cooked and served sandwiches.

And most of them knew him. Early on, Lenny was disturbingly demonstrative when one of his horses failed to meet his expectations. Slamming his *Racing Daily* down on the table, leaping about in anguish, shouting at his bad luck, he was the center of a scene. After a week, it took an intervention by a huge black customer known as Large to persuade Lenny to improve his manners. Large was a retired Teamster official with forearms the size of ham hocks. He had a serious talk with Lenny who, impressed, decided it was wise to modify his behavior.

After a string of dreadful betting days, he'd become known in the parlor as "Lenny the Loser." He heard the talk. Fuck 'em. He'd get this straightened out. Sooner or later. He knew it. But he knew enough to keep his mouth shut now, thanks to Large.

Lenny caught a big longshot who reveled in the Belmont Park slop that afternoon and raised his arms in triumph as he looked around the room. Didn't say anything. Large gave him a thumbs-up from his table across the room.

Chapter Seven

Moe Kellman reached across the table in his back booth at Dino's Ristorante, a major dining and socializing headquarters for Chicago's real and potential movers and shakers. He tapped Doyle on the wrist.

"Have you lost your fucking mind? You and me buy a horse? I'd never be able to get a racing license. Those bastards at the crime commission have labeled me 'an associate of known criminals.' They're talking about guys I grew up with from Taylor Street. So what? When you're a friend of mine, you stay a friend of mine. The only law infraction I've had in the last thirty-five years was a parking ticket on Rush Street. But they've still got me in their Black Book."

There was a lull in their conversation as Kellman shook hands with one of the city's police commissioners who had stopped by the booth to say hello to the little furrier.

"Moe, take it easy." Doyle smiled at his diminutive companion who, in his early seventies, was some three decades older than Doyle. Their friendship had its origin in the workout room of Fit City Health Club, where they both enjoyed cardiovascular challenges, talk of sports and politics. Right now Kellman's normally calm demeanor had been replaced by agitation that flushed his face. The overhead light glinted off the little furrier's Don King-like head of hair.

"Have another Negroni, Moe. Let me tell you about this horse." When Doyle finished his pitch regarding Plotkin, highlighting Ralph Tenuta's offer to train for only a percentage of winnings and to place ownership in his wife Rosa's name, Moe sat back. "You know, I've always wanted to own a racehorse. I saw how much fun my uncle Bernie Glockner, the guy called 'The Wizard of Odds,' had with his little stable when I was a kid."

Moe's reverie was interrupted by the arrival of owner Dino and two servers. The first one carefully placed a large bowl of pasta fazoli in front of Kellman. The other delivered a plate of calamari to Doyle. Dino said, "Gentlemen, enjoy. Your entrees will be beautiful."

Doyle said, "Your pal Dino hasn't changed much since I first came in here a few years ago. He looks just about exactly as he does in that big photo behind you, him and Frank."

Kellman smiled. "Sinatra loved this place, always came here when he played Chicago. I think," Kellman said after a spoonful of the thick soup, "either Dino is having that picture retouched, or himself."

"Have I ever asked you about Dino? How he got into the restaurant business?"

"Short version. Some of my friends started Dino, nephew of a made guy, out on a low level. He was a burgler. And he turned out to be terrible at it. But they knew he had smarts, so they finally decided to put him in the restaurant business. Lo and behold, Dino was at genius level in that field. He and his old sponsors now operate, what, four or five places in the city? All booming." Moe smiled over his Negroni glass. "A real American success story."

Doyle said, "Let's get back to this horse. I think we can do this. And do well with him. You can certainly come to the track with me and watch him train in the morning or run in the afternoon."

"What is this potential Pegasus' name?"

"Plotkin."

"*Plotkin*! Jack, spare me."

Doyle said, "The guy who bred and owned the horse was getting sick of having the names he suggested being rejected by the Jockey Club, which is in control of these things. They'd tell him, 'No, that name's been used. No, that name's reserved.' He got so disgusted that he decided to go with a name he knew had not been used. His own. Maurice Plotkin, a Skokie jeweler and horse owner, sent in his own last name. It was accepted."

Kellman was laughing now. "Jack, I don't know how you do it, but you continue to amaze me."

"Moe, I'm serious. There is a good side to this name."

"Like what?"

Doyle said, "A lot of people at the track, especially women, bet horses because they like their names. Beautiful Day…Girl Power…Pretty Pamela…and so on. That lowers those horse's odds."

He leaned forward, grinning, as he said, "There's no chance of that happening with a horse named Plotkin. Am I right?"

"Sometimes you are, Jack."

Two waiters approached the booth. One carefully presented Kellman's platter of rigatoni dotted by garlic slices under a vodka-laced tomato and cream sauce. Doyle looked appreciatively at his plate of ravioli stuffed with ground meat and spinach beneath a coating of marinara.

"Aw, Jack, what the hell? Let's give it a go. I'll have Pete Dunleavy drive over with the twenty-five to your place early tomorrow morning." He put down his fork and raised his glass toward Doyle's.

"Bumps," Kellman said as their glasses clinked.

"Confusion to our enemies," Doyle said.

"*Buon appetito*," Kellman replied, picking up his fork.

Chapter Eight

Ralph Tenuta led Doyle to a corner table in the crowded Heartland Downs track kitchen. He said hello to the many horsemen he knew. Doyle nodded to as many as he recognized. These were trainers who, he hoped, would give his client Mickey Sheehan rides on their horses.

Doyle stopped at one table. Horse owner Steve Holland looked up from his *Racing Daily.* "Morning, Jack. How are you?"

"Very well, Steve. And I'll be even better once you decide to use my ultra-talented young jock on one of your horses."

Holland said, "My trainer says take a wait-and-see attitude with your girl. I've heard she's pretty promising. And she gets the five-pound apprentice allowance, which is a plus. I'll keep my eye on her. I know you don't chase too many empty wagons, Jack."

"I try not to, Steve."

Tenuta had polished off the first of his two toasted cream-cheese- laden bagels by the time Doyle sat down across the table from him. He looked semisatiated, but worried.

"What's bothering you, Ralph?"

Tenuta took a sip of his coffee. "Earlier this morning, I let my vet go. Eric Allgauer. He took it badly."

"What about Ingrid, his partner, or assistant? You let her go, too?"

"No. I'm very impressed with that young woman and the work she does. Her 'horse communicating' stuff? That a lot of people laugh at? It works. You know that old brown gelding

Mister Sheridan? I started him three times this meeting on the main track and he wouldn't break a sweat. Beat one horse total. Then Mister Sheridan tells Ingrid, 'Please put me on the grass. I'm much better there.' I do. And the son of a gun wins his last two starts!

"Besides the communicating, Ingrid is a helluva vet . Every horse she's worked on has gotten better. Better than they were under Allgauer. I don't mean she has to talk to all of them. She tells me some horses just won't do that. But I trust her to do excellent regular vet work. She's got a gift."

Doyle said, "But didn't you use Allgauer for a couple of years?"

"Yeah. But he started to slide the last couple of months. The guy is a boozer. He started to show up late, or not at all some mornings, looking hung over. And surly, too. It took me awhile to figure out he was going bad before I decided to cut him loose. Funny thing, Jack, or maybe a sad thing, is that this is a talented young guy with a good feel for horses. But he seems to be throwing his life away. I can't afford to watch him do so. So, I let him go. I'm going with Ingrid, the communicator."

Tenuta sat back in his chair. He shook his head. "I never thought I'd ever be saying anything like that."

Doyle laughed, and Ralph did, too. Steve Holland looked up from his perusal of *Racing Daily's* past performances at his nearby table. "Ralph, you got a shot in the fourth today?"

"Mr. Holland, I've always got a shot." Holland smiled. "I guess your record bears you out, Ralph."

Doyle returned from the cafeteria line with a new cup of coffee.

"Ralph, how long did you say Allgauer worked for you?"

"Almost two years. My old vet, Ron Jensen, moved to California. Took a big job at a university there. Eric's first year was great. This season, he all of a sudden started not showing up when he was supposed to. Sometimes I could smell alcohol on his breath. I'm talking early in the mornings. Ingrid tried to cover up for him. I finally realized I had to get rid of him."

"Pretty hard-headed guy from what I saw of him. I can't imagine he took your decision in stride."

Tenuta said, "No, he didn't. If he'd have kept on taking care of business like he was supposed to, it would have been fine. But I've got these horses who deserve the best care to that I can provide. He wasn't up to it anymore. You know what he said to me? Kind of in a threatening manner. He said, 'Tenuta, you should think this over.'

"That made me kind of laugh, which pissed Eric off. He says to me, 'You think this is fucking funny?'

"I tell him, 'Nah, Eric, there's nothing funny about this. I was just thinking of something that happened in my car a few years ago. My wife Rosa and I were giving our daughter Julia and her daughter Cecilia, our youngest grandchild, a ride home from a kid's birthday party. Julia was steaming. She turns to CC in the back seat and tells her, 'Cecilia, you were very rude to several of those children. Pushing in front of them to catch the balloons. Knocking that one boy down when you were running to get cake. When Grandpa gets us home, Cecilia, you are going to your room. To think about how badly you acted at the party.'"

"I drive a mile or so," Tenuta continued. "The car was quiet. Then comes CC's big voice from her car seat in the back. She says, 'I don't have to go to my room. I thinked about it already!'"

Tenuta finished the remnants of second bagel. "Maybe I shouldn't have told Allgauer that story. But the guy really pissed me off. Lot of talent, no good sense in him. I wrote him a check for his last bill. I told him, 'I thinked about it already.' I'm all done with you."

"When Allgauer walked out of my office, he slammed the door so hard he knocked a couple of pictures off my walls. He can be a hot head."

Chapter Nine

Ingrid had not spoken to Eric that day. But she'd heard from Ralph Tenuta about his decision to dismiss Eric while retaining her as the veterinarian for his stable. She didn't pretend to be shocked, or even disappointed. She'd seen this coming. Eric should have seen it, too.

She had stopped to shop at Whole Foods on her way home from Heartland Downs. Purchased two porterhouse steaks, salad fixings, a pair of the twice-baked potatoes Eric liked, and a bottle of the Australian red wine he favored.

When she thrust her hip against the front door of their condo, heavy grocery sacks in each hand, the door was suddenly yanked open. Eric snatched one of the bags from her hand and threw it on the foyer floor. His eyes were red with fury, his cheeks flushed with alcohol.

"Shit," he said. "Shit shit shit." He stumbled into the kitchen and sat down heavily in a chair and began banging his large fists on the table top. "Those bastards," he shouted. "Those *bas*tards."

Ingrid bent to retrieve the scattered groceries from the floor and place them on the counter. For a moment she leaned forward, hands on the counter, back turned to Eric, bracing herself. Then she took the chair across from him.

"What bastards, Eric? I guess you mean Ralph Tenuta? I heard from him today. Who else?"

Eric reached for his half-full tumbler of Stolichnaya vodka and knocked it back. "Buck Norman," he spat. "Randy

McMillan. Trainers I've worked for since I came to Heartland Downs. They've all ditched me as of today. Bastards."

Ingrid took a deep breath. "Eric, listen to me. You can't tell me, or yourself, that you didn't see this coming. Jesus!"

She leaned forward, her tanned face tight with concern. "We've talked about how your drinking was getting out of hand. You'd say 'Yes', agreeing with me, but never changing. Eric, alcohol has taken over your life. Maybe it's your father's genes dominating you, I don't know, and I don't care. But I do care about you."

Ingrid got up and got a bottle of water from the fridge. Eric sat as if frozen, fists clenched, staring straight ahead. She sat back down. "Ralph Tenuta called me last night when you were out. He told me that he was going to fire you. He urged me to urge you to get some help, some counseling. He was very concerned about you, Eric."

She restrained herself from getting up and going around the table to put her arms around him. Instead, she said, "I was…I was going to try to talk to you about all this tonight. I'm very sorry it all happened to you this way today. I really am."

Eric jumped up, overturning his chair, shaking. He yanked open the freezer door of the refrigerator and reached in for the Stoly bottle. He raised the bottle to his lips, then brought it back to the table and sat down heavily, eyes slits. He looked across at Ingrid.

"You know what kills me the most?"

"No."

"Well," he said, "it's the fucking so-called horse communicating bullshit you have sold to these clients of ours. Used to be my clients. Then our clients. Now, they're yours. You have managed to fucking steal most of my practice from me." He slammed the vodka bottle down on the table. "Bitch!" He put his head down in his hands.

Ingrid stood up. "That's it."

Eric looked up at her, teary and bleary-eyed. "What the fuck do you mean?"

"I'm getting out of here. We're not partners in this condo, it's all yours. And you can have it. I'll take a suitcase tonight, be back for everything else I've got here tomorrow after work."

Eric looked at her in shock. "What? After, after all this time we've had together? What the hell do you think you're doing, Ingrid?"

"Doing? What am I doing? Trying to get back into a normal life. I can no longer put up with your drinking. You ridiculing my ideas about horse communicating. I just can't do it anymore."

She started to walk out of the kitchen to their bedroom for her suitcase when she turned and said, "You've become a replica of the father you told me you despised. You don't even know it. I can't take it anymore. And I won't."

Chapter Ten

Doyle pulled his Accord up to Tenuta's barn just as Ingrid McGuire's truck arrived from the other direction. She parked next to him. He got out, waved, and waited for her. She walked around the front of her truck with her head down, ball hat pulled low on her forehead, sunglasses on.

"What happened to you?" Doyle said kiddingly. "A night of serious carousing? You look a little wobbly."

She stopped in front of him and pulled off her glasses, revealing a large shiner under her right eye.

Doyle said, "Jesus, I'm sorry, Ingrid. Where'd you get that?"

Lips tight, she shook her head. "It's not a concern of yours, Jack. But thanks." She put her glasses back on and began to move around Doyle toward the office door. Doyle put his hand on her elbow to stop her.

"How about I make us some coffee in Ralph's office? He must be over at the track, watching the workouts. Okay?"

Ingrid hesitated. "Okay, Jack."

The story poured out of her in the next few minutes. "Eric gave me this shiner. Yes, Eric."

"What went on with you two?"

"When I got home last evening, Eric had been drinking. A lot. Again. I'd never seen him so angry, so full of rage. Out of control. He is so jealous of my success in working on horses that he just can't stand it." She put her head in her hands.

Without looking up at Doyle, Ingrid said, "I told Eric that he'd lost track of his real self. I said, 'Do you remember when you were on your bike in Urbana and picked me up during my morning run? How magic was that? How beautifully we started out, and how great it was for us after we'd moved up here? Until you started drinking so much. Letting alcohol take over your life and come between us.'"

"What do you think got him going this way. Changed him?"

"Beyond the alcohol, or maybe even behind it, is his damn jealousy of what I've done with my horse communicating. I mean, is that crazy? I believe I'm doing something useful, valuable. For anyone who truly cares about animals, this would be considered a major step forward. But," she said bitterly, "I guess Eric never really cared about animals. Or about me."

She sat back on Tenuta's old office couch. Tuxedo the cat leaped off the back of the couch onto Ingrid's lap, making her momentarily smile.

"It's still hard for me to believe," Ingrid said, "but when I started to go out of the condo door Eric jumped up from his chair and rushed toward me. He was stumbling. He looked like he was, well, nuts. First he grabbed me by the arms and shook me. Hard. I tried to break away. That's when he hit me with his fist. Then he backed off. For a moment he looked about as disbelieving over what he'd done as I did. He didn't say anything. He just turned and ran out the door.

"I didn't know where he went. I was so stunned I could hardly find one of my suitcases. I packed as quick as I could and got out of there. I hope I never see Eric again. He's not the person I thought I knew."

They looked up as they heard the cheerful voice of Ralph Tenuta as he returned from the track and strolled down his shed row, asking questions of some grooms, giving instructions to other grooms.

"Jack," Ingrid said, "I don't want Ralph to know about Eric and me. At least not today. Okay?"

She put her sun glasses back on, adjusted her cap, and got up from the couch and carefully positioned Tuxedo on the middle cushion.

"Sure," Doyle said. "I'm just very sorry this all happened. If there's anything I can do, Ingrid, let me know."

Chapter Eleven

Doyle was in the foyer of his condo building going over the past performances in *Racing Daily* when Moe Kellman's maroon Lincoln Continental, with Chicago police sergeant Pete Dunleavy at the wheel as usual, pulled up at the curb.

"Morning, men," Doyle said as he slid into the back seat next to Kellman.

Dunleavy said, "Hi, Jack. Good to see you."

Kellman was on his cell phone, looking agitated. He nodded to Doyle, but kept speaking into the phone. "Feef, you ordered that Persian lamb coat for whoever your current squeeze is. Your wife is still visiting family in Calabria, right? So is it for Doreen the hair dresser? Angie from Dino's? You said you wanted to surprise whatever broad it is when you take her to London for Christmas. I paid my people to get them started making this expensive item. Now you say you don't want it? Bullshit. Whether you want it or not, you owe me for it. Pay up, pal."

Moe listened for a few seconds to his boyhood friend, Fifi Bonadio, Outfit chief, before replying, "I don't care whether you have any luck getting Doreen back in your fold or not. It doesn't matter to me. If you'd stay at home, like a real Sicilian grandfather, you wouldn't get yourself in these jackpots." He clicked off the cell phone.

Moe sat back in his seat with a sigh. "I know this guy sixty years probably, and he still breaks my balls on a regular basis.

Anyway, Jack, good morning. Wait a minute," Kellman said as he fielded another call. There was a five-minute conversation that Doyle paid little attention to as he kept on reading *Racing Daily.*

Kellman closed his cell phone, smiling. "That was my grand-daughter, Sinead Goldstein. Wonderful kid, just turned ten. She's all excited because their prized dog Muggles had pups last night. They're keeping two of pups. One they've already named Huggles. The other one, Jamie. Can you believe it? Whatever happened to Rover? Queenie? Scout? Buster? Bowser?"

Doyle smiled out the window so his friend could not see it. "I think I recall you grousing about the Irish names that your prized grandchildren have been given. And some of their friends as well. I seem to recall a Sean Bimstein. Am I right?"

"Don't start me on that subject, Jack."

Dunleavy adeptly steered his way up the crowded Ohio Street ramp to the Kennedy Expressway. He swore softly as a Chicago Streets and Sanitation Department truck suddenly started up and came off the right shoulder, forcing him to yank the steering wheel into a sharp left. "Those jerks must have all of a sudden finished their morning loafing," he said. Minutes later Dunleavey had them in the clear on the Kennedy and heading north onto the Edens to the Willow Road Exit, where they turned west toward Heartland Downs.

Kellman took another cell phone call that he quickly dismissed. "Enough business," he said. "Jack, let's talk horses. How do we look in our race?"

"Moe, I can't look at past performances and handicap our race that way because they *are* no past performances. All ten horses in our race are making their first starts. One of them, number three, named Ronnie Ruble, was bought as a yearling last year for $280,000, the top price paid at the sale he came out of. He could be tough."

"And our Plotkin cost us just $50,000. I don't know if I like those numbers, Jack."

"Moe, Moe," Doyle said, "Do you have any idea how many of the big sales yearlings never do diddly? There was one a few years back that sold for a world record sixteen million! Can that register that on your meter? Sixteen fucking million! Turned out to be a complete bust. He couldn't beat an ant coming out of a fly trap. He never won a single race.

"But then you've got a horse like the great John Henry several years back. Sold for $25,000. Won about $7 million. Let's look on the bright side."

Doyle could see Pete Dunleavy smiling in the mirror, nodding in agreement.

Moe said, "And what exactly would that so-called bright side be?"

"Ralph Tenuta yesterday gave me money to bet on Plotkin for him and his wife Rosa. Ralph almost *never* bets. That's the bright side as far as I'm concerned."

The little furrier shifted in his seat. "But that name. Plotkin. Sheez."

Doyle patted his friend on the knee. "A rose by any other name…" he began before Kellman brushed his hand away.

"Don't give me that Shakespeare stuff, Jack. I'm starting to wonder why I agreed to this agreement."

Doyle leaned back in his seat, smiling. He could see Dunleavy looking at him in the rear view mirror. "Moesy," Doyle said, "not to worry."

Dunleavy gave Doyle a subtle thumbs up sign as Kellman fielded another business call.

Dunleavy dropped them off at the Heartland Downs clubhouse entrance. Doyle picked up a track program at the entrance gate. The oddsmaker for that publication had made Plotkin's odds twelve to one with the comment, "Relatively obscure breeding, but from a sharp barn." The five-to-two favorite was a colt named Chemistry King, trained by Tenuta's friendly rival Buck Norman. Second choice was the expensive purchase Ronnie Ruble.

Doyle led the way down the stairs to a spot on the paddock fence. They watched as groom Paul Albano walked Plotkin around the saddling ring.

Kellman said, "He's kind of small, isn't he Jack? Our horse?"

"So was the great John Henry. Relax. Ralph says this horse is ready to ramble."

The jockeys emerged from the tunnel leading to their room and began advancing toward their mounts, wearing their colorful silks, some snapping their whips against their polished boots. Doyle waved at Mickey Sheehan, but she didn't notice. She was walking purposefully to Plotkin's stall, where she shook hands with Ralph Tenuta and gave Plotkin an affectionate pat on the neck. The call came for "Riders Up." Tenuta boosted Mickey into Plotkin's saddle. The ten young horses began their final move around the walking ring on their way to the tunnel and its path leading to the track. A few were docile, but most were not at this point, the beginning of their racing lives. Plotkin, Doyle was happy to see, was striding forward in a very professional manner, looking all business, little Mickey comfortable upon his broad back.

That's when Doyle felt Moe grab his arm and heard him say, "Is that a leprechaun you've put on our horse? What the hell?"

Doyle patted his friend on the back. "That's my jockey, Mickey Sheehan, the girl from Ireland. She's like Plotkin, our horse. Small, but talented. Mickey's just about as tall as you are, Moe, and probably just about as tough. Jesus, I can't believe you questioning my judgment at this point. Relax. Tenuta's very high on Mickey. C'mon, let's go bet."

Tenuta joined them on their walk. He had overheard this exchange. He said, "Moe, you shouldn't worry. Mickey's been working Plotkin in the mornings. They get along great. Believe me, this 'little leprechaun' as you call her, can horseback. You'll see."

Walking up the stairs from the paddock, Doyle and Kellman found themselves behind a group of women, all well dressed, chatting away, all wearing red hats and obviously enthusiastic about their day at the races. "Must be some kind of club," Doyle said.

A woman immediately in front of Kellman said loudly, "And that horse called Plotkin? Who could bet on that poor thing with a name that ugly?"

Doyle nudged Kellman with his elbow as they reached the top of the stairs. "What did I tell you about names?"

By the time they arrived at Tenuta's box overlooking the Heart-land Downs finish line, Doyle had cooled off. Still a bit rankled, yes, having had his judgment questioned about Mickey. Kellman turned conciliatory. "I am not intending to denigrate our little leprechaun rider," Kellman said. He stopped to shield his face from the now riveting afternoon sun and reached into his sport coat for sun glasses. Tenuta had his binoculars trained on Plot-kin as the colt cantered around the first turn, Mickey Sheehan standing up in the stirrups. Moe said "Calm down, Jack. It's only a horse race. I'm sorry if I offended you."

"I'm cool, Moe."

They took their seats in Tenuta's box. Doyle fidgeted with his *Racing Daily*, track program, binoculars. Kellman said, "Jack, calm down."

Three minutes to post-time. Moe said, "I heard this one yes-terday. Irish guy from Chicago, visiting the old country, meets a leprechaun while he's hiking up in the Wicklow Mountains. The leprechaun says, 'Well, you're in luck, visitor. Today's the day that I can grant a visitor like yourself one wish.'

"The Chicago guy answers, 'I want to live forever.'

"'Sorry,' says the leprechaun, 'I'm not empowered to grant wishes like that!'

"The Chicago guy steps back to think this over. Then he says to the leprechaun, 'Fine. Here's my wish. I want to die when the Cubs win the World Series.'"

"'You crafty bastard,' says the leprechaun.'"

Tenuta, who had overheard this while watching Plotkin approach the starting gate, joined Doyle in the laughter.

They all heard rapid footsteps coming down the stairs to the box. It was Ralph's wife Rosa. Big purse swinging, a large Coke in her other hand, broad smile on her face. "Just made it," she said. She sat down in the front row of the box next to her husband. "How does our horse look?" She looked over her shoulder to smile at Doyle and Kellman.

"He's looking fine," her husband said.

The young horses danced and pranced and lagged back, some of them, on their way to the starting gate far across the infield on the other side of the track. Plotkin was acting, as Tenuta put it, "like an old pro. So far, so good. Mickey's got him all smoothed out."

Doyle felt his stomach muscles tighten. "God," he murmured, "I hope Neil Hanratty and Ralph Tenuta know what they're talking about." He raised his binoculars and saw Mickey Sheehan drop her protective goggles over her eyes as she guided Plotkin smoothly into his stall in the gate. The assistant starters quickly shut the doors behind them. Two other members of the gate crew were struggling to control Chemistry King and persuade this high-strung animal to begin his racing career.

Whether it was Plotkin's name, modest looks and breeding or the presence in his saddle of an unknown woman jockey, he went off at seventeen to one. The favorite, Chemistry King, refused to leave his stall in the gate, eliminating himself from the race.

Mickey Sheehan rocketed Plotkin out of the gate, putting him two lengths in front of his nearest rival after the first forty yards of the race. She guided him over to hug the rail. From then on, Plotkin easily increased his margin. He curved around the far turn right on the inner fence, changed leads like a veteran, all the while with his rider "sitting still as a statue," as Tenuta later put it.

"Moe," shouted Doyle, "he's going to win easy!" Plotkin did. "Wins by seven," Tenuta said, "and look at his time. Awful damn good." Rosa's face was flushed. In her excitement, she had dropped her Coke into the adjacent box to their left. It spilled upon the cuffs of the tailored trousers of Heartland Downs' perennial leading owner, Frank Cosentino.

Rosa, embarrassed and apologetic, started to say something to Cosentino.

"Hey, I can't blame you for being excited, Mrs. Tenuta," Cosentino smiled. "Damn impressive race by your colt. Nice going, Ralph," he added. "Have you thought about selling him?"

Doyle and Kellman were looking at each other in amazement, joy, and in Doyle's case, relief. Moe said, "Jack, you son of a gun, you'd pulled off another one!"

Doyle mopped his brow. Took a deep breath. Leaned over to the front row of the box to grip Ralph's hand, kiss Rosa on her cheek.

"C'mon," Tenuta said, "we've got to hurry down to the winner's circle."

Jack started to exit the box, then stopped, waiting for Moe, who said, "No, Jack. I don't want to give anybody any hint of my connection to Plotkin." He stood up from his seat smiling. "I got to give it to you, Jack. You were right about this horse, and right about the little jock. This is a hell of a lot of fun for me. Go get your picture taken. Tell everybody I want to take them to dinner tonight at Dino's. I'll meet you at my car when you're ready to leave. Pete will have it right in the center of the valet parking section."

As they hustled their way down the stairway to the Heartland Downs winner's circle, Tenuta said, "Jack, why doesn't Moe want to come down here to get his picture taken? That's what most owners that I've known love to be able to do."

"Ralph, it's not worth going into. Let's just say that Moe Kellman is kind of camera shy."

Doyle thought that he'd probably never seen Kellman as excited, as happy, as at the moment after Mickey Sheehan and Plotkin had flashed under the finish line in first. Well, maybe when Kellman's favorite boxer Manny Pacquiao won his most recent title, with Moe having bet heavily on the super-talented and magnetic boxer from the Philippines.

They reached the winner's circle just as Mickey brought Plotkin into it. A grinning Paul Albano put a halter on their winner. The veteran track photographer Bernie Greenwald, a perfectionist, was impatiently trying to arrange people for the shot. Doyle looked up at Mickey. The grin on Mickey's flushed and freckle- sprinkled face spread across the winner's circle.

Finally, everyone was positioned to the photographer's satisfaction. Doyle had nudged up his way to stand between Ralph and Rosa, putting an arm around each.

"Bernie, I want a half-dozen copies of this one," Doyle said.

Chapter Twelve

While their party was in the process of being seated at Dino's Ristorante, Moe was greeted first by one of Chicago's foremost aldermen, then an aged monsignor from the cardinal's staff, and, at a nearby table, Vito Lombardino, one of Moe's former grade school classmates before Vito eschewed scholastic pursuits and went directly into his uncle's street-loan racket.

Watching this tribute show, Doyle again thought how ironic it was that Kellman, who had obviously acquired considerable clout in this city of the big shoulders and hidden-from-view power pockets, couldn't get a racehorse owner's license.

He heard Vito Lombardino say, "Moesy, nice win today at Heartland. Lot of the guys bet Rosa's horse."

"You're looking tip top, Vito."

As Kellman prepared to finally settle down in his regular booth, he was interrupted once again by a large, worried looking man in a rumpled gray business suit. They spoke together in hushed tones. Moe finally sat down next to Jack on their side of the booth.

Doyle said, "Some of your various friends and acquaintances I recognize. But who was that last guy?"

"Ah," Kellman groaned, "I figured you would ask." He took a sip of the Negroni that had been placed before his plate before he was seated, Dino's staff always at the ready when Kellman came in.

Doyle waited. Moe said, "That schlub is Seymour Korshack. A very distant cousin on my wife Leah's family side. On the failure side of that family, I might add. Seymour somehow got through John Marshall law school after numerous repeated semesters. Passed the bar on his fifth try. Opened a minor-league law practice in Rogers Park. Now, he's managed, I don't know how, to get himself on the ballot in the fall for a minor Cook Count Circuit judgeship."

"What's that have to do with you?"

"Jack, even though it's distant, it's family. Seymour says he needs my help. With a donation to his faltering campaign."

Doyle said, "Will you do it?"

"For Leah's family's sake, a donation to Seymour's cause has been made."

Doyle said, "Why would you back this guy you describe as a loser? Just out of loyalty to Leah and her relatives?"

"Haven't you ever done anything like that, Jack?"

"Not willingly."

Moe sat back in the booth. "Actually," he said, "I would have given Seymour the schmuck a boost just because of his campaign slogan. I'm sure he didn't come up with it. Doesn't matter who did." He finished off his Negroni, signaled for another.

Doyle said. "What is Seymour Korshak's campaign slogan?"

"Put a Mensch on the Bench."

Jack laughed. "That's great. If Seymour is such a nothing, who came up with that?"

"Probably his nephew. Myron Goldstein. Very, very sharp young guy. He's made a fortune on the Internet."

"Doing what?"

Moe said, "Young Myron created a dating service to be used on computers. He located what he described to me as a 'niche market.' He was looking for some seed money. I listened to his pitch. I was impressed. The kid knows what he's doing."

"So, you invested?"

"Damn right. I've got twenty percent of Myron's action. And it's paying off very nicely."

Doyle said, "Moe, you've got your fingers in so many pies I can hardly keep track of you. I'm curious. What is Myron Goldstein's genius Internet business?"

"Jack, it's a discreet, on-line dating service. He's got subscribers from temples all over America. The enlistees are all carefully vetted by Myron and his growing staff of young, sharp people. You have to pay to belong. Myron's subscriber list bumps up every month. It's going gangbusters."

Doyle reached for a breadstick. "If I wanted to check this out, Moe, what would I look for?"

"I don't think you necessarily would, Jack. Although I'm sure I could use my influence with Myron to get you on board." He couldn't keep a straight face. Doyle was irritated. "What the hell is so funny, Moe?"

"Myron's dating/marital marketplace website is called 'The Jew for You.'"

Moe finished his Negroni and called for another refill. He sat back in the booth, smiling. Jack said, "What's so funny now?"

"You know what a boilermaker is, right?"

"Of course. The guys I used to work with during the summers on construction drank them every day after work. Shot of whiskey, glass of tap beer. Sometimes they did it before they started work in the morning. I was too young to go in taverns with them. I waited in the cement truck, eating my hard-boiled egg breakfast, while they prepped themselves for ten hours under a hot sun. So what?"

"This clever little entrepreneur Myron Goldstein has made quite a splash for himself on his website while promoting the value of what he terms 'the Hebrew Boilermaker.' This has created some controversy. Which, of course, Myron delights in. The kid's got a good sense of humor besides an excellent head for business."

Doyle plucked a breadstick out of the basket. "All right, Moe, you've got me. What the hell is a 'Hebrew boilermaker'?

"A shot of slivovitz washed down with a glass of Mogen David."

◇◇◇

Owner Dino hustled forward to hover over the Kellman booth like an obsequious butterfly, well aware he would be able to write a large number on the Kellman tab once this joyous gathering had eaten and ungathered. Moe, Jack, and Ralph and Tenuta sat on one side of the booth. Across from them were Moe's wife Leah, Rosa Tenuta, and the Sheehan sisters. Mickey said to Moe, "Thank you for giving me the opportunity to ride Plotkin."

Moe said, "You can thank your agent."

Kellman leaned over to whisper to Doyle, "My God, that little girl has a voice like a munchkin from the *Wizard of Oz*."

"Who cares what she sounds like? It's how she rides that counts."

Their drink orders taken, Leah asked her husband, as if she didn't know the answer, "Do you want to order for all of us?"

"My pleasure." Moe looked around the table. "We'll get something for everybody. Family style."

Minutes later from the kitchen came two large platters of fried calamari, three different pasta dishes, and a huge salad bowl. "Meat and chicken come later," Moe announced. He raised his Negroni in a toast. "Here's to Plotkin!"

Doyle went for the calamari, one of his favorite appetizers, dipping it in a horse radish- laden red sauce. He carefully observed the Irish sisters' approach to Italian-American cuisine. Nora took some salad and one small serving of two pasta dishes, pronouncing everything to be delicious. Mickey, meanwhile, was putting away sizeable portions of everything available. Leah said, "Moe, would you watch this girl eat? She's wonderful!" Leah patted Mickey's hand.

Moe said, "Mickey, how do you do it? Eat like that and keep your weight down for riding?"

"I've always been lucky along those lines, Mr. Kellman. Never had a weight problem." She stopped to take a forkful of pasta before saying, "I make 103 every day no matter what I've eaten. And this is wonderful food. We have nothing like this back home."

Nora sighed. "I don't know where Mickey's metabolism comes from. It sure isn't in my genes. Mickey's always been that way. When she ran mini-marathons as a kid in Dun Laoghaire, she'd wind up first at the top runners' table and eat more plates than the embarrassed lads she'd outfinished down on the strand. Me, if I look at a scone, I put on a half a stone."

"But in the right places," Doyle responded. He raised his nearly empty glass of Jameson's and reached across the table to clink it against Nora's wine glass.

Leah Kellman said, "Jack, sit back. Here come the waiters with the chicken Vesuvio and the veal picata."

Her husband nudged Doyle with his knee. Nodding toward Nora, Kellman whispered, "Jack, you never change, you rascal. Trying to romance one of the visiting Micks. Good luck with Miss Nora. She doesn't look like any pushover."

"I've never been interested in pushovers, Moe. What would be the fun in that?"

Chapter Thirteen

Rudy Allgauer, Eric's older brother, watched as his wife Michelle pulled into their driveway, parked, and began to extricate several bags of grocery from the back of their white Kia SUV. Rudy opened the kitchen door and went out to help her. As he reached for the largest bag, he gave her firm little ass an affectionate pat.

Michelle, black hair cut short, trim and fit at thirty-four, had spent a good deal of her adult life in pursuit of eternal good health. She jogged on a regular basis, was a Pilates enthusiast, a fan of acupuncture, cranial massages, colonic irrigation and, most recently, the addition of Chinese herbs to her vegan diet. That's what sent her into Chicago's Chinatown once every month to purchase supplies. She'd just returned from the city. As she had told Rudy, "These herbs really work for me."

Rudy did not complain. His horse-training business at Heartland Downs had gone from weak to dismal in the last half-year. But his sex life with Michelle was in the highest, finest gear he'd ever known. Maybe it was the herbs. Maybe it was because that was the only satisfaction he'd been experiencing lately.

That day at the track, Rudy had started two members of his seriously depleted stable. As he held the kitchen door for her, Michelle said, "How'd they do?"

"All they got was exercise. I'm in the slump of slumps."

"C'mon in the house, hon. I'll blend us some margaritas. She hefted two sizeable bags.

Rudy said, "I'm going to pass on drinks today."

"Why?"

"Saw brother Eric today. Depressing. He's acting more and more like the alky I think he's become. Runs in our family. I want that run to stop with me."

"But you don't drink much. Heck, nothing like Eric. Or your father, for that matter. What are you worried about?"

He closed the screen door and placed the heaviest brown bag on the counter. He said, "I'm worried because I think it's in the Allgauer genes. Our old man's a secret alky. Eric looks to me like he's following in those destructive footsteps. I don't want to go there, you know? Anyway, I've got other worries on the front burner right now. My top groom quit on me 'cause she was offered more money from Buck Norman. Hell, I can't blame Inez. She's a single mom with three kids to support. Still, it's another fucking blow. Ain't been a good summer, babe."

Rudy, the elder by four years of the Allgauer brothers, had not preceded Eric to college. Coming out of high school, Rudy went directly to work on the backstretch of Heartland Downs. He'd ridden show horses as a kid, always been intrigued by everything equine. At the track, he began as a hot walker and stall cleaner, advanced to groom, then assistant trainer to an aged curmudgeon named J. Paul Maslin. He worked for Maslin, doing most of the heavy lifting, for eighteen months before starting his own stable with horses mostly owned by people his veterinarian father had recommended. Rudy's first couple of years had gone great. The last two had been an increasingly slippery slope involving horses breaking down, owners pulling back having been caught up in the nation's financial descent, and the horses that remained in his care performing the far side of poorly.

Had it not been for the popular yoga classes Michelle conducted in their carpeted, mirrored, aromatic basement, this branch of the Allgauer family would be closing in on foodstamps and foreclosure.

Michelle said to him last weekend, "What about asking your Dad for some help here? He's got the money. You could tell him it's, like, temporary. A loan to help us through here. Hell, he's sitting on a pile of money."

"Forget it. I wouldn't give him the satisfaction. He's always had in the back of his mind that I would fuck up somehow. I'm not going to provide proof. Brother Eric's his golden boy," Rudy laughed. "Not me."

"Why are you laughing like that? What's funny about Eric?"

Rudy wiped his hand over his face, shaking his head. "I don't know why I said that. It's not a laughing matter. Eric, for years under the old man's thumb, finally rebelled against the famous Dr. Allgauer. But he has not rebelled against the booze. He's having a tough time with that. Losing Ingrid, losing most of his practice. Losing himself. I know that. I shouldn't be knocking him."

Michelle said, "Explain that to me after I start dinner. I've got a Wolfgang Puck frozen thin-crust pizza. That okay?"

"Not a speck of meat on it I suppose. Aw, sure, what the hell. I'll make a salad."

Michelle preheated the oven. Finished off the first half of her margarita. Leaned back against the counter, arms crossed, inquisitive.

"Rudy, what happened with Eric and Ingrid? Last time we saw them they looked to me to be very happy."

Rudy said, "That was weeks ago. I understand things have changed, mainly because of Eric's drinking. Guys I know at the track talk about Eric's drinking. But Ingrid, she's on the way up. Everybody seems to like her and her work. I don't know, I just think my brother is not taking that very well. I said to him the other morning, 'Man, you want to talk to me about what's going on?' He just turned away from me.

"I'm worried about him. And," Rudy added, "I'm worried about me and my training business." He walked to the refrigerator. "Maybe I will have a beer with dinner. Is that what Wolfgang Puck suggests for an accompaniment to his premier pizza?"

"Very funny."

Rudy reached into fridge. "A can of Old Style. Perfect." Michelle laughed and nudged him in the side as she carried the pizza to the cutting board. He put his beer down. Finished cutting up vegetables for the salad.

Michelle, after downing her fourth pizza slice, said, "A funny thing happened in Chinatown today. Well, maybe not funny. But interesting."

"What was that?"

"The herb place that I go to in Chinatown? I've told you about it. The man who runs it is Fred Yao Ming. Very nice old guy. Anyway, today when I was checking out at the counter, my Heartland Downs entrance pass slipped out of my wallet. He picked it up and handed it to me. He asked if I went to the racetrack. Sure, I said, my husband Rudy is in the business. He's a trainer.

"Mr. Ming smiled. He said there was another 'horse racing man,' that's what he called him, who came to his store regularly. 'Very good customer,' he said. 'Big shot trainer.'

"Naturally, I said, 'What is that trainer's name. Mr. Ming said, 'All I know is last name. Johnson. Mr. Johnson.'

"I said, 'Well, sure, I think I know who that is. Noel Johnson. He's the top trainer at Monee Park, where my husband sometimes sends horses to run. What a coincidence.'"

Michelle pushed her empty pizza plate aside and gestured to Rudy to hand her the salad bowl. No response. When she looked up, Rudy was up out of his chair, face as crimson as the red peppers in the salad. She was stunned. "What is wrong with you?" she said.

Rudy's put his hands on the table, glaring at his wife. He said, "Well?"

"Well, what? You look like you're ready to explode."

"Did you ask your Chink buddy what that son of a bitch Noel Johnson buys from him? To give to his horses?"

Michelle dropped her head. "I didn't think of doing that, Rudy. I'm sorry. I guess I should've."

Chapter Fourteen

"Jack, c'mon out and take a look at this," Tenuta said from his office doorway. Doyle was seated at the trainer's desk, poring over the new Heartland Downs condition book in search of possible mounts for Mickey.

"What's up, Ralph? I'm busy."

"Just get your ass out there and take a look."

Doyle grabbed his coffee cup and walked outside. Seven-forty on a bright, cool, June morning at Heartland Downs. Tenuta impatiently waved him forward. Walking ahead of the trainer was veterinarian Ingrid McGuire. Assistant trainer Paul Albano held a shank on the brown horse Frank's Fantasy. Ingrid, a look of delight on her tanned face, clapped appreciatively as Frank's Fantasy neighed and stomped his left forefoot on the ground.

"So what's going on?" Doyle said.

Tenuta said, "Jack, you remember how sullen and cross this son of a gun was before Ingrid started working with him? Frank's Fantasy wouldn't run, he'd hardly eat. Then, through Ingrid's communicating, she found out that Frank's Fantasy was in a funk because he missed that gelding Mister Twaggs who got claimed away. He and Frank were big buddies."

Albano offered, "This horse was such a pain in the as you had to pay grooms extra to deal with him. That was before Dr. McGuire started working with him."

"I'm telling you, Jack," Albano continued, "Frank's Fantasy had turned so mean spirited he reminded me of one of the first guys I worked with when I came on the racetrack. Old Jason Fennimore. Good horseman, but just a miserable s.o.b. Somebody said once that when Jason Fennimore died, they'd have to *hire* pallbearers."

Albano turned the compliant Frank's Fantasy in a small circle.

"What's Paul doing with this horse?" Doyle said.

Ingrid laughed. Her sun glasses were in the breast pocket of her denim shirt. Doyle was relieved to see that most traces of the Eric Allgauer-produced black eye had disappeared from her pretty face. "Paul will show you."

"Mickey worked Frank's Fantasy first thing this morning," Albano said. "Said he went great. He came back and got hot walked and cooled out. Went about it real nice, not like before Dr. Ingrid started working with him."

Tenuta said, "Frank's Fantasy has enlarged ankles. Not uncommon among racehorses. I hose those ankles down every morning with cold water. That's what the great trainer Frank Whiteley did with the great gelding Forego. Mr. Whiteley would spend an hour every morning doing that while Forego grazed on the patch of grass next to their barn. It sure as hell worked. Forego was Horse of the Year five times."

Jack fielded a cell phone call from trainer Buck Norman. "Saturday's second race on your horse for Mickey? Great. Thanks." He heard Tenuta say, "Paul, stop him there. We'll show Jack what we're talking about. Believe me, he won't ever see this too many places," Tenuta grinned.

Doyle shaded his eyes from the advancing sunlight. He watched as Frank's Fantasy moved in docile circles at the end of Albano's shank. He nudged Ingrid. "Are you communicating with this horse right now?"

"No. That's been done earlier this morning. Just watch."

Albano stroked Frank's Fantasy's neck as Tenuta picked up the hose. He sprayed the horses' ankles for a minute, Frank's

Fantasy standing stock still, head turned to the sky, luxuriating in the water treatment and the attention.

Albano held Frank's Fantasy's head. Tenuta took the stream of water off the horse's ankles. Lifted up the nozzle. Frank's Fantasy eagerly thrust his head forward and got the end of the hose in his mouth. Water shot up in the air. Then he aimed the spray directly at where Ingrid and Jack were standing.

They jumped back, Ingrid the quicker. Knowing what was coming, she ducked behind the surprised Doyle whose shirt and trousers were now soaked.

Frank's Fantasy let loose with a triumphant neigh while still maintaining control of the nozzle.

Tenuta and Albano bent over laughing at the look on Doyle's face. Frank's Fantasy shook his head back and forth creating a moist patch of ground at Doyle's feet. The horse abruptly dropped the hose and turned to look toward his stall. Show over. He waited for Albano to lead him back into his home place.

Walking back to Tenuta's office, Doyle said, "Ingrid, how can this kind of thing happen with a racehorse? I've seen videos of horse being taught to count, to maneuver any which way their riders want. Barrel racing, cutting horses, horses used for calf roping. Amazing stuff. But those are not highly bred thoroughbreds. How did you get Frank's Fantasy to come around the way you have? "

"What I've tried to do, Jack, is think about their lives from their angle." She shrugged, looked away. "I tried to go into this with Eric when we were together. He just dismissed my approach. I suspect he saw the value of it. But, because it was *me* and not him that came up with this, he spurned it. Very disappointing.

"My thinking was, and is, that what we are dealing with here on the racetrack backstretches today are thousands of genetically created descendants of herd animals. Our racehorses find themselves confined to stalls for twenty-two, twenty-three hours a day. Mother Nature made horses to be nomadic. Foragers. Social. That's been pretty much bred out of them."

She took a call on her cell phone. "Tell Buck I'll get to his horse by ten at the latest." Ingrid looked at Doyle, expecting him to say something. "Go on. Enlighten me."

"Let me sum it up for you, Jack. Through communicating I am able to tap into what's going on in some of their minds. By no means all of them. Some never respond. Others, well…yes. And that is very exciting and rewarding for me."

Ingrid got up, stretched, checked her watch, and smiled at Doyle.

"Pretty interesting morning, eh, Jack? You'd better get out of those wet clothes."

Chapter Fifteen

All the early morning fun of that June morning with the newly amicable and mischievous Frank's Fantasy was obliterated by a development in Heartland Downs' eighth race that afternoon. *Racing Daily* reported it this way the following day:

> Veteran jockey Wilfredo Gavidia was seriously injured in a riding accident at Heartland Downs yesterday afternoon.
>
> Gavidia was aboard Connie Can Do, the favorite in the eighth race, a mile and one-eighth event for fillies and mares on the turf course. Just after Connie Can Do entered the stretch three lengths behind the tiring leader, Gavidia guided her toward an opening next to the rail. At the same time, the horse running second, Loud Gina, under Billy Brinkley, swerved to the left aiming at the same hole. Loud Gina got there first. Despite Gavidia's efforts to haul back on the reins of Connie Can Do, the filly clipped heels with Loud Gina, and went down, throwing Gavidia heavily to the turf.
>
> Gavidia was taken by ambulance to nearby Holy Family Hospital. He underwent emergency surgery last night to fuse vertebrae in his spine. His wife Juanita said that the prognosis was "not encouraging." Her husband, it is feared, will be permanently paralyzed from the breast bone down.
>
> Count on Connie, suffered irreparable leg injuries in the fall and was humanely put down by a track veterinarian.

Gavidia, forty-two, is a native of Panama. He came to the US as a teenager and soon thereafter began his riding career in Florida. He has ridden some 2,700 winners. A long-time officer of the Jockeys' Union, he is one of the most respected leaders of that national organization. Pat McCarron, Union national president, said "Our prayers are with Wilfred, Juanita, and their three children."

Doyle read the *Racing Daily* story about Gavidia in his car after he'd stopped to buy the paper in the Heartland Downs track kitchen. "Damn," he said after he'd finished. He got out of his Accord and walked to Tenuta's office. Mickey Sheehan was already there, sitting on a downturned feed bucket near the door, her head in her hands. She looked up when she heard Doyle say, "Mickey."

Tear tracks were evident on her earnest, freckled face. "Jaysus, Jack, this thing with Wilfredo is a crusher. I don't know if I want to ride today."

He patted her on the shoulder. "Hey, kid, I could hardly blame you if you didn't want to."

Mickey gave him a fierce stare. "You don't think it's about fear, do you? I hope not." She took a deep breath. "It's about respect."

She jumped up off the bucket, which loudly overturned, and walked to the nearby first stall in the barn. "Plotkin," Doyle could hear her say, "how are you today, my friend?"

Plotkin eagerly poked his head out over the stall door. Mickey reached up and put her arms around his neck. Doyle could see her shaking with sobs. He stood still. Tenuta came out of his office, concerned. Doyle waved him back inside. Mickey gave Plotkin a final pat on the neck and walked back to Doyle.

"Jack, this is not about fear, me riding today or not. I'm sorry I was so angry with you. What I'm feeling today is all about Wilfredo." Mickey turned away to snuffle up another bit of weeping. Turned her head back to Doyle. Wiped her nose on the sleeve of her gray tee-shirt. "You're a patient sort, Jack."

"That's me all over."

Mickey turned the bucket upside-down again and sat down. She said, "Wilfredo is a great person. From the time I walked into the riders' room here, when nobody knew me, he was right away very nice to me. He told me where to go to get things I needed—a valet, a locker and bench, towels, so on. The other lads were cool, but distant. Wilfredo encouraged me to think I could do well here. Later, he introduced me to his wife and family and we've had dinners together.

"When I say other riders were cool to me, and that most of them under Wilfredo's leadership were at least respectful, that doesn't mean there weren't a few arseholes riding here. Men who hate the idea of a girl rider competing with them. Especially one from out of their country.

"Wilfredo never saw it that way. The first week I rode here, I'd be walking from the jocks' room to the paddock, and he would make it a point to come and walk beside me. Protective, like, you know? And encouraging after the races. He'd point out what I'd done wrong, or could do better. Made me think.

"The second race I rode in here," Mickey continued, "was for Ralph Tenuta. My horse won by a nose. Who do you think I beat in that photo finish? Wilfredo. When we were galloping out past the finish line, Wilfredo pulled up alongside of me and gave me a high five. I'll never forget that."

An announcement boomed over the track's backstretch public address system, the racing secretary's office declaring that entries were "About to close for Saturday's program."

Mickey stood up. "What I said before, about you taking me off my mounts today? Forget it. I'll ride today, Jack. Wilfredo would want me to."

That evening, driving home, Doyle thought of his client and said to himself, "What a tough little item is Mickey Sheehan."

She'd won three races that afternoon, leaping into fifth place in the Heartland Downs jockey standings.

He dialed Moe Kellman on his cell phone.

"Guess what our little leprechaun did today?" Doyle said.

Chapter Sixteen

Doyle and Tenuta sat on the bench outside the trainer's office the next afternoon. None of Ralph's trainees were running that day. Mickey had no mounts that day. She'd gone with Nora into Chicago to see the Michigan Avenue sites and the famous Bean in Millenium Park and do some shopping. All in an attempt to get their minds off Wilfredo Gavidia's condition.

Gavidia's physicians had concluded that their patient would be paralyzed from the waist down and wheelchair-bound for the rest of his life. Tenuta said, "Just like Ronnie Turcotte, who rode Secretariat. Turcotte has carried on pretty damn well. I hope Wilfredo can do the same."

Doyle said, "We should go to that fund-raising dinner they're having for Wilfredo in a couple of weeks. Should I buy us a table? I know Mickey would want to go. Probably Nora, too."

"I've already called us in and made the reservation. Lady running it said they were getting a great response."

"What do I owe you for, well, us. Me and Mickey and Nora. How much are the tickets?"

Tenuta said, "Seventy-five apiece. But this is on me, Jack."

Doyle took a call on his cell phone from Steve Holland, who said he wanted Mickey to ride his entry in the fourth race Sunday. "You've got her. Thanks, Steve. And good luck."

"Every once in awhile," Doyle said to Tenuta, "I think about what these riders do. It amazes me. Danger has to be in their minds. But they seem to ignore it."

"Jack, I've been around jockeys for more than thirty years. The ones that make a living riding don't let fear come into focus. It's the way they are. One of the older riders told me once that some people wonder which part of the racetrack is the most dangerous. He said, 'You can get hurt anywhere.' And that's the truth.

"Jocks have been killed in the starting gate when their mounts leaped up backwards and crashed their heads into the iron. That's how the great Alvaro Pineda died years ago in California. He was a friend of mine."

Tenuta paused, looking across the yard to where a horse was being carefully washed by a female groom as Ingrid McGuire looked on. Ingrid waved at Doyle and Tenuta.

"You heard about the fund-raiser for Wilfredo?" Tenuta called to Ingrid."You going?"

"Sure am." Then she turned her attention back to the nervous black filly she was dealing with. Doyle and Tenuta watched as she smoothed a hand down the filly's neck, calming her. The filly stopped squirming and stood still. Ingrid leaned close to the filly's left ear. After five minutes, Ingrid grinned and gave the now relaxed filly a slap on her rump as her groom started to lead her back to her stall.

"Man, I wish I knew how to do that, Jack," the trainer said.

"What do you mean?"

"I'm talking about that black filly of Buck Norman's that was over there. I've seen her act up crazy, throwing a fit morning after morning. Buck didn't know what the hell to do with her. Then I told Buck, 'Try Ingrid.' He did. Buck has been mighty damn grateful ever since. That filly won a race last Wednesday like breaking sticks. She's probably worth three times this morning what she was three weeks ago. You can thank Ingrid's work for that."

Chapter Seventeen

"That bitch. She's ruined me."

Eric Allgauer pounded one of his large fists against a wall in his brother Rudy's office on the Heartland Downs backstretch. "I can't believe this is happening to me."

Rudy said, "Eric, c'mon, calm down. Sit down. I think your knuckles are bleeding. What the hell's wrong with you? You look like shit. You haven't shaved. You're behind in your showering. I've never seen you like this, my brother. Damn!"

Eric wiped the blood from his hand onto his tee-shirt. He took a deep breath. Walked to one of the chairs in front of Rudy's desk and sat down, put his head in his hands. "She's ruining me," he muttered.

Over their years, Rudy had listened to many of his brother's tirades. Used to happen often when they shared their bedroom in the Allgauer's home. Eric would get lit up with some slight he thought he'd had from a chemistry teacher. From a bad interference call against him on their high school's vaunted football team. From losing that school's vice presidency of the senior class by less than a dozen votes to an opponent he derided as "that little nerd shit."

But, Rudy thought, in those days his brother would become angry, try and usually fail to get even, but always bounce back fairly quickly. Eric had graduated from high school with honors, six varsity athletic letters, gone off to vet school at the University of Illinois on partial academic scholarship, and thrived.

Rudy said, "Eric, you've gotten a bad deal from those trainers who dropped you. Ralph Tenuta. Buck Norman. A bunch of others. But you can't just blame all that on Ingrid. Let's be honest. You've been drinking too much, my brother. The word got all around the racetrack. You've been screwing up. Now, you've got to find a way back."

"And like you're doing so great?" Eric snarled.

Rudy said, "Believe me, I'm not saying that. I haven't saddled a winner in three weeks. I don't have very good stock here. You know that. I've never sunk so low before this season. I need help."

Eric looked appraisingly at his older sibling. "What kind of help?"

"I've got a horse going Friday that I need, I mean *need*, to win with. Friar Tuckie. Owned by one of the few remaining loyal owners I have, Mac Doherty. He's shown a lot of patience with me. But I can tell by talking to him, his patience is about to run out."

Eric said, "Is Friar Tuckie any good? Can he run?"

"Yeah, he's got some talent. Just not enough to win an allowance race."

"Why the hell don't you drop him down into a claimer?"

Rudy said, "Because the owner, Mac Doherty, won't let me. He named this horse after some old asshole buddy of his from college. He ordered me never to risk Friar Tuckie being claimed away from him."

Eric got up and went to the refrigerator behind Rudy's desk. "You got any beer in here? I didn't think so." He snatched out a can of ginger ale.

"What do you think, Eric? Have you got something that'll help this son of a bitch run faster?"

"Yes. I know of something new around here. It's called erythropoietin. It works to boost endurance."

Rudy said, "Say what?"

"EPO is what it's usually called. It's a blood doping agent. It boosts the number of red blood cells. Just like in humans, a horse's muscles need oxygen for fuel. Because red blood cells carry oxygen from the lungs to the horse's muscles, more red blood cells help the horse run faster. A higher red blood cell count equals more oxygen equals more muscle energy. Makes them run harder, faster, longer. It can impressively increase endurance. It's a very powerful performance enhancer. I've talked to a couple of guys who have used it. They swear by it."

"Shit," Rudy said, "I've never heard about this stuff. What do you do? Give it to the horse in its feed?"

Eric laughed. "No, Rudy, no. It has to be administered with a needle. Into the jugular vein. Horses are used to that procedure. When their blood work is taken to be checked, it's by means of a needle in the jugular. Don't worry. This magic stuff won't harm the horse. Just make him go faster."

"Do you need me to help you do this, Eric?"

"Hell, no. I'm a trained vet, remember? You know," Eric continued, "most vets, like ninety percent of the world's people, are right-handed. So they always use the jugular vein on the left side of the horse's neck. As you know, I'm left-handed. I'll use the other side of your horse's neck. Yeah, I know I have to be careful. Occasionally, the vein gets punctured and the horse can develop an infection. Not with me. I know what I'm doing. Not to worry, bro."

Rudy sat back in his chair, thoughtful, nervously twirling a pencil in his hand. He thought about Michelle's report of "Mr. Johnson" and the Chinese herbs. Coupled with that memory was one of his diminishing bank account and escalating late bill payments.

"Christ, I don't know Eric. I guess I'll have to have you try this. Can you fix Friar Tuckie up before his race next week?"

"No problem."

Rudy said, "Where do you get this stuff?"

"You don't need to know, Rudy. Let's just wait and watch it work its magic."

"Wait," Rudy said, "how about it being detected? What are the chances of that? Jesus, that's all I'd need, a drug-positive coming back on one of my horses."

"Chances of it being detected?" Eric laughed. "Just about nil. The testing labs aren't onto this stuff yet. You wait," Eric grinned, "you'll see Friar Tuckie flying to the wire when you send him out there next time."

Eric picked up his jacket and moved toward the door. "You know, Rudy, I've got something else that lights these horses up. It's called elephant juice. A *real* performance enhancer as they say."

"I don't get it, Eric. If it's so effective, why wouldn't you use this elephant juice on Friar Tuckie? Instead of that blood doping stuff?"

Eric said, "Because I don't want to use something on a horse of yours that would be detected by the state testing lab. And I'm damn sure the EPO won't be."

Chapter Eighteen

In his column of June 28, *Racing Daily's* Heartland Downs correspondent Ira Kaplan wrote:

> *"Injured jockey Wilfredo Gavidia has been transferred from Holy Family Hospital to the Chicago Rehabilitation Institute where he will undergo further treatment and begin a program of physical therapy.*
>
> *Gavidia's fellow riders and friends have planned a fundraising dinner for him. Heartland Downs director of relations Joan Colby said the date, time, and other details would be announced later this week.*
>
> *In other news today, Mrs. Ralph Tenuta's promising juvenile colt Plotkin will be traveling to Saratoga Race Course next weekend to compete in the historic Sanford Stakes. Plotkin's regular rider, young Irish jockey Mickey Sheehan, told* Racing Daily *that any earnings Plotkin might accrue from the purse of the race would be donated to the Wilfredo Gavidia Fund. Her jockey fee, too. "These are wonderful and generous people who own this horse," she said. "I'm praying we can do well in that big race."*

Mickey was across the aisle from Doyle, wide-eyed and excited as she settled into her seat in the first-class section of American Airlines Flight 1498 from Chicago's O'Hare to Albany, New York.

Nora sat next to her in the window seat. To Doyle's right was Moe Kellman, engrossed in that morning's copy of the *New York Times*, the little man comfortably settled in and buckled up in his window seat. In the row immediately behind these two sat Ralph Tenuta, obviously unnerved. As they had shuffled their tedious way through O'Hare Airport security, shoes and belts off, and on, Tenuta confided to Doyle his fierce fear of flying. "I've never understood how it works," Tenuta said as they sat in adjacent chairs, re-tying their shoe laces. "You're in this giant machine that goes up into the sky? What keeps it there?"

Doyle looked back over his first-class seat at the trainer's worried face. "Ralph, have a little glass of wine. Here comes the stewardess. Sit back, try to relax. Just put your mind on Plotkin's race Saturday."

Tenuta thanked the stewardess and took a gulp of his merlot. He tapped Doyle on the shoulder. "I don't know if this is going to put my mind at ease, Jack. I'm not sure we've done the right thing here."

Kellman put down his paper and took off his glasses. He reached around between the seats to pat Tenuta's trembling leg. "Ralph. This will all work out. One way or the other, we're going to have some fun. Relax. Enjoy."

As he picked up the newspaper Kellman said to Doyle, "You'd think this story would be in a supermarket tabloid, not the *Times*. You can't make up some of this stuff."

"Like what?" Doyle answered. He was ready to put his seat back after takeoff and take a nap. He'd been awake for hours helping to implement this excursion by Chicagoans to Saratoga.

Kellman said, "There's this guy in Russia they re-elected as head of the World Chess Federation."

"So? The Russians have always been big in chess, right?"

"Yeah, but this guy obviously had kind of different qualifications. He claims, according to the *Times* story, that he had been abducted by space aliens. That he'd later met with extraterrestrials wearing yellow space suits. In his Moscow apartment. That they convinced him chess comes from outer space." Kellman turned to look out his window. Said, "Hello out there."

Finally in the takeoff runway, American Airlines Flight 1498 roared down the tarmac and sliced into the sky. Doyle turned to give Tenuta a reassuring look. The trainer's hands gripped the arms of his seat. His eyes were closed, lips moving. "May the power of prayer help you out, my friend," Doyle murmured.

Doyle looked across the aisle at the Sheehan sisters. They were chatting about the upcoming on-flight movie choices, perfectly at ease.

"This Russian chess leader," Doyle said to Kellman.

"What about him?"

"Maybe he could launch his version of our Tea Party movement over there. Sounds like he's qualified."

He heard Moe chuckle as he moved his seat back and closed his eyes.

◇◇◇

After the amazing Plotkin, a fifty-grand purchase, won his first three starts, the latest a small stakes race called the Heartland Downs Juvenile, a member of the racing department at famed Saratoga Race Course left a message on Ralph Tenuta's office voice mail encouraging him to enter Plotkin in one of his track's upcoming big races for two-year-olds at his track. As Tenuta later related to Doyle, "I thought it was a joke. Being pulled off by one of my trainer friends here. I just kind of laughed it off.

"But this nice guy in the Saratoga office convinced me he was serious. That's when I mentioned it to you, Jack. Hell, I've never taken a horse to Saratoga. But then you talked it over with Moe. You told me Moe said, 'Life is short. Let's take a shot.'"

A quarter-hour or so after liftoff, Tenuta finally began to relax a little. He glanced around first-class. There appeared to be one other racetracker on hand, an intense, thirtyish man making multicolored notations in the margins of his *Racing Daily* past performance section. He wore a long-sleeved blue tee-shirt. The white writing on its back declared "The Maven Knows."

Tenuta smiled as he saw the Sheehan sisters discussing the luncheon menu card. All of them, co-owner Doyle and Plotkin's jockey, her sister, Plotkin's trainer, were riding this magic carpet to New York courtesy of Moe Kellman. "If we're going," he'd announced to Doyle, "we're fucking going in style."

En route to upstate New York in less glamorous fashion had been Plotkin, his departure two days earlier from Heartland Downs in a van from the Botzau Horse Transport Company. He'd walked up the ramp and into his stall like a seasoned traveler. Plotkin's lone companion was Tenuta's trusted groom Paul Albano. Paul had never been to this centerpiece of America's summer racing. He was asexcited as he'd ever been during his decades as a worker in the thoroughbred business.

Van company owner and driver Tom Botzau had carefully planned their journey. He pulled off the interstate the east side of Cleveland late the first afternoon into the back portion of a huge rest stop. Albano led Plotkin down the van ramp and into a nearby wooded area. Plotkin obligingly pissed powerfully into the weeds, shook his head, and looked for food. Paul gave him a half-bucket of honey-flavored oats. The oats went quickly.

By the time driver Botzau returned from the rest stop men's room, a small crowd of children had gathered around Plotkin. Their parents, munching candy bars and chips and sipping sodas from the rest-stop vending machines, looked on.

Paul said, "Folks, please stand back aways. This is a racehorse. He's not a pet." He led the docile Plotkin up the ramp to his stall and closed the van's back door.

Botzau turned from the driver's seat. "All set back, there, Paul?"

"Ready to go, Tom."

Botzau eased his truck and attached van up the exit path to the Interstate. He smiled into his mirror.

"You colt is a pretty damn good traveler."

They drove straight through, eighteen hours, more than 800 miles to Saratoga Springs, making a few more rest stops along the way. Plotkin nodded off a few times in his stall, Albano and driver Botzau not at all.

The Botzau van pulled up at the Saratoga Race Course back stable gate just before dawn on Friday. Botzau had to blink his lights to get the guard's attention. He showed the man their entrance papers and was directed to the stakes horse barn. Botzau had never been to Saratoga either. He very carefully drove down the still darkened gravel driveway.

Albano led Plotkin down the van ramp. Waited while the colt looked at his new surroundings and inhaled the new morning air. Following the guard's directions, Albano led Plotkin into his well prepared stall—hay on the floor, water in a bucket.

Botzau waited and watched. Dawn began to peek over the old track's eastern fringe of trees.

Chapter Nineteen

The white stretch limo Kellman hired was waiting for them at the Albany airport. The drive north to Saratoga Springs took less than an hour. Robert Karnes, the limo driver, engaged Doyle, who was in the front passenger seat, in conversation. Where was this party from? Who were they? What was their business in Saratoga Springs?

"Jesus," Doyle said good naturedly, "you are a nosey bastard, Robert." Karnes was impressed as Doyle told him of their connections to a horse that was one of the runners in the next day's Sanford Stakes.

But Karnes' eyebrows went up when heard the name. "Plotkin?" he said. "Never heard of him."

"You have. And you will," Doyle said.

Karnes efficiently delivered them to their downtown Saratoga Springs hotel. Kellman tipped the driver generously and asked him to return at six o'clock to take them to dinner at the famed restaurant adjacent to the racetrack. "That's a big deal, Mr. Kellman," Karnes said. "I guess you've got reservations?"

"Oh, yes," Kellman answered. "I have a good friend who knows the owners."

◇◇◇

The Kellman party of five was led to a table immediately after arrival. It was near the kitchen doors. Moe motioned to everyone not to sit down, to wait. The Sheehan sisters shrugged and looked around the jam-packed restaurant. Moe had a brief conversation with the maitre d'. Currency from the Kellman rubber-banded bankroll was offered, accepted, and swiftly tucked away. The maitre d', a veteran of the restaurant placement campaigns, led them to a table in the center of the large room. He pulled out chairs for the Sheehan sisters and left, smiling.

"How do people talk in here?" Doyle said to Moe. He had to learn forward and speak into his friend's ear to be heard. "Christ, there's more yapping going on in here than at the Westminister Dog Show."

"Jack, Jack, relax. Look around you. This is the cream of Eastern horse racing society on hand here tonight. Some well known owners from the Midwest and West Coast, too. It's good to check out the opposition once in awhile."

Drink orders taken, they listened to a dramatic three-minute recital of "tonight's specialties" from their young spike-haired waiter, who identified himself as Bruce.

Doyle sat back in his chair. To his right was the redoubtable furrier. Across the linen-covered table, the Sheehan girls. To his left, Ralph Tenuta, so relieved not to be airborne he actually seemed to be somewhat at ease, maybe even about to perhaps enjoy himself.

Mickey gasped when on the menu she read rack of lamb listed at 54 dollars. Nora was examining the choices and their stated values with similar wonderment.

Moe leaned forward. "Listen, my friends. Don't be put off by these ridiculous prices. You could probably get everything on the menu at half-price once the Saratoga racing season is over. But, we're here to do here what they do. Order whatever you want. I'm covering it." He raised his cocktail glass of Negroni to them.

"Whatever you order," he assured them, "it'll be good. Enjoy."

Doyle said, "I read a newspaper story about this place a couple of weeks ago. One of the owners was quoted as saying, 'Our vegetables were in the ground this morning, the fish were in the water yesterday.'"

"I think that's probably true, Jack," Moe said.

"I assume you've been here before?"

"I've been here and a lot of other places like it before." Moe raised his glass. "*Salud*, Jack."

Doyle passed the basket of rolls and bread sticks around the table. He said to his employer, "Mickey, what looks good to you on the menu?"

"Jaysus, Jack, just about everything." She took a sip of her club soda and whispered to her sister, "What are you having?"

Nora said, "I'll be having what's called here 'the Cassel Farms Rack of Lamb.' Courtesy of Mr. Kellman. Imagine, at that price they must hold it quite dear." She saluted Moe with her wine glass.

"Well, I'll have that, too," Mickey said. Putting her menu down on the table, she looked around the large room. "I don't believe I see another rider here," she murmured. The restaurant was replete with men wearing expensive blazers, many of their women chattering from beneath prodigious hats they'd worn to be seen with at the races that afternoon.

Nora smiled at Doyle. "We're a long way from Dun Laoghaire," she said. "This is great, great fun."

As they waited for their entrees, Doyle said, "Ralph, have you figured out how you want Mickey to ride Plotkin tomorrow?"

Tenuta winked across the table at Mickey. "She's going to ride to win."

Irritated, Doyle said, "I'm serious. Have you two come up a strategy of any sort?"

"Strategy can go out the window when the gate opens, Jack. Am I right, Mickey?"

The little jockey said, "You just never know at the start, Jack. You can get banged from the left or bumped from the right. The ground can break out from under your horse when he's leaping forward. Another horse could cut right in front of you without you seeing it coming."

She paused to take another sip of her club soda. Grinning, she said, "That's what makes it so exciting and fun."

"Jack," Tenuta said, "years ago I had an owner named Mary O'Hara Klein. Nice Irish lady married to a major Jewish real estate developer in Chicago. She knew a lot about horse racing, but not enough. Just enough to be dangerous.

"One day, in the paddock at Heartland Downs, Mary walked up to where I was saddling her horse. She was carrying a piece of paper. I tried to see what was on it, but she turned away. She was waiting for her jockey, Billy Hurtack. Good rider, veteran, dependable, I used him all the time. But he had his own way of going about things. Very, very independent guy.

"Anyway, this particular afternoon, Mary steps up to Billy and shows him this paper. It was like a map of how she wanted her horse to be placed, from the start to the finish. She's standing there, pointing at its highpoints, and I can see Billy Hurtack starting to steam. Before I can step into it, Billy yanks the paper, or the race map, out of Mary's hands and tears it to bits and throws it down on the ground. She's amazed. Billy says to Mary, 'This son of a bitch will win or lose the way I ride him.'

"The horse wins. Mary never gave any of her jockeys another map after that."

"Good for Billy Hurtack," Mickey said.

Moe leaned forward, elbows on the table. "An old friend of mine, a horse owner named Ray Freeark, a bigtime personal injury lawyer and a very good customer of mine, also had strong opinions about how he wanted his horses to be ridden. Ralph, you never trained for Ray, did you?"

"Nope. I heard he was a good owner, paid his bills, but was kind of a handful."

Kellman smiled. "Yeah, Ray could be that. He had a pretty good stakes horse named Noble Jack, a gray gelding, one with big ears, wore white blinkers, he looked like a giant running rabbit. One day I'm with Ray at Heartland. Ray's horse, Noble Jack, is in the feature that afternoon.

"Ray loved to bet, and he was good at it. But he was very, very disturbed that Noble Jack had not been ridden in the way Ray wanted him to be ridden in his races. Ray says 'Come with me.' He takes me downstairs and we walk into the paddock. We wait for the saddling to begin.

"The jocks come out of their room and Ray waits and shakes hands with, you're gonna laugh at this Ralph, none other than Billy Hurtack. Ray pulls a $100 bill out of his pocket. Tears it in half. Gives one half to the jockey. Tells him, 'Billy, just do what I say with this horse. Take him back early, wait and wait and wait, then make one run on the outside of horses, down the middle of the track at the sixteenth pole and, win or lose, if you do what I'm telling you to do, you get the other half of this $100 bill. Okay?'

"Billy Hurtack rode Ray's horse exactly the way Ray wanted him ridden. Noble Jack comes down the outside at the sixteenth-pole and wins going away. Pays $14.60. Ray, I knew, had bet a bundle.

"We go down to the winner's circle. Hurtack weighs out and smiles at Ray. Ray reaches over and gives the jock the other half of the $100 bill. Ray says, 'Tuck it in your boot, Billy. Good work'."

Mickey said, "Did your friend use that rider again on that horse?"

"Sure did, honey. Billy Hurtack won five more races that year on Noble Jack."

Bruce the waiter reappeared to ask if they were ready to order. They were.

Three or so furlongs away from the famously expensive restaurant, on the edge of the Saratoga backstretch, Paul Albano took a seat at one of the numerous long picnic tables under the large white tent. He had bedded down Plotkin, safe and sound and happy, in his stall in the nearby stakes barn.

Jose Moran, a groom with a horse in the stall next to Plotkin's, had introduced himself and told Albano "We're all invited to a free dinner tonight. All us backstretch people. That nice lady, Mrs. Whitney who lives up here, she and her husband put this dinner on every year before the Sanford Stakes. It's great. Come along."

Albano said, "Well, thanks. But how do I get into this dinner? I just got here with our one horse."

"You got an ID badge from security, right? That's all you need. Let's go. I'll have my little brother keep an eye on your horse. He was over there early and ate already. It's a big, buffet deal." Moran led Albano down the shed row.

Albano knew the Saratoga stable area housed some 1,800 horses attended to by nearly 2,500 workers, the majority of them Hispanic. At least half of that work force turned out enthusiastically for these free dinners, Moran told him.

Albano followed Jose into the tent and to the buffet line. Jose waved to several diners, already seated, who called out his name. It was a lavish spread. Paul was not a big eater, never had been. He picked up a slice of roast beef, a baked potato, a small scoop of mixed vegetables. Jose preceded him to a table in the far corner. He carried two plates for himself, both full. "How do you like this, Paul?" he smiled as he sat down.

Albano smiled. "I like it fine, Jose. Thanks for telling me about this."

"No problemo, man," Jose said. "Now, Mister Chicago, let me ask again, how do you like your horse in the big race tomorrow? And pass me that salt shaker, *por favor*."

Albano handed the shaker across the table. He said, "Does your owner have a horse in tomorrow's race?"

Jose smiled but kept chewing. He said, "Oh, yes, my friend. Mister Mosely's got a *bueno* colt in there. Called Go Yale Blue. He's started twice and won both times pretty damn easy. He'll be the favorite in that race tomorrow."

"Well," Albano said, "he'd better have his running shoes on. To answer your question, my friend, our horse can run."

Chapter Twenty

Kellman's party had just finished their hors d'oeuvres when a heavy-set middle-aged man approached their table. His face was flushed. His blue blazer was unbuttoned, providing relief to his protruding stomach. His club tie was pulled down from the collar of his white shirt. He stumbled slightly before positioning himself, chubby hands on the table between Moe and Jack. They all looked up at this intruder.

"So, you're the folks from Chicago? Heartland Downs?" he said loudly, slurring his words. "Brought a horse up here named Plankton or something. Some piece of junk from the hinterlands?" He turned his head to insure his party at the adjoining table could hear him. There was a sheen of sweat on his broad forehead.

Doyle rose rapidly to his feet and in the same motion gripped the man hard on his left wrist. "Our horse is named Plotkin. Who the fuck are you?"

Moe stepped in and attempted to pull Doyle back down onto his chair. "Jack, take it easy with this idiot. He'll go away." Doyle remained standing and did not ease up on his grip.

The man's jaw dropped when he heard himself described as an idiot. He shook his head in an attempt to clear it. "I'm Teddy Moseley. I own Go Yale Blue. I suppose the name doesn't mean anything to you hicks. My colt goes tomorrow in the Sanford. Against your horse."

Moe said, "What's your point, Moseley?"

Moseley again glanced back over his shoulder to the table that held his party of eight. They were watching avidly.

"My point, mister, is I think you're out of your league here," Moseley said loudly. "Because your horse was entered in the Sanford, my colt drew badly. Way on the outside. Your horse got a better post position.

"I wish you would have stayed the hell back in Chicago. But," he sneered, "you're not going to get anything here anyway."

Moseley steadied himself by grabbing the back of Tenuta's chair. He made an awkward reach for Ralph's water glass. Tenuta was on his feet now, fists clenched. Doyle moved in front of him. "Ralph, sit down. I'll handle this."

Doyle grabbed Moseley by an elbow and spun him around. "Get your drunken fat ass away from us, pal, or I'll kick you out the door." He shoved the now compliant Moseley toward his table. The maitre d' cautiously approached.

"No, no. Wait a minute," Kellman said. He walked over to Moseley. "You're very sure your horse is better than ours?"

"Goddam right," Moseley mumbled.

Kellman said, "Why don't we make a little bet on that? Man to man. Horse against horse. Plotkin against your Ivy League horse, Go Yale Blue. Elie Elie rah rah. 5,000 bucks. The horse that finishes before the other wins the money. What do you say?"

Moseley, aware that his party had heard this challenge, jerked nervously at his tie. One of his tablemates gave him an affirmative nod. "You're on," Moseley barked.

Kellman smiled. "Good. Looking at the box seat holder tag you're still wearing on that ugly jacket you've got on, I'll know where to find you at the track Saturday. Name tags," Moe said, shaking his head. "You'd think most of you would know each other by now. After all the years together looking down your noses at everybody outside your circle."

Moseley slumped down heavily into his chair, reached for his wine glass, drained it. Two of the women patted his hand supportively. One of the men signaled for the check. Breathing hard, Moseley said to his friends, "You want to come in with me? Bet horse against horse for 5,000? With that little guy over there with the funny head of hair? Looks like a Don King knockoff to me, but he's no afro. Isro, maybe." Moseley thumped the table in appreciation of his own wit. His friends did not respond. "Fine, then," Moseley bellowed, "I'll go it alone against the little sheeny from Chicago."

His wife slapped him on the shoulder. "For God's sake, Teddy, keep your voice down." She looked around the table. "I think we should leave."

Kellman sat down in his chair, well aware of the looks of astonishment on the races of the Sheehan sisters after the confrontation with Moseley. Tenuta grimaced, tense. He picked up his glass of pinot grigio, appearing almost as worried as he had before the American Airlines flight had set down safely at Albany airport.

Moe began grinning the grin Doyle had seen so many times after the little furrier had completed a set of fifty pull-ups in the Fit City gym. Or after he'd sold another expensive coat to his old friend Fifi Bonadio.

Moe gestured across the busy, buzzing room. Most of the patrons had turned their attention from his exchange with Moseley, and Moseley's retreat, back to their dinners. Entertainment over. The maitre d' responded to Moe's wave. At his signal the kitchen doors opened, unleashing a flow of food to the Kellman table. Smiling Bruce directed the placing of the plates by the three tray bearers.

"Go Yale Blue, eh?" Kellman said. "I remember a great comment on that educational pillar of privilege from a terrific novelist named Charles McCarry. He wrote 'All Yale alumni thought they had done everything that could ever be expected of them in life simply by being admitted to Yale.'"

Moe looked over at the table now being vacated by the Moseley party. Shook his head. "Tomorrow should be interesting. Let's eat."

Chapter Twenty-one

One of upstate New York's impressive summer rainstorms thundered out of the Adirondack skies and hit Saratoga Race Course shortly before Saturday's third race. Observing this deluge from their third-floor visiting owners' box, Moe said to Doyle, "What about Plotkin? Can he handle this kind of muddy track?"

"I don't know, Moe. Plotkin has never raced on an off track. But his dam ran some decent races over them." He stood up. "Nora, Moe, I'm going for a beer. You want anything? Sandwich? Peanuts? Popcorn?"

Nora said, "Not right now, Jack, thanks. I'm too nervous to be hungry."

"Are you saying Plotkin's mother was a mudder, Jack?" Mo laughed. "That's good news. Yeah, please, get me a Nathan's hot dog with everything."

Nora said, "I know Mickey has ridden over sodden trails worse than this one, anyway. No worries about her."

"Thank you, Nora, for the confidence booster," Moe said.

Doyle would have liked to consult trainer Tenuta for his views on the track condition. But Ralph was at the barn with Plotkin. And Ralph had never owned a cell phone.

The rain, reduced to a steady downpour, finally ceased one race before the Sanford Stakes, seventh event on the program. Nora was using the binoculars Doyle had brought. "Look at those poor jockeys coming back," she said, "all covered with mud. That must sting terrible hard when that wet dirt hits them in the face."

"All the more reason to be in front from the start," Doyle said. "I'll bet that's what Ralph will tell Mickey to try and do with Plotkin."

The post parade for the Sanford Stakes unfolded following an impressive version of "Call to the Post" by the heavy-set, bearded track bugler dressed in red jacket, black cap, black trousers. He bowed to the appreciative crowd after his last clarion note.

To the cheers of some of the more than 40,000 fans on hand, a rainbow rose in the sky to the south of the track. Some of the riders looked up at it and waved their whips in appreciation. Mickey, Doyle saw, wasn't doing any of that. She was concentrating on getting Plotkin to relax. She never looked up, her attention directed entirely to her lively little mount. Every few strides, Mickey bent over Plotkin's neck, saying something to him. The colorful silks Mickey wore had been selected by Rose Tenuta. They were the colors of Italy's flag.

Moe dumped his hot-dog wrapper in their box's waste container. Said to Jack, "What does asshole Moseley's Yale's horse look like?"

Nora handed Doyle the binoculars. "He looks like a big, tough, son of a bitch. He's warming up great, too. Aw, man." Doyle sat back down.

◇◇◇

The Sanford Stakes was completed in a minute and ten seconds, each of those moments pressurized for Plotkin's people. Nora gripped Jack's left arm so tightly he couldn't wave it to urge on their horse. Moe kept shouting, "C'mon, Mickey. C'mon. Bring him home." Moe was slapping his folded up *Racing Daily* against the railing of their box in rhythm with Plotkin's run. Doyle had never seen Kellman so excited, engaged, demonstrative.

Mickey had hustled Plotkin out of the gate in perfect stride, clearing horses on their inside and getting him quickly over to the rail where he took a three-length lead in the first quarter-mile.

Track announcer Trevor Durkin said, "That is a blazing first quarter, 22 seconds flat, on this kind of muddy track."

Tenuta said, "Mickey's not even pushing on him. She's sitting chilly. Oh, Jack, can they do it?" He had hold of Doyle's right arm. Nora clenched Doyle's left hand.

Plotkin led all the way to the final seventy yards when he was passed by a mud-spattered gray closer named Big Old Lew, losing by a length. Doyle watched closely as Mickey stood up in her stirrups rounding the clubhouse turn after the wire, patting Plotkin on his neck. Plotkin shook his head back and forth, obviously annoyed. The jock on Big Old Lew gave a respectful hand slap to Mickey.

"We came damned close to winning it," Jack said. Nora, hands clenched, kept her eyes on her sister as Mickey galloped Plotkin back to be unsaddled. "They did pretty feckin' good," Nora said.

Tenuta hurried from their box to join Albano down on the track as the groom began to unsaddle Plotkin. Ralph gave Mickey a big thumbs up. Albano's wide smile was very visible from Jack's box.

"Pretty damn good, indeed," Kellman said. "Plotkin ran great. Mickey rode him perfectly." He embraced Nora, then Jack. The little man's face was flushed with excitement. "How about that! We come to Saratoga with a longshot and almost pull it off. Great stuff. Great training by Ralph and great ride from Mickey. Who could ask for anything more?"

"Well, there's more," Doyle said. "Moseley's horse wound up finishing seventh, Moe. That jerk owes you $5,000. Think he'll come down here and pay?"

"No, Moseley won't come himself. He'll send somebody down here with maybe half of what he owes me. That keeps him kosher in the estimation of his pals."

Minutes later a young Moseley minion strolled down the steps to their box, smiled, and handed an envelope to Kellman. "That's for you, sir," he said before quickly retreating.

Kellman ripped open the envelope. He smiled as he looked up after a quick counting. "Half the money here, Jack. Why am

I not surprised? There's also a promise to pay note." Moe ripped up the note and threw it down.

Doyle said, "Wait a minute. Why would you settle for half of what he owes you?"

Kellman folded up his *Racing Daily*, offered his arm to Nora, and led the way out of their box. Over his shoulder, he said to Doyle, "Plotkin ran a terrific race. He earned second-place money of $40,000. And, at eighteen to one, he was a helluva good bet. I bet a thousand across the board. I'll have Ralph cash my tickets tomorrow. I'm not going to sweat the Yale blowhard shorting me. That was not unexpected, believe me."

Doyle laughed. He said to Nora, "I've never known my pal Moe to be so magnanimous. Must be this Saratoga Springs air."

Nora was glowing. "Whatever it is, it's brilliant. I want to hurry down and see Mickey."

"We'll walk over to the backstretch and congratulate Ralph," Kellman said. "And Paul Albano. And, of course, Plotkin."

Doyle said, "Nora, we'll meet you in the parking lot once you collect Mickey. Tell her how much we appreciated her ride on Plotkin. Your little sister is something else."

Doyle and Kellman made their way through the large crowd heading out the gate toward the stable area across Union Avenue where they would find their horse.

They pushed their way past tip sheet sellers claiming "Six Winners Today. Get Tomorrow's Winners Right Here." The ink had hardly dried on some of these recently manufactured spurious offerings. Doyle and Kellman stepped carefully around clumsily moving couples sharing opposite handles of coolers, picnic baskets atop them, neither the female or male bearer looking too happy.

Right before the traffic light changed and the patrol people in charge unleashed the impatient hordes, Kellman felt a tug on the arm of his sport coat. He looked down at a young Hispanic boy holding a small basket containing packages of peanuts.

"*Senor*, only one dollar a bag."

Kellman smiled down at this skinny little salesman. He said, "Can I have a sample?"

"*Si, senor.*" The boy looked up expectantly as he handed Kellman a peanut.

Moe sampled it. He said, "I'll take two bags of these good peanuts." He pulled out a twenty dollar bill. The boy's eyes grew large. "*Senor,*" he said, "I cannot have change for that."

Moe leaned down and folded the bill into to the boy's small hand. "I don't want any change. You keep this money. And take it home to your parents."

He patted the boy on the head. "C'mon," he said to Doyle, "let's go see our horse and our people."

They crossed Union Avenue. Kellman opened the bag of peanuts and offered it to Doyle.

"Pretty good," Doyle said after shelling one and popping the nut into his mouth.

Kellman waved him off when Doyle attempted to hand the bag of peanuts back. "Keep it, Jack."

Doyle said, "What, you don't like peanuts, Moe?"

"Never have. And never liked being poor and hustling when I was a kid like that little guy back there."

Chapter Twenty-two

Eric Allgauer still had access to the Heartland Downs backstretch even though he did not have any clients. As a licensed veterinarian, he could not be refused entrance. He took advantage of that fact. Also his ability to easily approach horses.

Tuesday was a "dark day," no racing, at Heartland Downs. Allgauer was waved through the gate and drove slowly to a parking area a couple of hundred yards away from the barn in which Ralph Tenuta's horses were stabled.

He sat silently in his truck until dusk, occasionally pulling on the pint of Stoly he'd brought with him.

After evening feeding time was over, and Tenuta's crew of workers had left for the night, Allgauer got out of his truck and carefully walked, unseen by the lone night watchman, to a horse he'd treated named Madame Golden. Eric knew she was entered in the seventh race the following afternoon.

This was Eric's second visit to Heartland Downs that day. Early in the morning, he had met his brother at Rudy's barn. They walked to Friar Tuckie's stall. Eric said, "What race is he in tomorrow?"

"The sixth."

"Perfect. I'll give him his 'booster shot' now. It'll make him good to go, go fast that is, for thirty hours. Hold his halter."

The brothers looked up and down the shed row before Eric slipped into Friar Tuckie's stall. Within seconds he had administered the shot of EPO.

Ten hours later, Eric was at Tenuta's barn moving quietly through the dusk.

"Hey, babe," he said. Madame Golden shuffled to the front of her stall, eager for the attention. Allgauer looked up and down the shedrow. There was no one in sight.

Allgauer reached into his windbreaker pocket. Took out the hypodermic needle he'd prepared that afternoon. Stroking the mare on the left side of her extended neck, he plunged the needle into the other side. Madame Golden neighed loudly and backed away, shaking her head from side to side.

"Run good, baby," Allgauer said as he left Madame Golden's stall. He walked unseen back to his truck and drove out of Heartland Downs. Near the exit gate, a young Mexican-American groom was walking a lively two-year-old around the training ring. Allgauer waved to the kid. Thought how much he'd always liked horses. Felt a surge of guilt over what he'd just done.

Another pull on the Stoly. "Fuck it," he said to himself. "I won races for Tenuta and that damned dago fired me. He deserves what he gets."

He drove down Euclid to his favorite restaurant, Tom's Charhouse, its motto emblazoned on the large sign at the front of the large parking lot: "No Beefs about Our Beef." Inside, Elisa the smiling hostess walked Eric to his usual table against the wall on the left side of the room. Where he used to entertain clients when he had them. And where he had frequently dined with Ingrid McGuire. Elisa recently had made two inquiries about the absent Ingrid and was met with gruff responses from Allgauer. She had stopped asking.

Rhonda, his regular waitress, smiled as she approached his table. "The regular, Eric?"

"That'll do, babe."

Forty-eight minutes later, Eric finished off the last of his New York strip steak, drained his third glass of merlot. Got up, leaving cash on the table to cover his bill, plus a fifteen-dollar tip for Rhonda.

◇◇◇

On his way home, Allgauer hit the ATM machine at the 7-Eleven store just blocks away from the condo he had shared with Ingrid. The condo that for him now was so empty and silent and depressing.

He withdrew $700 from the ATM machine. His balance had diminished, but was still decent. And it should soon improve.

Eric had apportioned his investment on Ralph Tenuta's trainee Madame Golden for the next afternoon. ""I'll make it $500 to win. Make it $100 to place. Just in case the elephant juice doesn't work. But I do believe it will," he said to himself. He reserved the other $100 for a win bet on Friar Tuckie.

Chapter Twenty-three

Racing Daily correspondent Ira Kaplan's front-page story in the Friday edition was headlined "Rash of Upsets at Heartland."

Heartland Downs, IL—Some longshot players cashed big here Thursday afternoon after the sixth and seventh races.

In the seventh, the previously undistinguished allowance performer Friar Tuckie suddenly came to life with a scintillating stretch charge, getting up in the final strides of the one-mile turf event to score by a length. He paid $48.80.

Friar Tuckie is owned by Mac Doherty, trained by Rudy Allgauer, and was ridden by journeyman Arnold Passman.

The following race saw a surprising wire-to-wire win by owner Hillis Howie's Madame Golden, trained by Ralph Tenuta.

Madame Golden, winless in her previous seven starts although finishing in the money in three, had previously lagged back far back early in her races. Not this time. Under a hustling ride by Mickey Sheehan, Madame Golden shot out of the gate and then widened on her field, winding up a four-length winner after leading throughout. Madame Golden returned $30.20 to win, $14.80 to place.

In post-race winner's circle comments to Heartland's in-house television interviewer Joe Kristufek, Tenuta said, "This is pretty amazing to me, Joe. I thought Madame Golden was training a little better recently. But I sure didn't see this

improvement coming. Glad it did, though. And Mickey rode
her great."

Friday evening, when Eric returned to his condo after going to
Heartland Downs to cash his winning tickets on Friar Tuckie
and Madame Golden, there was a message on his answering
machine. He heard the excited voice of his brother Rudy.

"Hey, Eric, thanks for what you did with Friar Tuckie." Rudy
paused. His voice was muffled as he spoke to someone he was
with. "Sorry about the interruption, Eric," he picked up. "I'm
at Tom's Charhouse, having dinner with Mac Doherty and his
family. Remember? The owner of Friar Tuckie?

"The man is riding high. Grateful for the win, buying dinner
for a bunch of us. He bet the horse good after I told him we
had a shot. 'A shot.' Ho, ho, in regards to that. Mac wants to
know if you'd like to join us. If you get this message in time. It's
5:40, Friday. Come on over if you can. After dinner, we'll be in
the lounge. It's karaoke night." Rudy's dropped his voice. "Mac
fancies himself as a singer. Who am I to discourage that, right,
bro? Thanks again."

Chapter Twenty-four

Early the previous day, Lenny Ruffalo had pushed his way through the crowded Metra train car to the rear where he spotted the lone remaining open seat. He elbowed out of the way a young pregnant woman carrying a small child in order to get to it. "You asshole," the woman snarled.

"Fuck you, lady."

During the forty-five minute ride from Chicago to the Heartland Downs station, Lenny busied himself going over his handicapping figures for the day's races. He really was interested in just two of the nine events, each with a horse trained by Ralph Tenuta.

Over dinner at her house the night before, Elvira said, "Lenny, with all your interest in this horse-racing stuff, you should go and meet Ralph Tenuta sometime. You know, he's a second cousin to you on your father's side." She passed the platter of lasagna to him. "Maybe he could give you a job at the track."

Lenny ignored the latter suggestion. He could not envision himself doing manual labor on behalf of one-thousand-pound animals that frightened him to be close to. But meeting Cousin Ralph was not a bad idea. He was well aware of Tenuta's impressive record of winning races. "Not a bad idea, Ma."

As usual, he pretended to agree with his mother. How could he not, being as dependent upon her as he was. His dismal betting results were carving up the money he'd saved from his former pizza delivery job. He'd begun lifting cash from Elvira's purse two, sometimes three, times a week. Just twenty bucks at a time. He was quite sure his lovingly indulgent mother was aware of this. But she never called him on it. And so he continued doing it, rationalizing "Hell, she can afford it." He had realized years before that Elvira was pretty much incapable of denying him anything.

◇◇◇

The racetrack crowd charged off the Metra train and up the long walkway to the track's entrance. Several men were running. "Got to catch the double," one hollered. Lenny took his time. Tenuta's first runner of the afternoon was Kenosha Rose in the third race. The other one, Madame Golden, was in the seventh.

Lenny didn't pay much attention to the finish of the second race. He slid his sandwich wrapper and empty beer cup under the bench where he sat near the railing to the racing strip. Picked up his *Racing Daily* and hustled to the paddock area. He positioned himself at the white fence as the third race entrants were saddled, walked, then mounted following the traditional cry of "Riders Up."

Tenuta, he saw, was a nicely dressed, stocky, middle-aged man, his Italian complexion made darker by years of working outdoors at racetracks. When Tenuta waved at his rider for the race, Mickey Sheehan, Lenny watched her stride toward her horse.

Lenny leaned over the fence.

"Mr. Tenuta. Sir. Could I talk to you for a minute?" he said forcefully.

Tenuta, concentrating on Kenosha Rose who was being saddled by Paul Albano, said, "About what, son? I've got a horse running here. I'm busy."

Lenny watched as Tenuta gave instructions to Mickey Sheehan. The horses circled the walking ring once more, then proceeded through the tunnel leading to the track. The paddock crowd dispersed.

Lenny grabbed his chance. "Mr. Tenuta, do you know you and I are cousins? I'm Bruno Ruffalo's son."

Tenuta, startled, stopped walking. "How about that? Nice to meet you, son. What's your name?"

"Lenny. Lenny Ruffalo. I'm a big fan of racing. And a huge fan of yours."

Tenuta smiled and nodded. Took Lenny by the elbow and began to steer him toward the grandstand. "Well, that's good to know, Lenny. What can I do for you today?"

Lenny grinned. "All I need to know is how you think your two horses will do today." He patted his jacket pocket. "I brought a bunch of money to bet on them. What do you think?"

Tenuta gave Lenny an appraising look. "Son, if any of us knew, on any given day, what our horses would do, we'd all be retired and wouldn't be working seven days a week. Hell, I think—I *think*—Kenosha Rose is going to run good for my new jockey Mickey Sheehan. My other horse in today, Madame Golden, I have no clue what she'll do. She's a puzzle. She trains great but runs terrible. I've had a new vet start dealing with her lately. The lady does horse communicating stuff. But I have no idea if it's going to work for Madame Golden today."

He pulled away from Lenny, saying "Nice meeting you," and walked rapidly through the doorway leading to his box. Over his shoulder he said, "Good luck, Lonnie."

"Lenny," muttered Ruffalo.

Lenny trotted past the first-floor mutual windows manned by clerks and went to one of the banks of automatic betting machines. He hated telling clerks what he was betting. The machines were fine with him.

Encouraged by Tenuta's assessment of his horses' chances, Lenny put most of his bankroll down to win on Kenosha Rose. The horse proceeded to run a dull fifth. Lenny disgustedly flung his *Racing Daily* down on the pavement in front of his bench. When Mickey Sheehan and Kenosha Rose, both splattered with dirt, came past him, Lenny shouted, "Nice ride, you dumb bitch."

A man next to him roughly grabbed Lenny's arm. "Watch your mouth, you jerk. I've got kids here with me."

Lenny walked rapidly inside the building. He bought a Bud Lite. Tried to calm down as he paced back and forth, calculating what he might do with the remnants of his bankroll. He finally decided to pass up betting on Tenuta's lesser entrant, Madame Golden. It was 4:24 p.m. He still had time to catch the 4:30 Metra train back to the city.

On the train platform he stood amidst a small crowd of obviously beaten-down bettors. One gray-haired old woman muttered over and over again, "Fuck horse racing and anybody who likes it."

Another senior citizen, a squat man wearing a battered Chicago Bears ball cap and Cubs windbreaker, said, "Sadie, you say that almost every afternoon you're here. And that's almost every afternoon." She gave him an icy look.

"See you tomorrow, Sadie?" he said.

Her smile revealed an amazing array of ugly and widely-spaced upper teeth. "'Course I'll be back, Barney."

With two minutes to go until the train's scheduled arrival, this motley crowd listened avidly to the track announcer John Tully's description of the fifth race. "And she continues to lead to the wire, Madame Golden, under young Mickey Sheehan."

The last thing this crowd heard before the Metra cars' closed was Tully's report that "Madame Golden returned $30.40 to win, $17.60 to place, $8 to show."

On the train, Lenny staggered to a seat near the door and next to a window. He felt as if he'd been punched in the stomach. Tears formed in his eyes. Passengers seated nearby gave him worried looks.

"Cousin Ralph," he said bitterly, over and over, "you fucked me up good this afternoon. God damn you."

Chapter Twenty-five

"Hey, it's me. Wanna get a beer after work?"

Teresa Genacro said, "Wait a minute, Lenny." She looked at the overhead mirrors above the aisles in the Berwyn convenience store where she worked as cashier five days a week, the late morning to late afternoon shift. A pair of furtive junior high boys were pretending to assess the packaged pastry items in aisle three. One of them slipped two cans of soup from across the aisle into the right pocket of his hoodie. "Hey, dipshit," Teresa shouted. "Put that back. You're on the video here, for Chrissakes." The boy dropped the cans of chicken noodle and scurried out the door, his buddy on his heels.

"What was that?" Lennie said when Teresa again picked up the phone.

"Business as usual here. Amateur hour. These little shits got no idea how to steal." She paused to punch out a multinumbered lottery ticket for one of the morning regulars. "Anyway, yeah, I'd like to go for a beer." She plumped down on the stool back of the register counter. "My feet are fucking killing me. The Den? Six? Cool."

Lenny arrived first at this aged Berwyn tavern and walked down the long, scarred wooden bar to one of the small, dark booths in the back of the large dark room. In early evening, The Den was crowded with construction guys just off work, plus remnants of the afternoon trade, oldsters who made their glasses of tap beer last as long as possible in order to delay them from returning to where they lived.

Some of the men nodded to Teresa as she strode past them. At five-ten, 155 pounds, she was what Lenny appreciatively termed "an impressive figure." She had responded to this intended compliment by saying, "What the fuck does that mean?" Teresa was from the neighborhood. Most of The Den's customers knew her. She was well remembered for throwing an obnoxious bricklayer through the tavern's front window one eventful Easter Weekend night two years earlier when the man had gotten more than usually out of hand.

On her way to Lenny's booth, Teresa said hello to Sid, the bartender, and swiped into her hand the bottle of Pabst Blue Ribbon he'd placed on the bar for her.

Seated in the booth, Teresa said, "So, how'd you do at the track?"

Lenny shrugged, looking down at the table. Tried to avoid the losing White Sox score blazing across the television set up on the wall behind Teresa. "I did good today. Only bet one loser. 'Course I only bet the one horse," he added sadly.

Teresa let out a sigh that ruffled the napkins on their table.

"You're still going that bad with those nags?"

"Bad as can be. But that's going to end," Lenny said, leaning across the table. "I've worked out some new speed figures angles, Treece. I'm gonna start using them tomorrow when I go down to the OTB parlor." He sat back, smiling.

"Lenny, Lenny, if you weren't such a hopeful soul I wouldn't be spending any time with you."

The tavern's dim lighting barely reflected off Teresa's large ear-pierced items. Lenny thought, by no means for the first time, how fine she looked with jewelry parenthesizing her broad face. He smiled as he remembered his favorite of her body ornaments, the one located in the considerable recess of what he considered to be her deeply enticing navel. He said, "I'll get us another round. Okay?"

They each had two more beers and split one of The Den's super-salty microwaved pizzas, Teresa on the leading end here. Lenny slipped into the nearby gents for a quick meth hit.

Teresa looked around The Den, the place that her widowed father used to bring her to as a kid after Sunday mass at nearby St. Stanislaus Church. He'd sit her on a bar stool, get her a pickled egg from the large bottle on the bar. Give her as many beef jerkys as she wanted. Owner Sid always had a cold glass of ginger ale for her.

Like Lenny, Teresa was an only child. Unlike him, she had been secretly sexually abused, by her father's brother Albert when she was a preteen. Too embarrassed to inform her dad, she had confided in Sister Mary Agnes at her parochial school. The nun informed her father, who proceeded to beat his brother Albert nearly to death. Albert was hospitalized, but he did not lodge charges against Stan. Teresa and her father never saw Albert again.

Teresa had never felt a meaningful connection to anyone other than her dad until she met Lenny, six years ago, in the detention center of their Pulaski High School. Lenny had been caught smoking pot in the gym locker room. Teresa, having admitted she'd "slapped the shit out of" a student hall monitor who had made an ill-advised comment about her weight, was the only other person in the small, airless room besides Lenny.

Seated on a long bench, head down, long lank hair drooping around his thin, frightened face, Lenny appeared close to crying. Teresa slid down the bench to sit next to him. "Stop that," she ordered. "That's what they want to see you do." She pointed at the ceiling corner where a security camera was aimed at the room.

She put her big right arm around Lenny's slender back. "Hey," she said, "we can get by all this shit. Just man up. Admit what you did. They'll just put you on probation. This isn't the end of the world for you, for Chrissakes." Lenny looked at her gratefully. Teresa was the first girl at Pulaski who had ever shown any interest in him. They'd been close ever since.

Lenny made a second meth run to the wash room. He returned walking jauntily, his eyes aglow. "Damn, Lenny, I wish you'd give up that stuff."

He shrugged. "Lot of days, if I don't get high I can't get by. Anyway, Treece, here's the deal. My fucking distant cousin Ralph Tenuta is going great at Heartland Downs. But when I bet his horses, they lose. If I don't bet them, they win. It's unbelievable. It's killing me. I talked to him today and he wouldn't tell me anything about what horses he's training that's going to run good. Says he doesn't know, which I think is pure bullshit. But I don't know how to get good info out of him. I gotta figure a way to do that."

Lenny got out of the booth. Sid was ready for him with another pair of Pabst Blue Ribbons. Back in the booth, he heard Teresa say, "Remember when we met back in high school. In the detention center?"

"How could I forget?" he smiled.

"Well, it was true that I beat that crappy high school rap by convincing the hall monitor, miserable little son of a bitch, to change his report. Not testify against me at the hearing."

"How'd you do that?"

"Simple. I grabbed him in the hall one day. Told him if he spoke against me, I'd go to his house some night and set it on fire." She took a swig of her beer and grinned in satisfaction. "It worked. He believed me."

Lenny leaned across the table. He said softly, "Would you really have done that? The fire?"

"Fuckin' A." She drained the Pabst bottle. Gave Lenny a long look. "What you've got to do, Lenny, is throw the fear of God into your Ralph Tenuta. Wait, no, I take that back. Not the 'fear of God.' The fear of you. Then he'll come through with the information, tips, inside info you're after. What you need to turn things around with your horse playing."

Lenny said, "Great idea, Treece. But what in hell could I do to make Ralph cooperate with me?"

"Let me think about it."

Chapter Twenty-six

As Doyle bounced down the Heartland Meadows clubhouse stairs, his cell phone rang. He recognized the caller's number. "Hello, Nora. Jack Doyle, ace jockey agent, here."

Nora laughed. "What happened today that makes you so bubbly?"

"Mickey had three mounts this afternoon. Won with two of them, finished third on the other. Damn impressive. And people are starting to take major notice. Ira Kaplan, the *Racing Daily* writer, wants to do a feature story on her. The sports announcer on one of the local TV stations called, interested in her. I've got her on five mounts tomorrow, another five the next day. Hey, business is booming."

He paused to look at his notebook. Mickey had earned a bit more than $3,000 that day. He was startled when Mickey burst out of the jockeys' room and snuck up behind him and hugged him around the waist, laughing. "Wake up, Mr. Agent. You never heard me coming."

Mickey was wearing white jeans and a black tee-shirt proclaiming, "Celtric Tigress—We'll Be Back."

"Great day, Mickey. I'm talking to your sister." She waved him a hurried goodbye and headed for the parking lot.

Doyle said, "Okay, Nora, I'm back on. That was Mickey. She's riding high. And very well, I might add." He smiled as he watched Mickey jump into Ralph's maroon 1992 Buick, a beautifully maintained reminder of topnotch American auto production. Ralph waved to Doyle as he pulled away. Ralph was taking Mickey to his Arlington Heights home with him for dinner with Rosa.

Nora said, "Mickey told me this morning she was invited to dinner at the Tenutas' house tonight. Ralph will drive her home after that. He and Rosa have been so very nice to the both of us."

"They're genuinely nice people. And what a cook Rosa is! By the way, what are you doing for dinner tonight?"

A short silence. "Well, I was going to warm some of the Irish stew I made last night. It's my culinary specialty. I made some good soda bread, too." She paused. "Would you like to join me?"

Doyle said, "What goes best with Irish stew? I'll pick something up at the Liquor Outlet."

"Don't bother. I've got some Guinness. And some Jameson's as a valued accompaniment." He heard her giggle.

"I'm on my way."

◇◇◇

"You're as pale as the moon. But much more lovely," Doyle said as he traced his finger down Nora's neck. They lay atop the spread of her bed, naked and satiated, an hour after they'd enjoyed the Irish stew and the brew and the Jameson's and each other.

They had moved quickly through the dinner, Doyle relishing all of it, telling her a few carefully edited stories about his past, then sitting back and getting her to similarly respond. He helped her clear the table. As Nora bent to turn on the dishwasher, he recognized a strain of possibility. He impulsively grabbed her around the waist as she turned toward the sink. Kissed her deeply. She looked up at him, eyes wide, smiling. Without saying anything, took his hand and led him to her bedroom. The night came alive for both of them.

◇◇◇

"That was good for me, Jack. It's been a long while since I've been with anyone. I could never lately set eyes on a man at home who sparked any interest in me." She turned and placed her head on his chest. Her long red hair spread in a tickling way across his skin that made him laugh.

"What's so funny, then?"

Doyle said, "Who would have thought that an Irish book-maker named Niall Hanratty would lead me to a young Irish jockey, and me into bed with the jockey's lovely sister?" He turned on his side, pressed her face against his chest, stroked her back. He heard her chuckle.

"Excuse me? What's so humorous to you, woman?"

"The fact that I had to cross the ocean with my little sister in order to find myself a place in bed with a useful man." She shook with laughter. Jack gave her a whack on her lovely firm butt. He smiled as she responded by kicking his foot.

They held each other and Nora continued to lay her head on his chest. Doyle looked up at the ceiling before saying softly, "Am I to assume that this, well, dalliance, won't lead to anything verging on serious?" He waited expectantly.

Nora said quietly, "Only to perhaps a few other similar 'dal-liances,' as you put it. If we're lucky. That would be fine with me, Jack. And, I'm sure, with you."

She sat up and shifted over in the bed to straddle him and leaned forward to put her mouth near his. Her hair framed Doyle's face as she whispered, "We're not the marrying kind, are we, Jack Doyle? And so feckin' what?

"Now put your hand there, dear Jack. And your other hand there. And your mouth here."

Never a man good at taking orders, Doyle took these.

Chapter Twenty-seven

Doyle had stopped in the Heartland Downs racing secretary's office to pick up Tenuta's mail. At the barn, he placed three envelopes on the trainer's desk. One was a letter from the Illinois Racing Commission.

It was a hot summer morning, and Tenuta was sweating when he came through the door. He took a bottle of water out of the refrigerator. Jack declined his offer of one. "I'm sticking with coffee."

Seated behind his cluttered desk, Tenuta reached for the mail. After he'd opened the envelope on top, his swarthy face lost color. "Ralph, what's the matter?" said a concerned Doyle. "You feel all right? You look terrible."

"Not as terrible as I feel, Jack. Here, read this."

The official notice from the Racing Commission informed Tenuta that his trainee Madame Golden had "tested positive for the illegal Class One Banned medication EPO, otherwise known as Elephant Juice." As a result, Madame Golden's purse earning would be taken away and distributed to the second-place finisher in the race in question. Tenuta was ordered to meet with the state stewards to determine why his "license should not be suspended for thirty days." He also faced a fine of $3,500.

Tenuta was baffled. "Jack, I've got no idea what this EPO is. Never heard of it. And," he said, "pounding his desk with a fist, "I've never given any of my horses anything but hay, oats and water. And, sure, some perfectly legal vitamin supplements. Everybody does that. Nothing illegal about that."

Tenuta sat back in his chair, face to the ceiling. "Thirty years in this business and I've never had a horse of mine turn up with a drug positive. I don't get it, Jack."

"Ralph, cool down. Maybe the lab chemists made a mistake. As I understand it, you can ask for an independent laboratory to test Madame Golden's blood sample. The commission has to allow you to do that. You just have to make a request when you meet with the stewards.

"You know, Ralph," Doyle added, "you'd probably be smart to get an attorney."

"An *attorney*," Tenuta said loudly. "What the hell for? I've done nothing wrong. There *must* be a mistake here."

Paul Albano leaned his head through the doorway. "Ralph, what do you want to do with Plotkin today?" Albano's surprise at the stricken look on his ordinarily good-humored boss' face was evident.

"Paul, check his workout chart. Use your best judgment. We'll talk later. I can't deal with workout schedules right now."

Albano carefully closed the screen door. Tenuta, head in his hands, said, "Rosa will not believe this is happening. *I* don't believe it is happening. Somebody screwed up in that testing lab. That's all I can think of."

Doyle said, "There's something else to think of, Ralph."

"What?"

"What if somebody got to Madame Golden and injected her with this EPO? Even though you know nothing about anything like that, under the famous 'trainers' insurer rule,' you're still responsible."

Tenuta said, "I've never given any thought to that rule, Jack. Never had to."

"Well, you better acquaint yourself with it. What it says, simply, is that you are responsible for your horse at *all times*. Doesn't make a damn bit of difference even if you're three states away at another racetrack with another horse. The horses back here under your care are all your responsibility. It sounds Draconian, but that's the rule."

"Sounds like Dracula? What the hell are you talking about?"

Doyle wanted to laugh, but held back. "I didn't say Dracula. Never mind about Draconian. The main thing is you've got to fight this ruling and suspension. Ralph, take my advice, you need a good lawyer to represent you."

The phone rang. Tenuta attempted to compose himself as he talked for a few minutes with an owner about her filly's next race. This was the aspect of training horses that most repulsed Doyle. Having to schmooze with many well- meaning but often idiotic clients. Most of Tenuta's owners were time-tested veterans who knew to leave things in their trainer's hands. But every year he was forced to add a few "fresh horses," as he called them, meaning their owners, not their runners. Tenuta was usually patient and accommodating in these phone calls. This morning, he cut this call short and slammed the phone down.

He leaned forward, crossed his arms, put his head down on the desk.

Doyle was angered. He hated self-pity, either in himself or others.

"Ralph, tell me one thing right now. Are you going to fight this case or not?"

Tenuta slammed his fist on the desk again as he stood up. "Damn right, Jack. But I don't know how to get a lawyer."

"I do."

Tenuta grabbed his jacket from the hook behind his desk. "I've got to go home, Jack. I can't break this news to Rosa over the phone. And I'll have to call my owners to let them know. We've got no horses running today, so I don't have to hang around. You staying here?"

"Yeah. Mickey's got mounts in the fourth and seventh. I'll watch those races before I leave." He placed a hand on his friend's shoulder. "You need anything, Ralphh, call me on my cell."

"What I need is a *Twilight Zone* moment where none of this actually happened today."

Doyle waited until Tenuta had left the office to dial Moe Kellman, who was at Fit City, in the middle of his daily workout. Moe picked up his cell phone. "Jack."

"Do I hear you breathing heavily, old fella?"

"I don't have time to fuck around, Jack. What do you want?"

Doyle quickly described the Tenuta situation. Kellman said, "I'm surprised to hear that. Everything I ever knew about Ralph Tenuta was that he was the straightest arrow in the quiver. Anyway, what do you want from me, Jack?"

"Do you know a good racetrack lawyer who would represent Ralph?"

Kellman paused to wipe the sweat off his brow. He'd just finished forty reverse-hand pull-ups. "Yeah. I do.

"Guy's name is Art Engelhardt. He's got a small law firm with an office on south LaSalle Street. Very sharp guy. Does a lot of racetrack business. Representing jockeys in their appeals of suspensions. Trainers like Tenuta in this case with drug positives."

Doyle said, "Is this guy real expensive? Ralph, God bless him, is a pretty close to the purse strings kind of man. I don't want to push him toward somebody who charges like Spence or Dershowitz or Valukas. He'd never go for it."

"I can help our friend Ralph come to an accommodation with a lawyer. People, if you ask around, are going to recommend another Chicago barrister with racetrack experience. Frank Cohan. Brilliant guy, but people I know refer to him as The Dip. Because, they say, he dips into the accounts he's supposed to be overseeing for aged widows. Forget Cohan. Engelhardt would be your guy."

"Moe, you know him good?"

"Jack, if I didn't, you think I'd even introduce him into this conversation?"

Doyle could hear Kellman instructing his driver Pete Dunleavy to "bring the car around in twenty minutes." He said, "Jack, I've got to shower and go. Any more questions?"

"This Engelhardt. Has he ever had any big cases? That he's won?"

"Do you think I deal with nebbishes? This guy is as slick as black ice. And mainly honest, too.

"I know you remember the great boxer Archie Moore," Kellman continued. "He had a brilliant, conniving manager named Jack Kearns. They made a pile of money together, even when Archie was at a very advanced boxing age. Archie once said about the old hustler Jack Kearns, 'Give this man a bundle of steel wool and he could knit you a stove.'

"Artie Engelhardt, Jack, is in that kind of category. Tell him I sent you."

◇◇◇

With Tenuta's okay, Doyle called Engelhardt's office later that morning. He set up a meeting with the attorney for that afternoon at 4 p.m. As soon as he had, the secretary called back and said, "If you don't mind, Art would like to meet you at Mother's Lounge. He does a lot of business out of there, especially later in the day. Do you know where that is?"

"I do. Thanks."

Chapter Twenty-eight

Minutes after Tenuta's departure, Doyle looked up from perusal of *Racing Daily* at the polite tap on the screen door. "Ingrid, come on in. What can I do for you?"

Ingrid McGuire answered, "How about coming out here, Jack? I'd like to sit on the bench. There's a nice breeze. I've already had a long, hard morning. One of Buck Norman's geldings started to colic, but I think we caught it in time." She paused to brush back a wisp of blond hair from her sweaty forehead. "I see Ralph's car is gone. Does he need me for any work today?"

"He didn't say. And, Ingrid, I guarantee you his morning was longer and harder than yours. Let me tell you about it."

When he'd finished, Ingrid said angrily, "This is preposterous. No way Ralph would hop one of his horses. No way. I think…" She was interrupted by a loud announcement from Paul Albano, who was standing midway of the shed row looking at a silver-sided food vendor truck that had just pulled up.

"Aqui viene al entrenador de las cucarachas," Albano shouted. The stable workers put down their rakes, brushes, and buckets and headed for the truck.

Doyle laughed at the puzzled look on Ingrid's face. "What did Paul just say? Do you know Spanish, Jack?"

"Very little. But I've learned what that statement means. Somebody here calls it out every noon hour. It means, 'Here comes the roach coach.' C'mon, I'll buy you lunch. The food is actually pretty good. And sanitary."

They stood in line behind the dozen of Tenuta's employees working their way forward to the truck's counter, chatting happily. Doyle bought a chicken burrito, Ingrid opted for two fish tacos. They took their food and cans of Dr. Pepper and walked to the south end of the barn to sit on the grass beneath an aged elm tree.

Ingrid said, "I'm sure Ralph is not responsible for this drugging. I wonder who is?"

"No idea. How about you?"

She finished her first taco. "Got to be somebody who is familiar with the backstretch. And who has it in for Ralph."

"Could it be another trainer?"

"I've never heard of anything like that around here. Couple of years ago, when I was still in vet school, I remember one prof talked about case in Oklahoma. One trainer tried to dope another one's stable star, trained by his brother-in-law no less. But he was caught in the act.

"It's certainly true," she continued, "that trainers are under tremendous pressure to win. So, damaging the chances of a rival might be tempting to some. Every trainer, you know, is like a small businessman. He's got obligations to the owners of the horses he trains, who are like shareholders. And he's got obligations to the people he employs who care for those horses."

Doyle said, "As long as I've been around here, I've never known Ralph to have any enemies. Everybody seems to like the guy."

"True. But there were a couple of problems he had with personnel earlier this year. There was a disgruntled groom Ralph fired for sloughing off and smoking pot. Hector Martinez. I was there at the barn that day. Martinez was furious. Took a swing at Ralph until Paul Albano got him under control. He's still around. Got a groom's job a couple of barns over.

"Then there was a real old veterinarian named Ambrose Pennyfeather. He worked for Ralph for many, many years before Eric and I came along. People thought Pennyfeather should have retired long before. But Ralph, loyal as he is, stuck with him until Pennyfeather completely misdiagnosed a promising filly Ralph trained. The filly almost died of colic. After that happened, Ralph let Pennyfeather go and hired me and Eric to replace him. I understand Pennyfeather was furious. Vowed revenge. Made threats. Nothing every came of it. Until, maybe, now."

She swallowed the last of the second taco and used a napkin to wipe her mouth and hands before gracefully getting to her feet.

"Thanks for the lunch, Jack. I owe you one. See you tomorrow."

Chapter Twenty-nine

Mother's Lounge was a venerable, popular watering hole for the LaSalle Street law brigades. Doyle had never been there, but he was familiar with what he saw once he walked through the front door. He'd been in joints like this before. Dark lighting, two busy bartenders roaming behind a long mahogany bar, a juke box featuring Sinatra, Tony Bennett, Miles Davis, Sarah Vaughan, Peggy Lee, Carmen McRae, Betty Carter, Mose Allison. Paused in the doorway letting his eyes adjust to the lack of light, he felt the clap of a heavy hand on his back. Doyle pivoted. Heard a deep rumble of a voice say, "Hello, Jack. I'm Art Engelhardt. Moe told me you wanted to see me. Follow me."

Doyle walked behind the attorney, who was wearing what looked to be a $2,000 suit that hadn't been pressed in weeks. He was a big man with a long stride. Arriving at a booth in the rear section of Mother's Lounge, he gestured for Jack to sit. Thinking of Moe's placement at Dino's Ristorante, Doyle said softly to himself, "All these hotshots take booths."

They ordered drinks. "A very cold, shaken, vodka martini, one drop of scotch at the start, no vegetables," Engelhardt told the waitress, saying to Doyle, "She's new. Doesn't know my regular order yet. How about for you?" Doyle asked for a Jameson's straight up, water back.

"So, Jack, tell me about your friend Ralph Tenuta's problem."

Their drinks quickly arrived, but Doyle didn't touch his until he'd finished summing up Tenuta's situation. Midway of his recounting, he said, "Art, aren't you going to take any notes about what I'm telling you?"

Engelhardt drained his martini glass and waved to the waitress for a refill. Jack declined another drink. A smile spread across Engelhardt's large face. He leaned forward. "Jack, if I have to take notes at this stage of my career, my career should be over. I've been doing this for forty-two years. Know what I mean?"

Doyle, at this point only half sold on attorney Engelhardt, said, "Have you had drugging cases like this before? Or alleged drugging cases, I should say."

Engelhardt smiled tolerantly, slowly shaking his big head from side to side. "Jack, I've had every kind of so-called drugging case you could imagine. One client last year was using cocaine for himself and on his horses. I couldn't win that one. But I've had many, many successes. One of my toughest cases was ten or so years ago." He paused to take a drink of his refilled martini glass. "A trainer friend of mine asked me to help with a drug violation in Louisiana. I'd known this guy for years. So, I flew down there to Baton Rouge. On expenses and with a decent retainer, I might add.

"I told my client, I'm not licensed to practice in this state. But I've got the name of a local attorney who knows the ropes. And the people. And what it takes. His name was Ed Bonnert. My client and I met him at the courthouse in Baton Rouge, where a judge was to be assigned to our hearing.

"Bonnert was a mighty crafty piece of work. One of those good 'ol boys with an aw-shucks facade. I listened to him for three minutes before I realized I wouldn't trust this guy to wind a cheap watch for me. But I suspected, and I was right, he was the man for us.

"Bonnert walked us through the door of the courthouse building to this long corridor of judges' offices. 'Wait here', he said. We watched. He went into the first door on the right. A few minutes went by. He came out and went into the second door on the left. Never looked back to us.

"Finally, he came out of the fourth door on the right. Came back to us, smiling. 'We've got the judge we want,' Bonnert said. My client's case was assigned to that judge, who dismissed it the next day. Only in Louisiana. It's a different world down there. Bonnert took us on a tour of the Cajun country. We passed a liquor store that had a drive-through window. These old pick-up trucks were lined up for half a block. They were offering a Friday afternoon special. 'Boilermakers three bucks, long necks a deuce.'

"Couple of blocks down the street from this liquor emporium," Engelhardt continued, "there was, I am not making this up, a drive-through crematorium. Their billboard advertised 'A Done Deal for $200. Urn Is Xtra. Cardboard Containers Free of Charge.' They weren't doing any business that day. But what an enlightening experience that was for me."

Engelhardt signaled for a martini refill. He said, "I remember barrister Bonnert told us his fee was ten grand. I'm sure he shared some of it with the helpful judge, man named Allen LaCombe, as I recall. But that was a bargain. Otherwise, my client faced a long suspension. He's a famous trainer today. If I told you his name, you'd sure recognize it. But I won't," Engelhardt smiled. He emptied his most recent martini glass and this time waved off the attentive waitress.

"My point is, Jack, I have experience in these cases."

Doyle said, "Art, with all due respect, don't tell me you can somehow grease the Illinois Racing Commission to forget this alleged Tenuta drug violation. I don't want to get Ralph in any crap like that."

"No, no, no," Jack. "That'd be impossible. Even if we had it in mind. As I've learned from some past experience. What we'll do, if Tenuta hires me, is we challenge the laboratory finding. Stress Tenuta's previously pristine record. 'Why would an extremely successful trainer like this, an officer of the horsemen's association, bulwark of the backstretch, etc. etc., resort to using an illegal drug on his horse', etc. etc.? I know I can get a stay order in circuit court if I have to. I know I can help your man," Engelhardt said. "And, obviously, as you know, he needs help."

"That he does." Doyle sat back in the booth, watching as Engelhardt fired up a silver, polished-from-use Zippo lighter to apply to his Marlboro in this, one the last bastions of smoking, not legally of course, in Chicago. Mother's Lounge was starting to fill up with late afternoon customers. Someone turned up the volume on the juke box so that Sinatra's version of *Chicago* layered out.

> *My kind of town Chicago is*
> *My kind of people, too,*
> *People who smile at you...*

Doyle said, "Okay, Arthur. Let's talk about money. Your fee. Tenuta is not planning on expending big bucks. He's just that way."

Englelhardt sat back, smiling. "Did you read the story in '*Tribune*' today about the court-appointed lawyers working to recover money that Bernie Madoff stole?"

"No, I didn't see it."

Englehardt said, "According to this report the 'average pay' of these recovering lawyers was $437.89 per hour."

"I hope you're not thinking along those lines for Ralph Tenuta," Doyle barked.

"No, Jack. I am mentioning these numbers only to be instructive. The key lawyer who billed over a thousand hours charged, are you listening to this, $830.43 per hour. That's what I call Attorney Hall of Fame chutzpah. And he's evidently going to get paid these obscene sums."

"The forty-three cents per hour at the end of this bill. What the hell could that be for?"

"Maybe postage?" Art said, sitting back in the booth, laughing. He listened as Doyle murmured, "You couldn't make up some of this shit."

The waitress hovered but was politely dismissed. "Arthur, give me a number. What would you charge my friend Ralph Tenuta?"

"One grand. Flat fee. That's it."

Doyle was surprised. "That's a pretty, well, modest fee. For a man like you. How come?"

"Moe Kellman is an old friend of mine, Jack. And friends of his are friends of mine. We take care of each other. Okay?"

"Fine with me, Art. I'll have Ralph Tenuta mail you a check tomorrow. When do you want to meet with Ralph?"

"I'm bringing some friends to the races at Heartland Downs Saturday. Let's say we meet in the Players' Room before the first race."

Doyle said, "I'll have Ralph there."

"Fine. Listen, Jack, you want to hang around awhile? They make a great hamburger here, prime Angus on a toasted Kaiser bun, plenty of garlic laced into the meat. I'll buy you one."

Doyle laughed. "That sounds like a sandwich right up Moe Kellman's alley."

"Oh, sure, Moe and I have eaten here many, many times. He's one of my main men."

"He's gotten to be one of mine, too. Thanks for the invitation, but I've got to go, Art. And thanks for the drinks and the advice. Ralph and I will see you Saturday at the track."

Doyle would have liked to hunker down in Mother's and schmooze with the colorful attorney, but he had promised the Sheehans he would take them to an early movie and dinner.

Chapter Thirty

Tuesday, the only day during the week that Heartland Downs was not open for live racing, was the day the track stewards met with alleged rule violators.

Their office was on the third floor of the large building that housed the track's various offices, down a long, carpeted corridor from the elevator. Doyle and Tenuta sat restlessly in the foyer of the stewards' office, awaiting Ralph's turn and also the arrival of attorney Engelhardt.

Doyle read that morning's edition of *Racing Daily*. Tenuta was equally silent, nervously tapping his foot. The receptionist, Lucinda Borland, a matronly exemplar of good manners after her nearly twenty years in this job, gave up trying to engage either one of them in conversation.

Earlier that morning, Doyle had run into blacksmith Travis Hawkins in the track kitchen. Hawkins said, "Jack, you got a minute? Let's sit." They walked to a corner table.

Hawkins, his heavily muscled forearms on the table, leaned forward. "What's going on, Jack? I know Ralph got some kind of ruling against him, but he won't tell me anything about it. I know it's killing him. When I was there yesterday morning, I heard Ralph holler at Paul Albano. Never seen that before. What the hell is going on, man?"

"Travis, I think this is a bullshit situation. There's no way Ralph Tenuta ever drugged a horse. No fucking way. He's got a meeting with the stewards later this morning. I've gotten him a lawyer. I 'm hoping we can get this mess straightened out."

Hawkins leaned back in his chair. "Damn, I sure hope so, Jack. Ralph Tenuta is a great guy. He was the first white man to give me a chance in this business as his blacksmith. I know he took some shit from some of those redneck trainers for using me. But he saw what I could do, and he let me do it. Ralph, man, he's as honest as they come. It kills me to see him in the bad spotlight like this. I agree with you, Jack. No way Ralph Tenuta ever juiced a horse of his."

◇◇◇

Waiting to be called into the stewards' office, Doyle and Tenuta continued to sit uneasily on a long leather couch, Doyle getting up to pace every few minutes, checking his watch every minute or so. "Art Engelhardt should be here by now," he said.

Tenuta said, "Jack, sit down. You're making me more nervous than I am." He folded up the *Racing Daily* and handed it to Jack. "Read that front page story about the problems these thoroughbred retirement associations are having."

According to Ira Kaplan's story, the numerous well-intentioned people who wanted to provide homes for retired racehorses had run into a tsunami of trouble. Major money from generous contributors had in some cases been misused, in other cases unwisely distributed, or halted. There had been ill-cared for horses found on some of the farms involved in these projects despite a generous endowment from the estate of one of the sport's most prominent sportsmen.

"Well, that's too bad," Doyle said as he returned the paper to Tenuta. "I know these people mean well when they try to provide for retired racehorses. I've just never understood the math."

Tenuta said, "How's that?"

Doyle sighed. "Ralph, every year, American breeders turn out between 20,000 and 30,000 potential racehorses. Maybe half get to the races. Maybe half of that half win a race. Then, when their racing days are done, where are they supposed to go?

"These nice people behind the retire-the-horse movement are not being realistic. Ain't no way any retirement organization can place, feed, and care for thousands of horses coming to them each year. Do the math."

Tenuta said, "I've been lucky. I've been able to comfortably retire most of the horses that leave my stable. Some are converted to riding horses, or hunters, or show horses. One mare, Nurse on Call, is the star of one of those therapeutic riding outfits out near Elgin. You know, programs for physically and mentally handicapped children. These kids really respond to horses. I've got a guy who specializes in these placements."

"Ralph, you can't tell me you've found a home for every animal leaving your barn."

Tenuta shook his head. "No, Jack, of course not. Some of them have been sold to what they call the horse knackers. They die in processing plants and wind up on French and Belgian and Italian dinner tables via Mexico. Or Canada. It's called humane destruction, as I understand it, Jack," Tenuta said, extending his hands. "What are you going to do with all of them? Let them gallop up and down our interstates? It's the way of the world."

Doyle retrieved the paper. "It says here that in Ireland the number of horses killed for human consumption has more than tripled in the last three years. It's blamed on the economy. The story says 'All the horses were slaughtered under strict veterinary and food hygiene rules. The French buy horse meat for 'steaks, barbeques, and stews…The Italians are the biggest consumers of horse meat in Europe. They like higher-fat marbled meat for processing into salami and sausage products.' I've got to remember that the next time I'm ordering at Giordano's Deli, 'Purveyor of Imported Italian Products,' as their slogan puts it."

"You probably wouldn't even know if you were eating horse meat, Jack."

"I'd know. Ralph, listen to this. These US do-gooders had a huge political movement that wound up getting horse slaughtering plants closed up in this country by the Congress in 2007. As a result, these herds of old horses are being shipped long distances out of the country. To plants in Mexico and Canada. Because the slaughter is taking place outside the States, they lose what were considered humane slaughter protections in the US.

"According to this article," Doyle said, "2006 was the last full year that equine slaughter took place in this country. About 140,000 domestic horses were slaughtered that year. The number is not dropping. It's just happening now beyond our borders, often under less humane conditions than our people had maintained. What a brilliant solution!" He tossed the paper down on the couch next to him.

Doyle looked up at the wall across from where they sat. There were striking photos of great horses such as Citation, Buckpasser, Secretariat, John Henry, Zenyatta, Rachel Alexandra. "I guess the great ones are the lucky ones," Doyle said. "They get to live long lives."

The door banged open. Art Engelhardt walked in, huffing and puffing, and apologetic. "Jack. Ralph. Sorry I'm late. There was a bad accident on the Edens. Truck turned over, wiped out two cars to the inside of him. Traffic didn't move for a half-hour. Did the stewards call our case?"

"Not yet, Art. But here comes their secretary."

"Mr. Tenuta," she said. "The stewards will see you now."

It was a large office with wide windows overlooking the racetrack. At a round table sat senior state steward and former jockey Henry Arroyo. To his left, young Joe Lynley. On his right the senior member of the panel, Peter J. Kosnicki, who was sucking on an empty pipe. He looked at Doyle. "Who are you?"

"I'm a friend of Mr. Tenuta's. And a licensed jockey agent. Jack Doyle."

"Take a seat, men," Arroyo said.

Engelhardt opened his brief case. "I have here," he started to say before Arroyo cut him off. "Art, forget the formalities. Let's talk realistically." He sat back in his chair looking at Tenuta.

"Ralph, I've known you for many years. Always admired your work and your horsemanship. That's why I was shocked when

Madame Golden turned up with a positive test. I would never have imagined anything like that. Is there any way you could explain how that happened?"

Engelhardt leaned forward. "Mr. Arroyo, I'm here to represent Ralph Tenuta. He believes that if, and it's a big if, Madame Golden did indeed prove positive for this Elephant Juice stuff, that he had nothing to do with her getting it. I am formally asking you today to send a split sample of that test to Cornell University's testing lab to see if they corroborate the findings of your Illinois lab."

Arroyo said, "I have no objection to that." The other two stewards nodded in agreement. "But," Arroyo continued, "we have no other choice than to suspend you, Ralph, in the course of this inquiry. You'll have your license taken away for thirty days. That's our rule."

Engelhardt was working his way up to an objection when Arroyo held up his hand, stopping him. "Counselor, I understand your feelings about this. You've got a client with an impeccable record over thirty-plus years. But the rule *is* the rule. If a horse turns up a positive test, it doesn't make any difference how that happened. It is the trainer, in this case Ralph, who is responsible. And that's that."

Arroyo got up and extended his hand to Tenuta. "We'll get this sample test off to Cornell by Fed Ex this afternoon. I wish you well, Ralph."

As they left the stewards' office and walked down the long corridor to the elevator, Tenuta's face was ashen. "What in the hell is happening to me here, Jack? It's a damned nightmare."

Engelhardt pressed the down button. "It's early days, Ralph," he said heartily. "We'll see what the Cornell lab comes up with. And, even if they validate the local finding, I'll get a stay order that will allow you to continue training your horses. There's something going on here that we haven't figured out. Give me a chance to try to do so. Count on me," he said, thumping Tenuta on the back.

They prepared to enter the elevator whose doors slid open. Emerging from it was Albert Greathouse, an apprentice rider whose horse had been disqualified as the result of Greathouse's reckless maneuvering in the previous day's sixth race. "Mornin', Mr. Tenuta," he said. Doyle looked at Engelhardt out of the corner of his eye, wondering how much "count on me" was going to be worth.

They walked to the parking lot. Engelhardt said, "Ralph, I'll call you as soon as I get the stay order. Jack gave me your office number. Do you want to give me your home number?"

"Mr. Englelhardt, I'd rather not. My wife Rosa is already so upset about all this, I don't want be taking any calls at home. She's not sleeping at nights. Neither am I. If you need to reach me, call me at my track office. Or call Jack."

Doyle said, "You've got my cell phone number, Art. Right?"

"Yes. I'll be in touch."

Engelhardt walked briskly to his gun-metal gray Mercedes 300 Luxury Sedan. He laid some rubber down as he aimed his auto toward the east exit gate.

Doyle said, "Ralph, how about I buy you some breakfast?"

"No thanks, Jack. I'm not hungry."

On their way to Jack's Accord, the two men passed groups of Latino workmen bent over their gardening tasks in the lush flowers that bordered newly-mown grass, a lawn that emanated one of Doyle's favorite smells. Ordinarily, he would stop and smile and breathe deeply. Not today. They trudged silently to Jack's car.

Chapter Thirty-one

Eric Allgauer knocked loudly on his brother Rudy's condo door. Michelle opened it. "Eric. What are you doing here? Rudy's not home. But he will be in a half-hour or so. C'mon in."

She led him to the kitchen, Eric admiring her tight-bunned walk as she preceded him. "I was just going to make some margaritas. Interested?"

"You bet."

They chatted about her yoga business, no mention being made of Eric's professional decline. Twenty minutes later Rudy entered through the back door with an armful of *Racing Dailys* and some Heartland Downs condition books. "Hey, bro. Good to see you. What's up?"

Rudy declined Michelle's offer of a margarita. "Hand me a Coke, will you hon?" He pulled up a chair at the centered counter. "Eric, what brings you here."

Eric smiled. Picked up his margarita glass and drained it. He motioned to Michelle for a refill.

"Couple of things, Rudy. Did you see in the paper today about that son-of-a-bitch Tenuta getting caught with a positive test on one of his horses?"

Rudy said, "Hey, everybody was talking about it. Couldn't believe Ralph Tenuta would do anything like that." He sat back in his chair, gave his brother an appraising look. "Should I presume Ralph didn't juice that horse?"

Eric smirked before knocking back most of another margarita. "Presume what you will, brother. Presume what you will. The fact that bastard got nailed has made my day."

Rudy sat back in his chair. "Could I presume that *you* had something to do with that bad test on the Tenuta horse?"

Eric shrugged. "Listen, let's get off that subject. You'd better be thinking about our next adventure with Friar Tuckie."

Michelle filled Eric's glass for the third time. "I'm going to leave you boys alone. I've got to do some billing in my office for some slow-to-pay clients. Nice to see you, Eric." She brushed a kiss on his cheek as she left the room and headed for the basement stairs to her work area. Then she stopped and turned back. "Eric, if you don't mind me asking, have you heard anything from Ingrid?"

"Ingrid who?" Eric snarled.

Michelle turned away and went down the stairs. The brothers sat in silence for several minutes, Eric tapping a forefinger on the table, Rudy regarding him with worry.

Finally, Rudy said, "You here for dinner, bro? Michelle won't cook tonight. We could order out. Or go out."

"No, not tonight. Thanks for the invite, Rudy. Your bathroom still in the same place? I need to use it."

When he reappeared, Eric had washed his face and slapped his cheeks and appeared to be at least semi-sober, Rudy thought. Rudy said, "So?"

"When have you got Friar Tuckie entered again? Is there a race for him?"

"Yeah. A week from tomorrow. Mac Doherty is all excited now after Friar Tuckie's win last time out. Mac wants to put the Friar into an allowance race." Rudy paused. "I don't know, man. Whether this horse can move up and do good at that level. But, I've got to go along with the owner's wishes."

Eric said, "Set your mind at ease. I'll have Friar Tuckie ripe and ready for that race. I'll give him his booster shot the night before. You'll have to meet me at the barn so that we can get this done safely. Okay?"

"You sure that you, or we, can pull this off again? The blood doping revving up Friar Tuckie?"

Eric said, "You know, Rudy, I don't think you've ever had as much confidence in me as I deserve."

He got up and opened the refrigerator door. "Jesus, Rudy, what's in here? It looks like a Whole Foods produce section. All veggies."

"Don't let Michelle hear you making fun of that. Have a goddam carrot, Eric."

They both laughed. Growing up, they had observed their mother Margaret's attempts to introduce vegetables to the nightly dinner table presided over by their overbearing father. But Dr. Allgauer was not a vegetable person, no matter all his well-intentioned wife's attempts. "Pass the fucking pork roast," was the single most memorable statement Rudy remembered from those mostly tense meals, followed by Dr. Allgauer retreating to his den, decanter of brandy in hand, slamming the door.

In the early morning hours eight days later, Eric arrived at Rudy's barn. The brothers walked the length of the shed row, Rudy glancing nervously about. None of his grooms or hot walkers had yet arrived, and he had dismissed his night watchman before his brother's arrival.

Rudy opened the door to Friar Tuckie's stall. He smoothed his hand over the horse's broad forehead. Eric stepped into the stall. Pulled a loaded syringe from his jacket pocket. He administered the shot of the potent blood-doping substance and was finished within thirty seconds.

"I hope this works, brother," Rudy said as he shut the stall door.

Eric said, "You talking to me? Or the horse?"

"To both of you. C'mon, I'll buy you breakfast."

"No, thanks. I've got some things to do this morning," Eric said. "And, you know Rudy, there's no reason why we couldn't help out a few more of your disappointing horses with the EPO."

◇◇◇

Ira Kaplan's story the following week was on page three of *Racing Daily*.

> *Owner Mac Doherty's resurgent runner Friar Tuckie scored his second straight upset victory at Heartland Downs yesterday. The former claimer beat a good field of allowance horses, winning easily and returning $28.40.*
>
> *Interviewed in the winner's circle, where the jubilant Doherty was joined by some two dozen friends and family, trainer Rudy Allgauer said, "Friar Tuckie has just recently come into himself. We always thought he had ability. Now, that promise is showing through."*
>
> *Owner Doherty commented, 'It's been a long while since I've made any money in this business. This is great. You know, we bought this horse as a yearling and named him for my oldest friend. This is a great thrill for all of us. Now, we hope we can move up the ladder with Friar Tuckie."*

◇◇◇

A week went by before Rudy called his brother. "Some worrisome news, man."

"Like what?" It was just after seven on a sultry August morning and Eric got out of bed and turned the thermostat down, activating the air conditioning. He was sweating.

Rudy said, "There's a story in *Racing Daily* that the Illinois Testing Laboratory is getting close to being able to identify this blood doping stuff you've used on Friar Tuckie. According to the story, they're not going back to re-test previously taken samples. But from now on, they'll try to identify them. Ain't that a kick in the head?"

Eric leaned his head back against the kitchen wall, phone at his side.

"Hey, Eric. You still there?"

"Yeah, Rudy, I am. I guess I knew this was going to be coming some day. Hell, the shady chemists come up with some magic potions, then it takes the regulatory labs a few years to uncover them. That's what's going on here. But, Rudy, 'getting close' isn't getting there. I think we've got a little more time to carry out these EPO capers."

Rudy said, "Mac Doherty wants me to run Friar Tuckie in a little stakes race next week. What are his chances?"

"Without the magic juice?" Eric said. "Are you kidding? That bum Friar Tuckie could hardly beat me in a dash across the parking lot. I won't go near Friar Tuckie again once they perfect their testing procedures. You better figure out how to prepare Mac Doherty for a coming major disappointment."

"Shit."

Eric bristled. "Listen, I've managed to revive your career. At least temporarily. Don't overlook that fact."

"You're right, Eric. I am grateful."

"And I've got some planning to do, Rudy. I've got some unfinished business with that bastard Ralph Tenuta."

Chapter Thirty-two

They met at the end of the East Pier, the long granite extension that stretched from Dun Laoghairie's shore into the Irish Sea.

Kieran Sheehan walked briskly through the early morning haze. He wore a black windbreaker over a black turtle neck sweater above black jeans. With his dark glasses and black ball cap pulled down low, he was as unidentifiable as he could be.

Twelve hours earlier, Kieran had lain on the riders' room massage table in the basement of the Curragh Race Course's large building. He'd won two good races that afternoon. He was being administered to by the German-born masseuse on staff, Hilda Schulte.

Trainer Aiden O'Malley came through the door. Walked to where Hilda was working on Kieran, nodded a hello to her. O'Malley smiled as he heard the pounding of Hilda's hands on the jockey's heavily muscled back. Sheehan's head was face down, but he was aware O'Malley had approached.

"Hilda, my dear, hold off for a moment, will you? Why don't you get me a bottle of water. Aiden, what brings you here an hour after the races ended?"

"Kieran, I wanted to let you know right off that my owners want to send Boy from Sligo to the Heartland Downs Million Juvenile in late August. This is quite exciting for me. I've never been over there to that great track. I don't believe you have, either."

He pulled up a short stool next to the head of the massage table so that he could directly address Sheehan. "First, of course, Boy from Sligo has to run well next week in the Healy Handicap at Leopardstown. I do believe he will. He's been absolutely brilliant on his gallops in the mornings, all last month."

Sheehan cocked his left eye up at the trainer, his frequent employer. Sometimes even now, after his years of riding, the excitement of being involved with a very good horse could be contagious. O'Malley, a brilliant horseman, was only in his early thirties, but he was well on his way to becoming a legend. Sheehan marveled at and could not help but envy O'Malley's enthusiasm.

Sheehan had lost most of his some years earlier, though he persisted in carving out a memorable riding career.

"Well, Aiden, we'll have to see how Boy from Sligo does in the Healy, won't we? He's got the talent, all right. We've known that since he went unbeaten after his first three races. But I'm not convinced this colt has the mind for stern competition. He can be a feckin' flake. Remember when he jumped the tractor path at The Curragh in June and almost tossed me?"

O'Malley smiled. "Of course I do. You did a brilliant job of hanging on and straightening him out and winning. You've got a great gift, Kieran."

Hilda Schulte returned with the bottle of water for Sheehan. She said, "Mr. O'Malley, can I get you anything?"

"No, thank you, Hilda. I just need a couple of more minutes here with Kieran." She walked over to a bench on the far side of the room and sat down.

O'Malley said, "Kieran, I've spent many hours working with Boy from Sligo in these last two months. No doubt about it, he's got that hot-blooded, impetuous Nasrullah breeding in his pedigree. Very fast and talented horses, but very hard-headed horses, challenges to handle. Demanding their own way.

"But I believe, Kieran, that I've got this colt settled down and now serious about his racing business. As they say in America, he can 'run a hole in the wind.'"

"Yes, Aiden, he can. When he wants to."

"Well, I want to try him over there on that dirt track. If he runs well, his owners would like take a shot with him in next year's Kentucky Derby."

"That would be brilliant," Sheehan enthused.

O'Malley got up off the stool and patted the jockey on the arm. He nodded a goodbye to Hilda. She was a tall, sturdily built woman with close-cropped blond hair and the largest, strongest-looking hands he'd ever seen on a woman. She began working on Sheehan's legs. Eyes closed, head down, Kieran moaned, either in pleasure or in pain, O'Malley could not tell which.

Walking to his auto, O'Malley considered strong, sturdy Hilda, thinking of her in terms of an hilarious satirical movie his parents had laughed about long ago titled, *Ingrid, She-Wolf of the SS.*

◇◇◇

Early as he was for this 6:30 meeting, Kieran saw that the person he was there to meet had once again arrived before him. A big, broad-shouldered man wearing a gray overcoat and felt hat. He had his back turned to the shoreline as he gazed across the roiling gray waters, but nevertheless was aware of the jockey's arrival.

"Morning, Kieran," Martin McCluskey said, smiling as he turned.

"Morning, Martin." Kieran paused. "Christ, what is that creature you've there alongside you?"

"My new dog, Behan. I'm training him to stay with me as I go about my business."

Behan was a brindle-colored Irish wolfhound. About three feet in height, 130 or 140 pounds, a member of the tallest of all breeds of canines. Saliva was stringing out of both sides of his huge muzzle. "Jesus, Martin, he's big enough to run in the third race at Leopardstown tomorrow."

McCluskey said, "Just be careful with him a bit. He's only eleven months old. He's got a bad habit of thrusting his nose into peoples' crotches. Quite embarrassing at times. Although not to him, so far."

"Well, I suppose that would be," Kieran said, watching the dog warily.

Behan ambled up to Sheehan, who thought, *This is one of the stupidest-looking animals I've ever seen.* Sure enough, Behan poked his snout at Kieran's private parts. Kieran responded by giving Behan a hearty kick with his right boot into the stomach. The dog backed off, whining. McCluskey stayed quiet, observing. Then he said, "Well, maybe that's the way to train the poor young fella." He leaned down and patted Behan's head. Went into his overcoat pocket for a dog treat, which was eagerly accepted. Behan struggled to his feet, shook himself, and ignored Kieran Sheehan.

Kieran and McCluskey had been doing business for a few years. McCluskey's employer, one of European racing's biggest bettors, a financier and secret arms dealer known as a brilliant, ruthless opportunist, was Padriac (never Paddy) Hanrahan. He was known, nevertheless, behind his back, in the Irish underworld, as "Paddy the Man."

Hanrahan had selected Kieran Sheehan as a potentially valuable accomplice, or "usable tool," as Hanrahan described him to McCluskey. And he had been proven correct. The careful Hanrahan never directly dealt with Sheehan, always using his muscle man McCluskey for that.

Their association began when Hanrahan learned that Kieran had fathered a son named Liam. Out of wedlock. And never to be in wedlock, according to the boy's mother, an independent young nurse from Donegal named Maureen Hogan, one of Kieran's numerous sexual partners. She'd gone to the Galway races one afternoon, met Kieran in a nearby pub late that night, and they began their often contentious relationship.

Shortly after being born, Liam was diagnosed with cerebral palsy. Sheehan was not present for either the birth or this alarming announcement. Maureen, sobbing on the phone, had called Kieran. He felt both appalled and responsible. After hanging up the phone, Kieran said to himself, "Why did I not use a condom with that girl?" He sat down, remembering the first of their sex experiences, in this attractive woman's tiny rental apartment. She was so lovely to him. He treasured that memory for a week. Then he got on a plane to France, won two major races at Longchamps on a beautiful Sunday afternoon. Had a great evening in his hotel that night on the Isle St. Marie with two adventurous and attractive Air France stewardesses.

Maureen and Kieran agreed to place Liam in a very expensive private hospital just outside Dublin. And there the child had remained, his parents communicating only by phone or checkbook. Maureen visited Liam every week.

She well knew Kieran would never marry her. He had made that clear from the time of Liam's birth. She considered, then rejected, the thought of taking this story to one of the frothing English tabloids. She trusted Kieran to keep his promise regarding Liam's care.

Kieran had made just one visit to what he considered the depressing facility in which his son was housed. He'd taken a quick look at this small, damaged child, and, tears in his eyes, brushed past Maureen on his way to the exit. "I'll never be back," he said to her over his shoulder.

Not wanting to impinge on his comfortable life style, financed by his racetrack earnings, Kieran had listened to McCluskey when they first met on the East Pier. McCluskey made Hanrahan's offer of major, not-taxable or reported money. Kieran accepted. He intentionally lost seven races designated by Hanrahan in the first year they did business. For this he earned 80,000 Euros, which he used to pay for Liam's care.

Maureen Hogan telephoned Kieran on his cell once a month to report on Liam's progress. There was little. Kieran always thanked her and sent an envelope of cash to her apartment. Some nights, Kieran dreamt of Liam. His twisted little body, palsied limbs. Kieran would awaken in a sweat and churn the covers of his bed. More than eager to get up and go to Aiden O'Malley's training center, where all he need think to about was the refreshing early morning air, the horse between his knees.

◇◇◇

McCluskey and Sheehan both looked up at the blaring sound of a nearby foghorn. Behan stayed with his head down, apparently sleeping. "Let's talk now, Kieran.

"You're set to ride Aiden O'Malley's Boy from Sligo next week in the Healy Handicap. Am I right? He'll be a powerful favorite, I'm told. Mister Hanrahan wants you to lose with that horse. There'll be huge wagering on Boy from Sligo. Mister Hanrahan is taking a large position against him winning in the exchange betting."

Kieran slumped forward on the bench, head down. McCluskey stood in front of him. "Are you hearing me, now, Kieran?"

There was a foghorn repeat that again startled them both. So did a colorfully dressed female skateboarder as she zipped past them to the end of the pier before stopping with an accomplished move. They waited. She turned back and passed them, waving. Behan briefly raised his head, then laid it back down between his paws.

"Feckin' unbelievable what some of these youngsters do on those skate things," McCluskey said. "But that's not our concern here this morning."

He reached into an overcoat pocket and took out a bulging envelope. Handed it to Kieran. "Mr. Hanrahan calls that a down payment. On Boy from Sligo Down failing in the Healy as a result of your clever efforts. Considerable money for one small afternoon of work, I would say. Are we clear on this now, Kieran?"

Kieran turned the envelope over in his hands, not opening it. They sat in silence on the bench. They watched as two middle-aged women swimmers walked bravely from the strand into the frigid waters of the Irish Sea. Kieran shivered thinking about what they must be feeling. He gave them a congratulatory wave they never saw as they fully immersed themselves and stroked forward.

He got up off the bench. Said to McCluskey, "If I lose on Boy from Sligo, his owner might just decide not to send him to America, the big race near Chicago that Aiden has set on his schedule. I've never ridden in the States. That would be a huge opportunity for me. Something I've always wanted. Jesus, man, could you not get that across to the Big Pat?"

McCluskey chuckled. "Like he gives a shit about what you want? Try to be serious, Kieran."

Behan unleashed a thunderous fart. He turned over on his back. McCluskey quickly went to the dog's side and rubbed his chest. "I think he needs to be taken for a little walk, now." Kieran did not answer. He thought what he'd most like to do right now was throw this big, ugly beast far out into the water.

McCluskey said, "Think of it this way. You don't have to do anything to harm Boy from Sligo's reputation. You could just do one of your acrobatic bailouts when you come out of the gate. Like you did last year, at Epsom, on that big filly favorite of O'Malley's. Sister Sinead. That was a grand piece of work."

"I don't know. I'm still sorry I did that. The filly didn't deserve it, and Aiden didn't deserve it. He had his heart set on winning that race."

McCluskey sighed. "Sentiment doesn't enter into this, Kieran. It's just business we're about here, not your tender feelings. You must realize that by now. Mr. Hanrahan had his heart, not to mention his money, set, too. On a big score. You were paid, as I recall, 30,000 Euros for that bit of work."

Kieran walked over to the railing. "I was paid. I still regret that I did that." He paused. "I don't know if I can do the same thing to Aiden and his owners with Boy from Sligo."

"Well, Kieran, you'd better know soon. Mr. Hanrahan has laid his plans for a betting coup dependent on you doing your part."

Kieran looked up angrily. "And what if I don't agree to carry this one out for you people?"

"Ah, Kieran, don't try to venture down that path again." McCluskey rubbed his big hands together. "You'll do what you're told. Just like you've done the past three years. Mr. Hanrahan depends on you." McCluskey leaned down and adjusted Behan's enormous collar. "Otherwise, Kieran, you'll be facing major trouble."

Kieran laughed bitterly. "What are you saying, man? If you or your thugs hurt me, your feckin' crooked game is over."

McCluskey turned away, gazing at the roiling gray waters. "Kieran, if you don't go along with us, the hurt would be in a different direction. We know where your poor damaged son is housed. And where his mother lives."

Kieran's face drained of color. Fists clenched, he stood chest to chest with McCluskey, who smiled and used one large hand to easily push the jockey away from him. "You've crossed the line here into blackmail," Kieran shouted. "You and your man Hanrahan."

McCluskey patiently looked down at the enraged jockey. "And how many lines have you crossed, Kieran?"

McCluskey snapped his fingers. The giant dog struggled to his feet, shaking his head, spurts of saliva coming out of each side of his mouth.

"I hate that feckin' dog," Kieran said.

McCluskey leashed Behan and started off the pier to the auto parking lot. At the end, he turned around. Kieran trailed him by a dozen yards.

"Do it right, Kieran. The money will be there for you."

Chapter Thirty-three

Doyle hated Fridays at Heartland Downs. In an attempt to attract a younger crowd than its usual complement of seniors, the track hosted locally based rock-and-roll bands, offered beer and pizza at bargain prices. It was a strategy that seemed to work. The park area was full of twenty-somethings in casual dress, eager for a good time, which Doyle considered to be encouraging. With the average racetrack attendee eligible for membership in AARP, an infusion of youth was a good thing.

But the afternoon's racing program did not start until three, too late, in Doyle's view. He had Mickey booked on just two mounts that day. One in the first race, the other in the ninth and final race. As a result, he was stuck there for the long afternoon and early evening.

He sat in Ralph Tenuta's box, nursing a beer, attempting to ignore what he thought of as the raucous ruckus from that day's featured band, Humpty and the Dumpties. They were thrashing their way through a long set. The voice of their lead singer, rarely on key, seemed to grow even more ear-shattering as the afternoon went on.

Doyle, a dedicated jazz fan, had never been much interested in rock and roll. He ignored the Rolling Stones, none of whose musicians he thought could actually play worth a damn despite, or perhaps because of, their on-stage antics. His parents were huge fans of the Beatles. Listening to that group at home in his formative years, he was bored to death. Their song "In My Life" was the only one lodged in his memory. There were a few rock performers, Janice Joplin, Bob Seger, Eric Clapton, Bruce Springsteen, some of whose work he enjoyed. But that was about it. Sipping his beer, he smiled as he remembered the story about the late, great jazz drummer Buddy Rich. Hospitalized and seriously ill, Rich was being rushed on a cart toward an operating room when a nurse, running alongside the cart, said, "Mr. Rich. Are you allergic to anything?"

"Country and western," Rich responded.

Doyle felt pretty much that way about rock music.

Mickey cleverly rode the winner of the ninth race, coming from mid-pack after seemingly being pinned down on the rail down the backstretch to shoot through to the lead in the upper stretch. Nora had joined Doyle in the Tenuta box, so they walked down together to await Mickey. She burst through the jockeys' room door twenty-five minutes later. Her hair was still wet from her shower. "Now, how was that, now?" she grinned.

"A great ride, sister," responded Nora.

"That's for sure," said Doyle.

He took the sisters to dinner at the nearby Panino's Ristorante. Doyle had the large Italian salad, as did Nora. Mickey enthusiastically worked her way through a huge plate of lasagna. It did not take them long to finish their dinners.

Doyle drove the sisters to their apartment. Mickey jumped out of the back seat. "Thanks for dinner, Jack. I want to hurry in and make a call."

Nora, sitting next to Doyle in the passenger seat, gently laid her hand on his. "That's to Mickey's lad back home. She's very much in touch with him."

They kissed. "I've missed seeing you," Doyle said. "How about you come with me into the city Saturday night? We can have dinner. The great Chicago piano player Willie Pickens will be at the Jazz Showcase. Then you can stay over at my place."

Nora brushed her hand across his mouth. Her eyes were merry. "As you people say over here, 'sounds like a plan to me.'" She turned back at the doorway to give him a final wave.

Chapter Thirty-four

Doyle drove rapidly to his Chicago condo that evening after the races. He grabbed a Harp's out of the refrigerator. Turned on his television, feeling restless and lonely.

The American Movie Channel was showing one of Doyle's favorites, *The Commitments*, a film about a collection of talented Dublin misfits who come together to make a successful entrance into the world of popular music.

One of the best scenes came up. A young man was leading a fairly good-sized horse into the freight elevator of a Dublin public housing project, whose Irish residents earlier had been described as "the niggers of Europe in this Third World country."

The young man, holding the horse's halter, is asked what he is doing taking the horse into the elevator. The reply was, "Sure, the stairs would kill him." Where the horse was going was never explained, which Doyle thought was great.

Doyle's phone rang. He recognized Kellman's number on the screen.

He said, "Yes, you've reached the hotline for unhappy purchasers of items made of animal skins. Do you have a question?"

"Very funny, Jack. Is that the end of your humor for tonight?"

"Probably," Doyle said. "What's happening, Moe?"

Kellman said, "Sunday evening. I want you to go with me to talk with Fifi Bonadio. Can you make it? I'll have Pete Dunleavy pick you up around six."

"Meet where? Why?"

"On Feef's yacht in Belmont Harbor. Jack, this is important. Otherwise I wouldn't be calling when I should be sitting with my wife Leah in front of our television drowsing myself through another *Masterpiece Theater* rerun."

"Okay, Moe. I'll see you there. At Belmont Harbor. Anchors away."

Doyle smiled at the ironic conclusion of *The Commitments*. Made himself a Jameson's nightcap. Went to bed wondering what Fifi Bonadio had on his mind.

Doyle and Kellman walked up the short gang plank to Fifi Bonadio's massive yacht in Belmont Harbor.

"Most of these big boats, of which there are not all that many around here, have to anchor farther out in the harbor," Kellman said. "Feef got around that arrangement. Like he gets around a lot of things."

A pleasant breeze stirred the nautical flags on the long, white, motor yacht. It was an impressive craft with an aluminum hull, carefully swabbed and polished teak decks, gleaming brass. The retreating evening sun glinted off the wide top level windows in the pilot house. Looking up, Doyle saw one of Bonadio's bulky assistants waiting for them so he could open the gate onto the boat. Doyle smiled up at the man. His smile was not returned. "Why does Bonadio keep using these bozos?" he said.

"Is Feef still alive and well? After all these years? Maybe that's why."

Once aboard, the assistant said, "This way, Mr. Kellman." He ignored Doyle. Led them to the front of the motor yacht on the first level. It was a large area with comfortable wrap-around leather seating, a table in the middle that held an elaborate variety of snack items. Cavier and crackers, plates of cheeses and vegetables, assorted fruit, cocktail meatballs and wieners. They sat down.

Kellman plucked a toothpick from its holder, impaled two of the small wieners and swiped them across the bowl of hot mustard. He chewed appreciatively. "This reminds me," he said, "of the phone survey call I got today at the office. This very polite woman says, 'Do you know the approximate shelf life of a Hebrew National hot dog?' I couldn't believe what I'd heard. I asked her to repeat the question."

He paused to pluck a piece of mango from the fruit platter. "I told her, 'My dear, when I was a kid and my old man once in three blue moons managed to bring home to his large, hungry, poor family, a package of those hot dogs, the 'shelf life' of the Hebrew Nationals was about fifteen seconds. We didn't wait for them to be cooked."

"How big is this boat, Moe?"

"No idea. I try to stay away from boats and water. How do you measure something like this? In square feet or length? Or what it cost?" He picked up a celery stick from the table. "I've only been on this thing a couple of times. I think Feef said it has a permanent crew of four, sleeps eight, has a restaurant-worthy kitchen. He takes it to Florida every winter. Then flies back in the spring. The crew brings it back up here. An expensive project. He can afford it."

"Gentlemen! Welcome aboard." It was their host coming nimbly up the stairway from below.

Bonadio went right to Moe and embraced him. He nodded at Doyle. "Take a seat, men," he said expansively. "I've got to make one quick phone call. I'll be back shortly. Raul will be here to take your drink orders." He walked to the rear of the boat, cell phone in hand.

Doyle looked at the retreating Bonadio, a wry smile on his face. Bonadio wore full nautical whites, shoes, trousers, shirt, under a blue blazer, a gold-braided cap on his large, handsome head. His face featured a large nose that would have been appropriate on an ancient Roman coin.

Doyle said to Kellman, "Who does your pal think he is? Commodore Vanderbilt? Ted Turner?"

Kellman shook his head, refusing to reply. Doyle persisted. "With that sailor's tan Bonadio has overlaying his natural Italian coloring, he reminds me of a couple of my mother's favorite movie stars. Rozzano Brazzi. No, maybe Ricardo Montalban." He was chuckling at his own wit. Kellman sighed and looked off into the sunset. "Keep quiet, Jack," Moe advised.

Raul came hustling up the stairs from the galley, adeptly bearing a Negroni for Moe, a Jameson's on the rocks for Doyle. He carefully placed the glasses on the table. Right behind him toting a tray with napkins and bottles of water sashayed a gorgeous, young, wonderfully tanned woman wearing a sailor suit of considerable briefness. The skirt was short, the blouse revealing. She smiled at Kellman and Doyle. Placing her tray down, she displayed impressive cleavage, before pivoting and shaking her impressive ass on the way to the stairs.

Doyle laughed. "All right, Moe. I've got to ask. Who was that dusky beauty?"

Kellman drank from his glass of Negroni. "I don't know, Jack. These knockout young women seem to come and go here on Admiral Bonadio's flagship. They are never mistreated as far as I know. He has a full roster of applicants for this, what would you call it, nonmarital maritime duty?"

"He's still married, right? To that beautiful woman who looks a lot like Sophia Loren?"

Kellman said, "Of course. Italian Catholics for the most part don't favor divorce. The Bonadios have a marriage of what you could call convenience. She conveniently spends most of each year back with family and relatives in Calabria. Feef keeps about his business here. Pass me the caviar."

Doyle said, "Whatever happened with Bonadio's son? That nice, kind of dumb kid who was a very good football lineman at Wisconsin?"

"He's in the family business."

Bonadio joined them, apologizing for the delay. "You fellows need anything else?"

"Yes," Doyle said. "An explanation, if you don't mind, as to why I'm here."

"You know, Doyle, I've only met you what, maybe, three or four times. You've always impressed me as being a major pain in the ass." He paused to empty his glass of wine, signaling to Raul for a refill. "And I wouldn't be looking at you here now unless I had an excellent reason for doing so. Believe me."

"So, what's the reason?"

Bonadio said, "I know you're close with Ralph Tenuta. The Tenuta family and mine go back a long way. Came over from the same Sicilian town and settled on Taylor Street. Eighty years ago or so. I think maybe once, at a christening or a funeral, I met Ralph Tenuta. But our grandfathers were goombahs even though they hardly spent any time with each other. Dario Tenuta, Ralph's grandfather, made a good living in the produce business on South Water Street. My grandfather, Emilio, got into a lot of different enterprises. But they stayed friends. When you come from a dirt-poor place like they did in Sicily, and make it in Chicago, there's a bond. *Capice?*"

"Yeah, I can see that. But what does any of this have to do with me?"

Bonadio leaned forward. "Ralph has a young cousin named Lenny Ruffalo. This douche bag is on a mission to hire a killer to take out Ralph Tenuta. I told Moe about this, I mean it was so crazy it was almost funny. But maybe not. Then Moe told me about your connection to Tenuta. So, I figured I should talk to you about this situation."

"If I'm supposed to be flattered, I'm not."

Bonadio ignored this jibe. "Actually, I'd had an inkling about this. A guy that gathers information for me, no need for you to know his name, just believe that he's been ninety-nine percent accurate over the years, came to tell me last week about a young punk who was looking to connect with a hit man. This was before this Ruffalo came to my home a couple of nights ago. He bullshitted his way past my two night security men. Former security men, I should say. Those knuckleheads have been replaced. Anyway, when Ruffalo was brought to me, I listened to him for about thirty seconds before having him tossed."

Bonadio took a sip of wine. The sun continued to descend behind the tall high-rise buildings to the west of the Outer Drive. Raul trotted up the stairs from the galley to look expectantly at his employer and his guests. Moe said, "I'll have another Negroni."

Doyle said, "Make mine a double Jameson's." He took a deep breath and stood up, and looked at the Chicago shoreline and the impressive buildings behind it. The sky was now a mixture of light purple and orange. The air was clear and cool, a slight breeze from the East causing water to slap gently against the hull of the huge craft. There was a pause in the conversation as their drinks were being prepared. Doyle walked to a railing. Leaning over, he tried again to process what he'd learned about Ralph Tenuta evidently being in danger.

When he sat down again, Bonadio and Kellman were engaged in whispered conversation. Doyle laughed silently as he thought of himself, where he was this beautiful Chicago evening, with the furrier-to-the-mob and the head of the mob, aboard a million dollar craft on Lake Michigan. I wonder what the Sheehan sisters would say if they saw me now, he thought.

Doyle said to Bonadio, "What did your guy tell you about this Ruffalo wanting to kill Ralph Tenuta? Why would Ruffalo want to do that?"

"I've got no idea about motive, Doyle. The connection I've had with the Tenuta family over the years, that's the reason I was informed about this. Like I said before, I've probably spent less time with Ralph than I have with, well, the Pope. But that doesn't mean I don't want him protected."

"Ralph Tenuta is being fucking wrung through the ringer," Doyle said. "He's got the medication violation against him, which I know is bullshit. I can't figure who would want to destroy Ralph's business. And reputation. But somebody's trying. Then there's this threat from this Ruffalo.

"Ralph is one of the nicest people you'd ever meet. Great friend of mine. Whatever I can do to back him up, I'll do," Doyle said. "Believe me."

Bonadio nodded appreciatively. "Okay, Doyle."

"So what have you got in mind?"

Bonadio reached into his blazer pocket and pulled out a small slip of paper. "My people have located the whereabouts of this punk. Ruffalo lives in his mother's basement in a Berwyn bungalow. He was very briefly in the U.S. Army, which flushed him out. Never married. Never had a long-lasting job.

"Nobody I know knows how seriously to take this whack job. And, at this point anyway, I don't want to get any of my people involved in dealing with him. The Tenuta family and mine go back is why I'm looking into this. And asking you for this favor."

A motor boat with a half-dozen half-drunk passengers roared away from the adjacent dock. Its driver waved at Bonadio, who ignored him. Bonadio shook his head. "They're letting a helluva lot of riff-raff into this harbor. Coke-sniffing traders from the Mart." Bonadio was obviously offended.

Efficient Raul arrived with another round of drinks. Doyle put his aside. Poured much of a bottle of water into his Jameson's glass.

"As you might know," Bonadio said, "there's a new, very ambitious federal prosecutor here looking to make his mark. He's put me high up on his list of targets. I don't want to do anything to make myself vulnerable. Such as sending any of my men to deal with this Ruffalo punk.

"So, Doyle, I am proposing that you make a visit to Lenny Ruffalo. Convince him to forget about trying to get his cousin Ralph killed. I know all about your reputation as being able to handle yourself in tough situations. Like the creep you killed with a pitchfork at Monee Park. Would you do this for your friend Ralph Tenuta?"

Bonadio put his wine glass down on the table. He said softly, "I would be in your debt, Jack Doyle, if you would."

Doyle said to himself, "The last fucking thing I need is to have the head of the Chicago mob in my debt." He glanced at Kellman, who was giving him a nod to say yes.

"I'll do everything I can," Doyle said. Bonadio leaned across the table and tapped Doyle on the hand. "I'll expect that."

"It might take me a day or two."

"I understand," Bonadio said. "But don't take too long. Who knows what this nutcase Ruffalo's got in mind."

Bonadio turned to Moe and patted him on the knee. "C'mon, old friend. Let's go down below and have dinner. It'll be good."

Jack and Moe followed their host down the stairs to a large stateroom that had a linen-covered dining table placed in its midst. Raul appeared from the galley and pulled out Bonadio's chair at the head of the table. Bonadio motioned for Moe to the chair to his left. He said, "Doyle, you can sit at the other end."

Doyle wondered why he was not assigned to sit across from Moe when the dusky beauty emerged from one of the ship's bedrooms. She had changed her sailor ensemble for a stunning, black, off the shoulder dress. She took the seat next to Bonadio across from Kellman.

"This is Marcella Greco," Bonadio said. "A great friend of mine."

The wall behind Bonadio was almost completely covered by a large mirror. What Doyle saw next, in that mirror, made him wonder if he'd had too much to drink. For walking past him to take her place at the table next to Marcella was either an apparition or her twin sister.

Bonadio chuckled at Doyle's reaction. "This lovely young woman is Marcella's sister, Gina Greco. You are looking at the Greco twins. They've been on staff here for, what, girls, four months?" Getting no response, he repeated his question in Italian. Gina smiled and evidently said yes, for her employer patted her hand. His other hand was under the table apparently on Marcella's thigh, for she scowled and reached down and slapped that hand away.

Bonadio sat back in his chair, laughing heartily.

"The Greco twins," he said, "are what you could call spirited."

Marcella Greco indicated to Doyle she would like him to pass the basket of breadsticks. He did so. Heard her say in a soft, low voice, "*Grazie, Signore* Doyle, sir."

"How does this woman know my name, Bonadio?"

"Because I told her your name. Be nice, Doyle. Something good could come to you with the Greco twins if you handle yourself right."

Raul and another waiter came into the room and placed bowls of steaming seafood soup before the five of them. Kellman leaned forward over his bowl, inhaled, and said, "Nice work, Feef. You still have Luigi Pingatore cooking for you?"

Bonadio tapped the service bell next to his place setting. Gave it another tap. Out from the kitchen hurried a white-aproned, middle-aged man so wide he barely fit through the doorway.

Bonadio rapidly said several words in Italian. The Greco twins giggled. The huge man doffed his chef's cap and bowed. Bonadio said, "This is my longtime cook aboard this craft. Chef, I should say. Luigi Pingatore, from Palermo." He fired off another couple of sentences in Italian, concluding, in English, with "Let's eat."

The chef snapped his fingers and two busboys, herded by Raul, hustled forward bearing platters of steaming Italian food.

Moe had been quiet for minutes, sitting back in his chair, smiling at this scene and at Jack's reaction to it. Bonadio was talking in Italian to the glowing Greco twins, both competing for his attention. They smiled and, occasionally, each one shot Doyle a quick, interested glance.

Moe, having appreciatively worked his way through the soup course, sat back in his chair. Muffled a burp.

"What do you think, Jack?" he said. "Do I take you to interesting places?"

"No question about that."

Marcella was talking excitedly in Italian to Bonadio, who barely looked up from his soup. Doyle said to Moe, "I can't believe how gorgeous these girls are."

Bonadio must have heard him. "Hey, Doyle, gorgeous is the standard here." He laughed.

"Which of the twins do you think is the most beautiful?" Bonadio said. "It's a dead heat as far as I'm concerned," Doyle answered. "What's your opinion?"

Bonadio translated Doyle's response. The Grecos giggled, both blushing. "Some nights it seems to me Marcella. Other nights, Gina," Bonadio said. "The answer probably lies somewhere in between. Where, on special nights, I place myself."

Chapter Thirty-five

Kellman and Doyle were ushered off the yacht shortly before ten. Pete Dunleavy was in the parking lot, waiting for them. In the Lincoln town car, Moe said, "Pete, drop me off first. I've got some calls to make. Then you can take Jack up north."

"No problem."

Dunleavy drove south on Lake Shore Drive toward Moe's residence, a two-level condo at the prestigious 1100 North Lake Shore address. Jack sat in silence.

Moe said, "Why so glum, my friend? That wasn't a bad night out for us."

"Yeah, except for the news about Ralph Tenuta. Jesus. You couldn't make this stuff up."

Two blocks later, Moe said, "Can I tell you something? Might change your mood? Pick you up?" He was smiling as he turned in his seat to face Doyle.

Doyle shrugged. "Do your best."

"I was in Los Angeles last week. Dealing with some of my oldest customers."

Doyle interrupted him. "Who needs furs in LA?"

"Jack, be patient. Women can be living on islands in the South Pacific, or on desert oases, they still want furs. The items I supply for my LA customers are much admired. If I say so myself."

"You just did," Doyle said, turning to face his friend. "What do you want to tell me?"

Kellman said, "Let me tell you a story. I was at Hillcrest Country Club last week, meeting with a couple of my clients. You ever hear of that place?"

"Sure. They have a big professional golf tournament there every year. It's on TV."

"Correct. But Hillcrest is not as important as a golf course than it is as a societal statement. Back in the 1920s, Jews were not admitted to Christian or WASP or whatever you want to call those pricks, country clubs. So, they built their own. Hillcrest. Right in the middle of Los Angeles. All the big Jewish movie people chipped in major money. They wound up with a membership that included not just the studio moguls but famous performers like Milton Berle, Jack Benny, Danny Kaye, both Georges, Burns and Raft, Al Jolson. So on. The membership costs were way up there. $150,000. And they didn't accept for membership non-Jews."

Doyle said, "What was that? Reverse discrimination? "

"Fair is fair," Moe said.

"Not always."

"Ah, Jack, I know how you love to try and rattle me. It wasn't what you say it was, 'reverse discrimination.' It was adjusting to life as it was."

"Moe, I don't need a history lesson here. What are you getting at?" He stirred restlessly in his seat.

"This. When I was there last week, I had lunch with several men including one of Hillcrest Country Club's earliest members. Gus Greenberg. Great guy. Been there from way back. A scratch golfer in his younger days they say. Made his money in apparel. He's up in his eighties. Wrinkled like an old brown envelope. But still sharp."

Dunleavy turned onto Chestnut Street, preparing to slide the Lincoln to the entrance of Kellman's building.

"Gus tells me this story," Kellman continued. "Swears it's true. Back in the forties or fifties, there was always a big poker game in the Hillcrest clubhouse, usually on Tuesday afternoons. The heavy hitters showed up for these games after other members had played morning golf. One of the members had invited a famous actor I'll call Robert M. there for lunch and poker. You remember him?"

Doyle said, "My old man showed us the video of that movie he was in, *Night of the Hunter*. Who could forget that? Yeah, I know who he was. So what? And you mean they let non-Jews cross the Hillcrest threshold?"

Kellman said, "Yes, as guests. Robert is at a table with the famous comedian Milton B., who is killing them all with wisecracks and raking in pot after pot in the poker game. Robert starts drinking heavily. Getting in a worse mood with every hand he loses. Finally, he says to Milton, 'I'm told you've got a big dick. You're supposedly the best hung man in Hollywood. Well, I think I've got you beat on that. Even though I'm not beating you at cards today.'

"Milton says to him, 'Bob, I think you're wrong. And I'll bet you $500 that you are.'

"Robert checks his reduced bankroll. He says, 'You're on. Let's go to the men's room. We'll measure.'

"They both get up from the table. As they're starting down the hallway to the john, Milton's agent shouts out, 'Milton. *Only show him enough to win.*'"

Doyle was laughing now. He said, "And?"

"A few minutes later, the two of them came back to the card table. Robert peels off some bills and tosses them down in Milton's direction. And stalks off. End of story."

Dunleavy stopped the Lincoln next to the entrance to Kellman's tall building. A uniformed door man popped out. Moe opened his door. "This has been quite a night, Jack. I'm sorry that Feef asked you to see this Ruffalo kid. Laid some responsibility on you. But I don't know anybody else he could have asked that could handle this matter better than you."

"What high praise," Doyle said derisively. "You and your old buddy Bonadio have more confidence in me than I have in me. I'll think about all this, Moe. I'll get back to you."

Kellman gently closed the car door. Dunleavy drove Doyle to his condo on the north side.

Doyle picked up his mail and newspapers in the foyer of his condo building. Checked his phone. No messages. Watched the late news on WGN anchored by Mark Suppelsa. Suppelsa had moved a couple of times from channel to channel. Doyle always kept track of him. He liked Suppelsa's work. He wasn't as fond of the weathermen on these various channels, with their psychedelic screens and over the top reports. He'd never developed an interest in dew point readings or rainfall levels.

Doyle considered making himself a Jameson's nightcap, then thought better of it. He was afraid he'd toss and turn tonight dealing with Ralph Tenuta's problems and the challenge of this punk Lenny Ruffalo. He thought about calling Nora. Decided not to. Lay back on his couch, the television on mute. Smiled as he thought of the Greco Twins. And fell into a wonderfully deep sleep.

Chapter Thirty-six

Doyle walked rapidly from his Accord to Tenuta's office. The trainer was talking on his phone. He waved Doyle to the couch. Doyle waited impatiently as Tenuta concluded his conversation by saying, "We'll run that filly back in two weeks, Steve. Sure, we can use Mickey on her again. As a matter of fact, Mickey's agent is sitting here in my office right now. Yeah, I'll say hello to him for you." He hung up the phone, smiling.

"Steve Holland," Tenuta said. "Said he was mighty pleased with the winning ride Mickey put up on his filly Dazzling Diane yesterday. Wants Mickey to ride her back."

"Fine. Glad to hear it. But that's not what I'm here for. You have a relative named Lenny Ruffalo?"

Tenuta frowned. "Yeah. That's my cousin Elvira's loony son. I hadn't seen him since he was a little kid until he came up to me near the paddock one day a week or so ago. Showed up out of the blue. Asked how my entrants would do that afternoon. The way he acted kind of bothered me. So, I asked around about him in the family.

"Lenny got into the Army a year or so ago," Tenuta continued, "when they'd lowered their standards. He was out of high school, out of work, had always been crazy about those soldier video games. I'm told Elvira was happy he enlisted because she thought, or maybe hoped, he'd found a place in life. But the Army gave him the boot after a couple of months. I understand he's back home, living in Elvira's basement in Berwyn. Goes around wearing camouflage outfits. His Dad died years ago. I feel sorry for his mother. The little bum is mooching off her. According to the family grapevine, he's gotten into betting horses in a serious way.

"A month or so ago, Lenny called me a couple of times, pestering me for tips. Then he comes up to me here that day in the paddock. I kind of brushed him off. He was pissed off when he stomped off away from me. I could see that."

Doyle said, "Pissed off is an understatement, Ralph."

"What do you mean?"

"Your cousin Lenny showed up the other night at Fifi Bonadio's mansion in River Forest. He somehow talked his way past security and got into see Bonadio. You know who Bonadio is, right?"

"Supposedly a big mob guy." Tenuta's surprise was evident. "Lenny at Bonadio's home. What the hell for?"

"Lenny told Bonadio, who thought he was a raving asshole and probably on some kind of drugs, that he wanted to hire a hit man. That he wanted a man killed. Bonadio's security guys finally got Lenny quieted down and their boss got some information from him. Then Bonadio had Lenny tossed out on his ass."

Tenuta stood up and leaned his hands down on his desk. "I figured Lenny was trouble, Jack. But I never imagined he'd be nutty enough, or have balls enough, to approach Fifi Bonadio. Jesus! This kid's off the rails." He sat back down heavily in his creaky old desk chair, shaking his head.

"Maybe you'd like to ask me something, Ralph."

"Like what? You've given me enough information already to spoil my morning. Although I'm not blaming you. I'm glad you told me about Lenny and Mr. Bonadio. What should I be asking you?"

Doyle said, "When Lenny Ruffalo told Fifi Bonadio he wanted to hire a hit man, that he'd pay $3,000 for such a service, Bonadio gave the signal to his men to have Lenny rapidly removed. But as they were hustling Lenny to the door, Bonadio stopped them for a moment. He said, 'Who do you want killed?'"

"Well, that's a good question," Tenuta nodded. What did Lenny say? Who does he want killed?"

"You."

Chapter Thirty-seven

Doyle took the Edens onto the Kennedy, tussled through the late afternoon rush hour traffic before turning west on the Eisenhower Expressway. He arrived at 1815 Gunderson Avenue in Berwyn nearly thirty-five minutes later.

Gunderson was a quiet street of sturdy bungalows and well-tended lawns. Across the street from where Doyle parked, an elderly man wearing an old-style white undershirt, à la Stanley Kowalski, watered his lawn. Kids were playing kick ball in the street four houses down, their excited shrieks piercing the early evening air.

Doyle rang the front doorbell at 1815 Gunderson. Waited, rang it twice more. Nothing. He walked down the front steps to the east side of the bungalow where he saw a small stairway leading to a basement door. "Maybe that's where this asshole lives," Doyle muttered.

It was. Doyle knocked loudly and Lenny Ruffalo yanked the door open. The sounds of rock music and a racetrack announcer's voice came from inside. "Yeah?"

Doyle didn't immediately answer. He paused to regard Ruffalo, who was wearing fatigue pants, brown boots, a cut-off tee-shirt that exposed his pale, skinny arms. The inscription on the tee-shirt read "Alice in Chains—Greatest Band Ever." Doyle estimated Ruffalo to be about five-foot seven, maybe one hundred fifty or so ill-conditioned pounds. His dark, greasy hair was brushed back from his forehead, ending in a tattered-looking pony tail. Ruffalo's black eyes skittered from Doyle's face to the nearby wall, then back again. This mother's on some kind of drug load, Doyle thought.

Doyle leaned forward, hands on the sides of the doorway. "I'm Jack Doyle. A friend of your cousin Ralph Tenuta. I want to talk to you."

Shock was apparent on Ruffalo's face. He attempted to shut the door, but Doyle stopped it with his foot and pushed his way into the basement apartment. The major item in that long, red-carpeted room was a giant television screen tuned to one of the national horse racing stations. A battered Barcalounger was positioned in front of the screen, behind a table holding a laptop computer, copies of *Racing Daily*, a yellow legal pad laden with scribbled notes. The walls of the room were covered with posters of various heavy metal bands plus *Penthouse* and *Biker Babes* magazine foldouts. Several empty pizza cartons lay next to a haphazard stack of Bud Lite beer bottles. To Doyle, not himself a fantastically fastidious man but no slob either, the odor of unwashed clothes and at least one unwashed body was noticeable enough to make him wince.

Ruffalo glared at Doyle. Then he turned his attention to the television screen. There was a three-horse photo finish in the fourth race at Del Mar. Its result was apparently not satisfactory as far as Ruffalo was concerned. He howled, "You pinheaded jock. You just cost me another one. Mother fuck." Lenny's sallow face was flushed as he pounded his fist on the back of the Barcalounger.

Doyle grabbed Ruffalo's left shoulder. Spun him round. Threw him down in the chair. Ruffalo attempted to rise, but Doyle kicked his feet out from under him and slammed him back.

"I don't have time to fuck around with you, Lenny. Stay down. Turn off that fucking TV."

Ruffalo smirked. Defiantly handed Doyle the remote control. Doyle hurled it as hard as he could against the back wall. Lenny yelped, "What'd you do that for, man? That's expensive." Shaken, he sat up straight in the chair.

Doyle stepped back. Took a long look at this poster-child for loserdom. He briefly thought, What am I doing here dealing with this societal remnant? The answer came when he thought about his friends Ralph and Rosa Tenuta.

Ruffalo made a lunging attempt to get up from the chair. Jack gave him another slap, this time a slighter one, right side of Ruffalo's unshaven face. Yanked him back down by his pony tail. The pitiful look on Ruffalo's face almost made Doyle soften his attitude. He squelched that inclination.

"Lenny, keep this in the front of your screwed-up mind. Do not ever again think about hiring someone to kill your cousin Ralph."

Clearly surprised, Ruffalo started to deny having sought a hit man. Doyle gave him another slap, this one harder. "Sit still."

Doyle walked to the little sink. After some searching, he located a somewhat clean glass and filled it with water and drank it down. Ruffalo shifted in his chair, Doyle watching him in the mirror over the dirty dish-laden sink. Doyle barked, "Sit the fuck back down."

Turning back to Lenny, Doyle said, "If you ever try anything like that again, I'm here. You won't see me coming, either. Things will get very fucking ugly for you. Get it?" He gave a tug on the pony tail that pulled Ruffalo's now tear-streaked face up.

"Okay, okay," Ruffalo said. "Jesus, how did you know about what I was doing?"

"That's not the main question, how I know. The main question is why would you want to have Ralph Tenuta killed?"

Ruffalo jumped up from the chair, enraged.

"Because," Lenny shouted, "your buddy Ralph, my relative, won't ever tell me about any winning horses he's got. He stiffed me good with one named Madame Golden. I was going to bet her if he'd given me any sign I should. Nothing. She won and paid a fucking bundle."

He slammed his hand on the arm of the chair. "Isn't blood supposed to mean something?" He slumped back down, head in his hands.

"Ralph is using this new rider from England, Ireland, wherever the fuck she's from," Ruffalo continued, "and she's doing great. She's new here. Nobody ever heard of her. I always bet against her, any race she's in. But the little bitch keeps winning. She's killing me in my betting. And so," he added bitterly, "is cousin Ralph."

"Lenny, you're breaking my heart. I'm not concerned about what you bet and lose, get it? If you are such a loser, why not give up betting? Get a real job. Get out of your mama's basement. 'Off the maternal teat,' as my Uncle Pete used to say."

Ruffalo made another attempt to reach up and strike Doyle. Jack slapped on both sides of his face. Ruffalo moaned, but looked up defiantly. "I won't forget this, you son of a bitch," he snarled.

"I hope you don't, punk. You ever try to do any harm to Ralph Tenuta, you won't live to regret it."

Ruffalo muttered something, but Doyle walked past him and up the basement stairs into the Berwyn evening, slamming the door behind him. He took a deep breath. "What a fucking day!"

Doyle curved around the side of the bungalow toward the front and the street where he had parked. An older woman came up the front walk toward him, head down, toting two heavy grocery sacks. She looked exhausted. But when she sensed Doyle's presence, she stopped, startled, and put down the bags.

Doyle said, "Mrs. Ruffalo?"

"Yes. Who are you?"

"My name is Jack Doyle. I was just down in the basement, having a talk with your son Lenny."

Elvira Ruffalo smiled. "Well, that's nice. My son doesn't have many friends. Or visitors. Pardon me. Your name again?"

"Jack Doyle. Tell your son not to forget what I said to him. Good evening, Mrs. Ruffalo."

Stumbling around his apartment, Lenny managed to locate the TV remote control his menacing visitor had thrown against the wall. Amazingly, it still worked. He walked to his mini-fridge and took out a Mountain Dew. Back in the Barcalounger, he turned on the horse racing network that showed night programs from the East Coast. Shuddered when he thought about the way this Doyle had pushed him around. Wondered how in the hell Doyle had found him. Remembered one Bud Lite-ridden afternoon when he'd asked a couple of OTB shop so-called buddies how he could lay a hit on Cousin Ralph. He thought he could trust those guys, especially Large. Maybe not. He winced as he thought of his contemptuous dismissal by Fifi Bonadio, his painful expulsion from the River Forest mansion by Bonadio's goons.

He'd have to come up with something else to convince Cousin Ralph Tenuta to help him with his wagering. He sat back in his chair. Took a slug of Mountain Dew, followed by a small dose from the large stash of meth he kept in the slit right arm of the Barcalounger.

Elivira opened the upstairs door to Lenny's basement lair.

"Can we eat, Lenny? In about a half-hour?"

"Yeah, Ma. I'll be up. I gotta make a phone call first."

He dialed Teresa Genacro.

Chapter Thirty-eight

Ingrid McGuire parked her green Chevy pickup truck in her allotted slot behind her Arlington Heights apartment complex. It was nearly 7 p.m. She had put in another twelve-hour day treating horses on the Heartland Downs backstretch. She was exhausted.

Ingrid walked slowly into the building's lobby and toward the elevator. Its door opened. "Why, hello, darling," said a stocky, elderly woman, Ingrid's next-door neighbor on the third floor of the building and one of the nosiest humans Ingrid had ever known. Samantha Gutteridge wore one of her several bright green pants suits, low-heeled shoes, earrings large and luminous enough to magnify light, and the look of expectation she always had when she was about to board the shuttle bus that would carry her to the Joliet, Illinos casino. She went three or four nights each week. Which was fine with Ingrid, because then this pest wouldn't be knocking at her door wanting to talk about horse racing. A well-off widow, Samantha loved the races almost as much as the slot machines.

Ingrid managed a "Good luck, Sam," before she opened her door. She was bone-tired. Another taxing day dealing with, and sometimes talking to, a series of one-thousand pound clients. Working this veterinarian practice by herself following Eric's departure had turned out to be much more than she'd bargained for. As soon as she had a chance, or time, she intended to advertise for a partner to join her in the growing practice. These days she never seemed to have the energy to do that at the end of her arduous days. Maybe after the Heartland Downs meeting ended....

She stripped off her work clothes and tossed them into the washing machine. Put a frozen chicken pot pie dinner in the oven. Ran a hot bath. Poured herself a glass of white wine, which she placed on the tub's edge as she slid into the water and lay back, gratefully feeling tension and fatigue draining out of her.

At 8:11, the phone in her living room rang. She wasn't about to leap out and answer it. Minutes later, her cell phone, which she had placed on top of her bedroom dresser, rang. Stopped. Rang again. "Got to be Eric," she said.

Every few days in the recent weeks since the breakup of their relationship and business practice, Eric had been phoning her, usually at night, usually late. At first he had been his old charming self, jocular, persuasive, as he attempted to lure her back. Her refusals made him increasingly angry. Ingrid changed both her landline and cell phone numbers in order to avoid his calls. Somehow, he had managed to find the new numbers. And his messages, left on voice mail after she had told him she would never talk to him again, became more and more threatening.

One morning at Heartland Downs, she had talked to Jack Doyle about this situation. He said, "Maybe you should get a restraining order against this guy."

"How would I do that?"

"Well, you'd need an attorney. I know one who could maybe help. Name is Art Engelhardt. I'll get you his phone number."

She called Engelhardt the next day. "Honey," he said, "I'm a racetrack and personal injury lawyer. I represent jockeys and trainers who have been unjustly accused and maligned. I got out of that crappy civil stuff years ago. But I can give the number of a Chicago attorney who's pretty good in that area. Frank Cohan. You want it?"

Ingrid had written down Cohan's name and number, but hadn't called him. Memories of her early days with Eric in

Urbana, later when they first came to the Chicago track, when he was not drinking heavily and, she thought, were in love, created a barrier to that kind of legal action.

She ran some more hot water into the tub. Sipped her glass of wine. Lay back and recalled what Eric had spoken to her about his "affection for," not his addiction to, alcohol.

"I stole my first drink from my father's nearly empty Manhattan glass when I was about ten," she remembered him saying. "My old man drank every night when he got home from his vet clinic. I loved the buzz I got off that taste and tried to do it again, couple of nights later. He caught me. Thumped the crap out of me. Grounded me for a week.

"My old man was not only a highly functioning alcoholic, but a bully. It wasn't until I was sixteen and big enough to start pushing him around that he stopped his late night rampages against my mother, me, and Rudy. One night, he was screaming obscenities aimed at my mother. I jumped out of bed. Ran into the corridor and into him and pushed him down the stairs. He was hurt, but not bad. He got up and looked at me and I could see the hate in his eyes. That was the end of all that shit from him.

"In high school, I played football and hung with a bunch of guys who were big beer drinkers. One of them, Freddie Bongard, also had secret access to his old man's liquor cabinet. His dad wasn't much of a drinker. Not like mine. Freddie would sneak out a fifth, whiskey or scotch or rum, we'd polish it off, then fill the bottle back up with tea and put it back. Took almost a year for Freddie's dad to get onto this hustle."

Ingrid took another sip of wine. Placed her head back on the rim of the tub. Tried to think of something other than, first, the good times she and Eric had at the University of Illinois, then the hints of disaster to come. Eric rarely drank much during the week. He zoned in on his studies and gleaned top grades. But he binged almost every weekend. Suffered monumental hangovers that encouraged him to dry out for the next five days. Then, he would be back at it again. Trying to justify this regimen to Ingrid, Eric laughed off its implications. "I'm in control of this," he insisted. He quoted a writer named Alexander Woolcott, who had famously remarked that he drank "in order to make other people interesting."

"I know where Woolcott was coming from," Eric said one evening. He reached out to hug her on the couch where they sat, watching the Urbana sunset through their condo's west window. "But I don't need booze to make you interesting, my dear."

The memory of him holding her, stroking her and kissing her, his wide smile and laughing eyes, their many shared interests, lingered. Painfully. She missed him badly. The old him.

After nearly an hour, muscle soreness and fatigue erased, Ingrid stepped out of the tub. In the floor length mirror on the back of the bathroom door, she noticed a nasty looking bruise on her right thigh. She toweled off, even managing to smile at the memory of Ralph Tenuta's newly arrived two-year-old filly, Betty the Blur, who had kicked her in the course of the examination Ingrid was providing. The blow had hurt for a few seconds, then been forgotten.

"They sometimes know not what they do," she said to herself. "That's why I've gotten some of them to listen more closely when I communicate with them."

Ingrid walked into her darkened bedroom, pulled a long white tee-shirt from the dresser drawer. In the kitchen, she took her dinner out of the oven. Poured a half-glass of pinot grigio. Heard both her phones ring in sequence, land line first.

Had to be Eric, damn him. The phone ringings bounced back and forth as she refused to answer. She took the landline off its hook, picked up the overcooked pot pie and threw it down into the disposal. Furious, she answered her cell phone. "You asshole," she shouted, "you're pitiful. Leave me alone." She banged the phone down on the counter. Felt tears forming. Picked up the phone, saying, "After all we had...that you completely blew off with your jealousy, your drinking..." She turned her head so he would not hear her sobs. "You need help I can't give you."

"Hey, dear Ingrid," he slurred, "you think this is all over between us? Wrong, baby, wrong."

She heard the rattling of ice cubes in whatever nearly glass was in Eric's hand. The sound of the glass being slammed down. Then his voice, low and hard.

"It ain't over," he said and hung up.

◇◇◇

Two nights later when Ingrid got home, there were several voice mail messages from clients. She held off listening to Eric's until she'd finished with the others. She was surprised to hear him talking so calmly.

"For your information," Eric said, "I've made an appointment with an alcohol addiction counselor. I'll go there Thursday. I hate living like this without you," he said softly. "Wish me luck."

"Well," she said to herself, "that's at least somewhat encouraging."

She made herself a sandwich before sitting down at her computer. Wiped out several generic emails before reading the one sent by her client, Buck Norman. "Ingrid, please come by the barn tomorrow or the next morning. I need you to try and 'communicate' with Myra, my old stable pony. For some reason, she's soured on life in general. She's only fifteen. That shouldn't be happening.

"On a better note," Norman continued, "if you haven't seen it, check out the YouTube video about a former, no-good racehorse named Lucky Lucy. She was rescued by this woman trainer. Taught to do all kind of things. Pretty amazing."

Intrigued, Ingrid located the video in question. A trainer named Sharon McCoy was shown running the formerly recalcitrant Lucky Lucy through an extensive routine that included nodding 'yes' or 'no.' Catching, fetching, kissing. bowing, staying and coming, counting up to five, and much more. Ingrid was entranced as she watched Lucky Lucy distinguish among three colors and, on command, rearing, pushing a barrel, performing a curtsy.

"Horses can do so much more than we ask them for," she said to herself.

Ingrid turned off the computer. Thinking about Lucky Lucy, and Eric's promise to seek counseling, she quickly went to sleep for the first time in many weeks. Hoping for the best.

Chapter Thirty-nine

Eric was on his way to a small office in a small office building just off Golf Road in Skokie. He parked in one of the spaces reserved for visitors. Laid his head on the steering wheel for a minute. Should he go through with this? Finally, he got out of his truck and went up the short walkway and hit the front door directory panel and was buzzed in. He looked at his watch. He was a few minutes late. He hurried down the carpeted corridor looking for number three. A door opened in front of him.

"Eric?"

"Yes."

"Welcome. I'm Rita Doty. Please come in."

She was a tall, attractive woman, in what Eric estimated to be her early forties. She wore a stylish black pantsuit over a white blouse. No lipstick or jewelry except for a sizeable wedding ring. Her hair was cut so short as to make her look on the verge of severe. A serious looking broad, he thought.

Her phone rang. Rita motioned him to the couch placed against the wall. As she engaged in a short conversation, Eric reviewed the diplomas and certificates on the walls. A University of Chicago undergraduate degree in psychology. Master's degree from Northwestern in the same field. A document testifying that she had completed three renowned courses in the counseling of alcoholics.

She replaced the receiver on her desk and sat down in a chair across from the couch. "I'm glad you decided to come here this morning, Eric. Let me ask you a few questions."

Rita made notes on her clipboard during the next twenty minutes when she elicited information about Eric's family background, education, job experience. She made a check mark at the section where Eric described, without much evident emotion, his father.

He was jittery. Sat forward off his couch seat, feet moving up and down, fingers tapping on his thighs. It was 10:27 a.m. "Why in the fuck am I doing this?" he muttered.

This was a question he had asked himself as he drove to Skokie. His motivation had been Ingrid's threat that if he didn't make this effort, keep this appointment, she would be forever through with him. Motivating this final threat of hers was the stupid, drunken, abrasive phone call he'd made to her earlier in the week, a call of which he was ashamed. He knew she cared about him. And he cared for her. Maybe, he had to admit to himself, loved her.

With so little work to do at the racetrack, Eric had begun drinking more than usual. Starting early in the morning, lasting until late at night. Deep down he knew it was getting away from him. But he didn't want to admit it to himself. He spent hours at his computer, betting horses and the stock market. Amazingly, he was doing quite well in the latter gambling game, not so well with the horses. He frequently woke up in the middle of the night. Tossed and turned. Got up to play some music and have a glass of brandy before, finally, sleep became possible. He had lost weight as well as energy. He knew he was going downhill. So he had decided to meet with Rita Doty.

Rita said, "Eric, I want to make something clear." She paused and took off her glasses and laid them on the desk. "I am a recovering alcoholic. I can speak to you about alcoholism from experience. Mostly bitter experience. Some of my drinking I considered enjoyable, a form of escapism. But the large majority of it, though I was for years determined not to admit it, was by far very, very bitter. I began drinking in junior high school, eighth grade. Hung with a bunch of people who also drank.

Continued in high school. Went on partying during college. I fought to not let it derail my scholastic progress.

"Finally, one late winter day, I admitted to myself that my life was out of control. I was now ignoring obligations and deadlines. And people I cared about who cared about me. Alcohol had taken control of me. I felt battered. Desperately unhappy. That is when I finally decided to enter a rehab program." She paused to take a sip of tea. "That decision saved my life, Eric."

Eric, uneasy, glanced restlessly around the room. "What has that got to do with me? Sure, I drink. Probably more than I should. But I don't feel it's ruining my life."

Rita leaned back in her chair. Smiled. "Unfortunately, that's what all alcoholics want to believe. 'Not ruining *my* life,' they tell themselves. How does an alcoholic's drinking affect others? He, or she, ignores that question. I know this from experience."

"How long has it been since you stopped drinking?"

"Twenty-two years and five months. When I did, I put my life on the right track. I married. My husband and I have two children. I've established a very useful practice helping people like the person I used to be to become a different, happier, better person, like I am now."

He got up from the couch. "That's quite a claim." He walked over to the small room's lone window. An Hispanic gardening crew was aiming loud blowers at piles of leaves and grass cuttings toward the parking lot curb. He stood with his arms crossed on his chest, right foot tapping the floor. Feeling an immense sense of threat to the way he now lived. To who he really was. There was a boiling feeling in his chest until he finally took a deep breath.

Seated back on the couch, under control, Eric said, "Look, I appreciate the fact that you have gone through what I've heard called the 'tunnel of alcoholism" and come out the other side. I admire that. But I just don't consider myself to be in that tunnel."

Rita waited. Eric said, "Okay, what would be your advice for me?"

"First, commit yourself to embracing change. I run a program here I call 'Life Retrieval.' It aims to remove alcohol from its ability to barricade your true self from life. Sound corny?" she said, leaning back in her chair. "So be it."

"Life Retrieval," Eric said. "Please. Sounds like some kind of infomercial crap that's on an obscure television channel late at night."

Rita looked down at the notes on her clipboard. "Eric, have you considered joining Alcoholics Anonymous?"

"Oh, yeah. I went to one meeting a couple of months ago. Right at Heartland Downs. Run by the Racetrack Chaplaincy in their little building on the backstretch."

"What did you think?"

"I was surprised at some of the people I saw there. A few guys my age, a couple of punk kids, many older guys, some of them horse owners, a couple of trainers, a few young women grooms."

Rita said, "It sounds as if you were observing them pretty closely."

"This meeting went on for more than two hours. People drinking bad coffee and smoking cigarettes. Getting up to make their public confessions of weakness. Yearning for appreciation for their candor. I thought it was embarrassing. A lot of crap."

"There are hundreds of thousands of men and women all over the world who would disagree with your assessment."

"That's their business," Eric snapped. He thought she was looking at him condescendingly. He could feel anger again churning inside of him. What he really needed right now was a stiff drink. He got up from the couch and walked to the office's little water cooler and filled a small cup. Drank it down. Then another. The midmorning sun was coming through the dark window blinds. He took a deep breath as he looked out. Reviewed his situation with his brother Rudy, his dilemma with all the goddamned clients who had dropped him, led by Ralph Tenuta. Thought bitterly of Ingrid's retreat from him.

He reached into his jacket pocket for his checkbook.

"What do I owe you?"

Startled at his abruptness, Rita got up, put her glasses on, shaking her head in frustration. "Seventy-five dollars, Eric.

Although you didn't use your fifty-minute hour." She went behind her desk and moved some papers around.

He quickly wrote out the check and placed it on her desk. He waited until she looked up at him.

"Nice try, Rita. But this kind of thing is just not for me. Nice meeting you."

Rita went to the window and watched Eric walk across the parking lot, open his car door, get behind the wheel, and slam the door closed. He sat for a minute or so. Arms extended on the steering wheel, head between them. The gardeners motioned for him to move his car so they could collect the piles of leafy debris.

Eric jammed his car into reverse. Turned and gunned it toward the entrance leading to Golf Road.

Rita sat down behind her desk. She had nearly twenty minutes before her next client. It had been an unpromising meeting with Eric Allgauer. She hated results like this. But she knew there was nothing to do but accept them.

She booted up her Mac. Pulled up his name. An entry she had made the day before when she thought he might turn out to become a client.

Rita hit "delete." She knew Eric would never be back.

Chapter Forty

Carrying a sack of takeout from the hamburger joint around the corner from his condo, Doyle was fumbling for his key to the front door when he heard a noise to his right. Pivoting, he dropped the food as he saw a ski-masked individual leaping toward him, swinging a piece of lead pipe at his head. Doyle's boxer reflexes enabled him to evade the wide swing as he simultaneously unleashed a crushing right cross on the jaw of his attacker, who tumbled backwards into the bushes.

Almost at once, Doyle felt a glancing but painful blow on the back of his head. It knocked him to his knees. He fell flat and rolled over onto his side. He recognized the voice of Lenny Ruffalo saying, "Theresa. Theresa. Are you all right?"

The figure in the bushes struggled up. Doyle realized he had punched a tall, sturdy woman with his quick right cross. He tried to stand. Out of the corner of his eye he saw Lenny raising a baseball bat.

Ruffalo kicked Doyle in the stomach twice. Doyle gasped. He could see Lenny reaching back for another kick. Doyle swiveled onto his left hip and kicked the feet out from under Ruffalo whose head bounced off the concrete. Doyle managed to get to his feet.

Lenny was helped up by his companion. Blood dripped from his scalp where it had landed on the concrete stair. The woman said, "We gotta get out of here." She picked up the bat Lenny had dropped.

"That's what you get, Doyle, you son of a bitch, for threatening me in my house. And there'll be more you ever do that again," Ruffalo screeched. The woman grabbed Lenny by his elbow and hustled him down the entrance walk and around the corner. Doyle heard the loud rasp of an old car's engine, then the screetch of tires.

Doyle, dizzied and in pain, leaned over the curb and vomited into the gutter. A couple of jaunty joggers swept past him, laughing, one saying, "Can't hold your booze, buddy?"

"Fuck you," Doyle mumbled. He retrieved the brown sack with its now flattened cheeseburger and fries, walked slowly to the rear of his condo building, and deposited the bag in the dumpster. He briefly considered an emergency room visit. Instead, he stumbled through the back door of his building and into the elevator and rode to the second floor. Before making it to his couch, Doyle got a towel, filled it with ice, and held it to his bloodied head.

"This," he vowed, "will not go unanswered." He slept. Four and a half hours later, he woke up, sore as hell, mad as hell.

It was almost noon when he arrived at the Ruffalo's Berwyn home. His knock on Lenny's door as well as his knock on the front door went unanswered. As he started to leave, neighbor Pat Sena leaned across the fence. "If you're looking for Elvira, she's at her flower shop."

"Actually, I came here to see Lenny."

"Well, you're not going to have any luck there. Lenny and his lady friend left about an hour ago. Said they were going on vacation."

"Did they say where?"

Pat Sena said, "No, they did not."

Chapter Forty-one

Doyle made his phone calls, lining up mounts for Mickey Sheehan in the upcoming weekend races. He'd gotten her on some
decent mounts. He walked out of Tenuta's office onto the patch
of grass bordering the barn area.

Raised his face to the early morning sun. Breathed in the air
pungent with the odor of hay and horses. Listened to a pair of
Mexican-American grooms trying to sing along with the salsa song
playing on the boom box they had positioned on the railing at the
north end of the barn. A procession of female hot walkers followed
with their horses, not at all into the music provided by their co-
workers. The men were on their toes while leading their horses,
bopping up and down. The women looked tired as they trudged
behind but they were chatting happily. Doyle knew a couple of
them. Single mothers rearing young children working their asses
off to get by. He gave them what he hoped was an encouraging
smile. "*Hola*, Jack Doyle," answered one of them.

The two lead men, both in their late twenties, continued
down and around the large barn. Their singing was so awful as
to be comical. And they knew it. They laughed as they passed
him by. He gave them a grin and a thumbs-up. As a survivor of
the corporate account executive wars, he was always delighted
and appreciative when he observed people at work who liked
their work, no matter what the hell it was.

Doyle saw Ingrid McGuire approaching, groom Paul Albano
beside her.

"Ingrid," Doyle said, "when you're done here this morning, can I see you for a minute?"

She gave him a long look, then a lengthier laugh. "I've never seen you wear a ball cap before. Much less one turned backwards."

Doyle said, "I'm working on changing my image." Actually, he had put on the cap to conceal the still sizeable lump on the back of his head from Ruffalo's bat attack the night before.

"Do you want to interrogate me about horse communicating, you skeptic? I'll give you maybe half a minute." This was the most relaxed he'd seen Ingrid on her backstretch rounds in several days.

"I'll be in Ralph's office. Come in when you can."

An hour later, as they sat in Tenuta's office, Paul Albano poked his head in the door. "Jack, I'm going home to kick back for a couple of hours. I'll be back before the first race. When you leave, lock the door."

Doyle said, "Ingrid. Coffee?"

"No, thanks. Does Ralph have any bottled water in that battered old mini-fridge?"

"As a matter of fact, he does. That appliance," Doyle said as he stepped toward it, "looks like it dates back to the early days of electricity. But it still works." He handed Ingrid a bottle of water. Reached deep into the second shelf and extracted one of the bottles of Dr. Pepper he had placed there.

Ingrid opened her water bottle. "Thanks, Jack." She drank a third of it. Said, "Tell me, how is Ralph dealing with his suspension?"

"According to Rosa, he's 'pacing his house like a panther. Wearing a path in the carpet.' In other words, driving her nuts. I went there last night for dinner. Great meal as usual. But fun was not had. Ralph is depressed, and pissed, and bewildered and puzzled. He had nothing to do with Madame Golden's positive. But here he is, stuck with the results. The time away from his job, the smear on his record, it's killing him."

Doyle answered the phone. Relayed Tenuta's instructions to blacksmith Travis Hawkins for the following day about the horses that needed to be reshod. "Take care, man," Doyle said as he hung up.

He turned on the ancient desk fan. It whirred weakly. He said, "Look, Ingrid, I'm sorry I ragged on you the other day about your horse communicating. I was, well, not myself."

"Maybe you were yourself," Ingrid smiled. "But I appreciate your apology. A hard guy like you, you probably don't do much apologizing."

"You've got that right," Doyle grinned. "But I'm working on improvement in that area."

"I think you've got work to do," she laughed.

Ingrid sat back on the couch and lay her head back. "My communicating with horses is a special thing in my life. As, for the most part, horses are. I find them fascinating. Last week I read about what some researchers in France had recently determined. Amazing stuff."

Doyle said, "Like what?"

"Well, they did acoustic analyses of whinnies and the reactions of horses to various recorded whinnies. It all suggested that vocal calls play a very important social role. The whinnies appear to be unique to each individual horse. The researchers described the whinny as a three-part call, having an introduction, a climax, and an ending that varies according to sex. Stallions have low-pitched frequencies. Mares and geldings have higher-pitched frequencies. Horses apparently recognize the voices of their social partners, as the researchers termed them, even when they can't see each other. That explains their reactions when they're separated. If these buddies, or social partners, are still within hearing range of each other, which is up to six-tenths of a mile, their reactions are vocally strong."

The reclusive cat Tuxedo spurted out from behind a turned-over cushion and leaped onto Ingrid's lap. Ingrid patted her absently. "I'm kind of used up this morning. Taking over the whole practice from Eric is more than I had bargained for. I'm doing the work, hard work, of two people. But," she sat up and smiled, "it's got its rewards. Most of the horses I treat are all doing well and running well. And I'm making more money that I ever have in my life. I've actually started to make major inroads into my student loan debt."

"Do you have any contact with Eric?"

"Not that I enjoy. He's so angry and bitter. I just want to stay away from him. He said he went to a counselor on alcoholism and that it was 'a fiasco.' People tell me he spends his afternoons in that Big Players Bar at the track. Drinking and betting. Losing money. They'd had to call his brother Rudy a couple of times to take him out of there he was so obnoxious." She turned her face away from Doyle and looked out the window. "God, it's just so pitiful what this man is doing to himself. I first knew him when he was a much different, better person."

Doyle restrained himself from declaring he'd long considered Eric Allgauer a premier asshole. He changed the subject.

"Has Plotkin had anything to say for himself lately? That's what I wanted to talk to you about."

She sat up. "Plotkin is a happy little colt. We're lucky, you know, that horses can communicate in ways we have yet to imagine. People keep considering them dumb animals. If people would take their time and look into this, they would lose their prejudicial attitude I guarantee you, Jack.

"I saw a film the other night about a famous cowboy horse trainer named Brannaman. The man holds clinics all over the country on educating horses. He says something early in the movie that struck home to me. 'A lot of times, rather than helping people with horse problems, I'm helping horses with people problems.' I know exactly where he's coming from."

Ingrid checked her watch and stood up. "I'm due over at Buck Norman's barn. Gotta go. I've got to worm that new filly he just bought. Thanks for the conversation, Jack."

Doyle walked her to the door. "You've succeeded in making a believer out of me as far as communicating, Ingrid. And I know you're doing the best for these animals that you treasure and treat. I sure as hell respect that."

"Thanks. Maybe you're more open-minded than I thought."

"People have started to say that a lot about me," Doyle kidded.

Ingrid climbed into the driver's seat of her pickup and keyed the ignition. Doyle leaned into her open window. "Listen. Be very careful how you deal with Eric. From all I've heard, he's running off the rails."

"Thanks, Jack. I know enough to be careful."

She started the engine but didn't drive off. "Jack, do you ever think about reincarnation? No, no, don't laugh. I'm serious. I've been thinking about it a lot lately. There are millions of people who believe that after dying and leaving this life, they will return as something other than what they were."

"This is a little early in the day for me to tackle serious subjects. I didn't know they included philosophy in the University of Illinois vet school courses. That's where you went, right?"

Ingrid said, "I know you're being facetious, Jack. That's probably ingrained in what you are." She pulled her hat down on her head. He could see she was angry.

"Ingrid, I didn't mean to insult you. It's just that I have many doubts about many practices. Whether they be religious. Philosophical. Hell, culinary, for that matter. I have a hard time trying to determine who is right on a lot of things. Freud? Jung? Noam Chomsky? I lived with a woman for a year and a half who was trying to fight her way through that maze. Had to leave her."

"Why was that?"

Doyle said, "She wore me out."

A breeze came up and kicked dust into the parking lot.

Ingrid put her truck in gear. She said, "It's not even ten in the morning and I'm asking you probing questions. I've got to get going. See you."

He leaned back from her truck window. "If I had my choice of animals to return as, I'd be a popular thoroughbred stallion. Good food, good care on some beautiful Kentucky farm. Active sex life lasting for years, with a variety of mates."

"Jack, you are something else." She was still laughing as she turned onto the roadway leading to Buck Norman's barn, where she had succeeded Eric Allgauer as the chief vet. Doyle waved as she pulled out onto the asphalt roadway.

Five days later, the horse Keno Chemist, trained by Buck Norman, won the ninth race at Heartland Downs. Four days after that came the positive report of the drug elephant juice discovered in Keno Chemist's blood and urine tests. The winning purse was ordered to be taken away and redistributed.

Despite his protests, Buck Norman, another trainer with a previously unblemished record, joined Ralph Tenuta on the thirty-day suspension list.

Chapter Forty-two

Doyle drove to their apartment and picked up Mickey and Nora to take them to the Wilfredo Gavidia fund-raising dinner at Heartland Downs. The sisters sat in the back seat of his Accord. He looked in the rear view mirror. "Ladies, you both look great. Save a dance for me."

He could see Nora in the mirror nodding to him. Mickey was silent, looking out the window. Doyle said, "Mickey, anything new on Wilfredo?"

"No. His condition remains the same. I talked to his wife just before you came to get us. She's having a terrible, terrible time."

They sat at a table that had been reserved for them by Moe Kellman. Tenuta had reserved the tickets, but Moe insisted on buying a table. He had told Jack he was unable to attend, but wanted to participate. Doyle read the program. Among the $5000 donors was M. Kellman. Jack sat between the Sheehan sisters. The other two chairs at the table were vacant.

It was bounteous dinner served buffet style, courtesy of Heartland Downs owner R. L. Duncan. All ticket proceeds would go to the fund for Wilfredo Gavidia and his family.

A country and western quartet worked assiduously from the temporary bandstand. Every twenty minutes or so, they played a number that lured some of the jockeys and horsemen and their wives or dates to hit the dance floor and line-dance the Texas two-step in impressive fashion.

Nora watched avidly. "Jack, have you ever done that dance? Looks tricky to me."

"It is. And I don't. I made a fool of myself when I first tried it. Even with all my good footwork carrying over from my boxing days." He sipped his glass of beer. "When they play one of those slow, mournful country numbers, involving heartbreak and trucks and booze and guns and dogs, deceit, and desertion, I'd be happy to guide you gently and gracefully around the floor."

Mickey returned to the table carrying a mounded plate. "Fantastic food display up there, Nora. And Jack. You should give it a go."

He followed Nora in the buffet line. She was wearing a well-cut light brown dress. Short enough to show what Doyle thought of as "her excellent wheels." She was getting admiring glances from several of the nearby males as she talked animatedly to the two women in front of her in the line.

Back at their table, Mickey had quickly eaten everything on what had been her full plate. "I've got my eye on that dessert table," she said seriously. "Looks feckin' brilliant."

"Your sister is an amazing little person," Doyle said.

"I wouldn't argue with you about that. I love her dearly. She is, well, completely open and enthusiastic. Not like most of the rest of our family."

"You're referring to brother Kieran?"

"I am indeed."

Another couple came from the buffet line to claim the two open seats at their table. Doyle got up, shook hands with the man, and introduced himself and the Sheehan girls.

The man, medium height, husky, well dressed, said,"I'm Mel Benbow. I'm a customer of Moe Kellman's. He was nice enough to invite us to share his table. This is my wife Melody. Nice to meet you."

Benbow dug into his his laden food plate. He said, "Jack, I think I remember you. I used to work in television. Now, I produce a lot of product for various Internet sites. I saw those clips of you at that racetrack balloon disaster a years ago. Am I right? You're that guy, right?"

"Yes. That was me." Nora was looking at him. Surprised and expectant. Waiting for an explanation. Doyle gave her a look suggesting that he would explain later. "Yes, Mel, that was me. If you don't mind, I'd rather not talk about it."

Melody Benbow laughed dismissively. She looked to Doyle as if she'd had at least a couple of visits to the open bar to rev up what appeared to be her unpleasant attitude. "He'd rather not talk about it," Melody said. "What a hero." She drained her glass of Scotch and soda. Challenged him with a snarky little grin.

Melody's makeup was draining in small rivulets down her obviously surgically remodeled face. Jack turned to talk to Nora, but Melody would not let go. "So what kind of hero were you?" Doyle knew she was being contentious. "I was not a hero," Doyle said. "All I did in that moment was get the hell out of the way of being killed. Hero. It's a much overused word these days. It's thrown around without a lot of regard for accuracy."

"What do you mean by that?" Mel Benbow said.

"I'm sure we all recall the plane that went down in the Hudson River after leaving that New York airport. I don't remember if it was from Kennedy or LaGuardia. A few years back. Whatever. The media repeated again and again that the pilot was a hero. Bullshit."

Melody said, "Why wasn't that pilot a hero, Doyle?"

"Because a hero is someone who *risks* his or her own life to save another or others. This pilot, adroitly landing his plane on the river with no damage to his passengers, was not a 'hero.' He was saving his own ass as well as all the people on his plane. What he was was an extremely efficient practitioner of his craft. God bless him. A remarkable man. Very good pilot. But no 'hero' by my definition."

Melody, angry, said, "Well, who do you consider heroes, Mr. Doyle?"

"Heroes? The soldier that falls on a live grenade to protect his platoon. Firemen who charge into burning buildings. Cops who get into gun fights with armed criminals. In other words, people who voluntarily risk their lives and well being. There was nothing voluntary about what the Hudson River pilot did. He *had* to try and do what he did." Doyle stood up. "If you'll excuse me, I'm going to get a beer. Nora, you want anything?"

Benbow began talking to his wife, both of them ignoring the Sheehan sisters. Nora said, "You know, Mickey, I think Jack makes a good point. About words being inaccurately tossed around. Like this morning, when I got on the computer, there was a news item about a famous actor quote secretly losing his hair unquote. What can be 'secret' about it if it's on the Internet?"

Mickey laughed and patted Nora's hand. "What do you call these things? Sermantics?"

"No," Nora said. "I think you mean semantics."

"I'm sure you're right. I just didn't go far enough in school," Mickey said.

Mickey excused herself, the Benbows paying her no attention whatsoever, and walked to the next table and invited fellow apprentice jockey Calvin Bolt to join her on the dance floor. She was nimble. He was earnest. They embraced as the song ended. Turned out, Mickey was a natural at Texas two-step dancing. When the music stopped, Calvin Bolt bowed deeply to Mickey, then raised her right hand in the air. The jockeys and their dance partners looking on roared their approval. Bolt led her back to her table, where they sat and watched Nora and Jack move around the dance floor to "The Tennessee Waltz."

Jack smiled at his enthusiastic partner. "You're quite lithe on your feet," he said, giving her a twirl.

"Lithe? Or light? Oh, Jack, we Irish dancers are both." He hugged her as the song ended and they returned to the table. The Benbows had departed. It was just Mickey there with young Calvin Bolt.

Bolt rose from his seat to introduce himself to Nora. Jack said, "Hello, Calvin. I know who you are. You take some mounts away from my client Mickey. Good to see you."

Calvin, Doyle had observed, was yet another impressive jockey talent from out of Louisiana's Cajun country. Many of his predecessors from that unique section of America had been voted into racing's Hall of Fame. They were introduced at early ages to 200-yard, bare-backed dashes on unsaddled horses charging down brown dirt chutes on Sunday afternoons filled with encouragement from friends, family, and beer-drinking bettors. Calvin, Doyle knew, had his first ride in that colorful world of competition when he was six-and-a-half years old.

"Mister Jack, I'm happy to meet you, sir." Like most of his predecessors and contemporaries, Bolt was given to forms of formal address. A man's name was always preceded by Mister, a woman's by Miss or Mrs. It was a Cajun thing, reflecting how he was raised. Doyle always marveled at this polite practice that was so alien to most American athletes.

Mickey, her face flushed from the exertions of dancing, reached for her water glass. She said, "Calvin, tell Jack about the trail rides with music down from where you're from. They sound like terrible great fun."

"Well," Calvin said, "there's one that drew, I don't know…2000, 3000 people last year. Called the Pineywoods ride. They ride their horses on this long, winding trail. End of the day, they wind up at a big farm where there's food and music. And dancing. This is near my home town, Lafayette. It's great, Mr. Jack. Folks are real friendly. If you horse has troubles, they'll lend you a trail horse for you to take. They'll hand you a beer real quick, too," he smiled. "And a good boudin sausage to go with it."

He turned to Mickey. "There's another real popular one out of St. Landry Parish. That's in the fall. Called Step-and-Strut. I did that once. Also great, Mr. Jack."

Doyle was intrigued. "Who supplies the music? Bands or tape? And what kind of music?"

"Oh, bands, or small groups of players," Calvin said. "We got two kinds of music. Both from Acadiana. We've got Cajun music, a lot of it. Kind of sad, slow, but pretty, you know? They have to have good fiddlers to make this right.

"Then, you've got zydeco. A lot of black guys from the Creole area do this. They use accordions, washboards. It's kind of a bit livelier. But," Calvin said, "both kinds of the music lead to a lot of fun."

The band stopped playing. Overhead lights dimmed to signal the start of an intermission. Melody Benbow stumbled her way back to her seat. "Have you seen Mel? I'm ready to go home."

They said no. Said goodbye to her, Nora even giving Melody a pat on the shoulder as she passed.

"That was nice of you," Doyle said.

"She's kind of a sorrowful person," Nora said.

"Well," Doyle said, "the songs are over. But Melody lingers on. Jesus, she seems like a sour little bitch to me." He got up. "I need a drink. Can I get you ladies anything?" They declined.

"I'll have a glass of wine later, Jack," Nora said.

Chapter Forty-three

Drinkers were stacked three deep at the temporary bar. Doyle recognized his friend from the track, the bartender Las Vegas Lou, who nodded to him over the heads of the two short women in front of him.

"Jameson's, Jack?"

Lou expertly poured a healthy measure and handed it to Jack over the heads of the chattering women. Doyle tried to give him a five-dollar bill. Lou shook him off. "On me, my friend."

"Thanks, Lou."

As he started back to his table he felt a tug on his sleeve. Irritated, he spun around. It was horse owner Steve Holland. "Sorry, Jack. I just wanted to say hello," Holland said apologetically.

Doyle relaxed. "Steve, please remember never to grab a man by the arm with which he's holding his drink. It's an old Irish saying."

Holland smiled and looked around the large room. "It's a very good turnout here tonight. I'm glad to see it. Racetrack people stick together."

"Agreed. I hope they dig down deep for the Wilfredo Gavidia cause. Catch you later, Steve."

Shortly before nine, after the dessert table had been thoroughly utilized, Heartland owner R. L. Duncan made his way to the front of the room where a microphone had been set up. People began to quell their conversations. Duncan tapped the mike. The room became quiet.

Duncan, a multimillionaire businessman who had bought Heartland Downs a dozen years before and a prominent figure in thoroughbred racing, said, "I'm so glad to see you all here tonight. Your presence is a great tribute to Wilfredo Gavidia, one of our finest jockeys, and gentlemen, and a friend of so many of us."

He paused to drink from a water glass. "As you know, Wilfredo faces a long, long, uphill battle. A battle that will be expensive both in emotions for him and his family, and in medical bills. We are here tonight to help Wilfredo and his lovely wife Juanita and their young son and daughter face the financial challenges. We are depending on your generosity.

"Very few people outside of our sport," Duncan continued, "understand the consequences of what is so often a very dangerous athletic pursuit both for horse and rider. Our jockeys, needless to say, are extremely talented people athletically. But by the very nature of what they willingly do, they are often in jeopardy. They accept that reality. And they live with it.

"In an attempt to emphasize this to some of the non-racetrackers who have joined us here tonight, I have asked Dr. Louise Gendel to address us. Dr. Gendel is one of the major practitioners at the Chicago Rehabilitation Institute, the world renowned institution devoted to aiding seriously injured members of our society."

Dr. Gendell got up from her chair at a front row table and walked to Duncan's side. A middle-aged, heavy-set woman, she held a fistful of note cards in her slightly shaking hands. Duncan gave her the microphone. Doyle shifted in his chair, having an empathy moment for this nervous woman. She glanced down at her note cards. Slid her glasses up higher on her slightly sweating face. After shuffling the note cards one more time, she plunked them down on the lectern. Removed her glasses. Took a deep breath. Finally smiled and looked out at her audience.

"Good evening to you all," Dr. Gendel said. "I am by no means a practiced public speaker. I'm a physician. And a researcher. I had prepared a long presentation of statistics, background and foreground, an elaborate PowerPoint presentation describing the work we do at the Institute. I've decided not to go into all that detail here tonight."

Dr. Gendell paused. Took a deep breath. Looked increasingly more at ease. "Many of you know the saying that when jockeys are at work, riding horses in their races, theirs is a job that sees them always followed around by an ambulance. Every race. Every day in this country. Unfortunately, there is a very good reason for that. Theirs is a dangerous occupation that demands it.

"The studies we have done at the Institute over the past several years have produced some pretty amazing statistics involving jockeys. At least sixty percent of them, during their careers, suffer multiple fractures resulting from falls. Of those fractures, fifty-three percent occur in the upper body and chest. A depressing percentage of those injuries result in either deaths or lives spent as quadriplegics. These are depressing statistics that we must ponder and attempt to improve while we care for those already impaired. We urge you to be generous in contributing to the Wilfredo Gavidia Fund tonight. Thank you."

Doyle glanced across the table at his little employer. Mickey had listened raptly to Dr. Gendel, her hands clenched. Nora had an arm around her sister. A pang of fear shot through Doyle. Could such a terrible thing happen to Mickey? He knew the answer was, of course it could. To any one of these brave, determined little athletes. On any given day, at any given racetrack.

He turned his attention back to the front of the room where Duncan was thanking Dr. Gendell and encouraging "everyone present to donate as much as you can to the Fund. There are envelopes on tables near the exits. Thank you all very much for coming here tonight."

◇◇◇

Doyle drove the sisters to their apartment. Nora sat in front, Mickey in back, chin propped in her palm, looking out the window. There was little talk. Finally, as he steered the Accord up to the entrance of the building, Mickey said, "That was pretty depressing stuff from that doctor there tonight." Doyle said, "I guess it's better to know those facts than not."

Mickey tapped him on the shoulder. "Jack, I heard everything there tonight that you heard. All the sad statistics about what happens to riders. What I want to say to you is, don't back off on me. I want to go on riding here. I love it. I need it."

She opened her car door. "You're kind of what at home we'd call an 'old soul' when it comes to me." He could see her in the mirror, smiling. "Don't be," she said emphatically.

"I know Ralph has me riding three tomorrow. And Plotkin's coming up to that little stakes prep for the Futurity. I'm looking forward to that. See you tomorrow, Jack. Later, Nora." She sprinted up the walk to the doorway.

"Mickey's in a hurry to call her back-home honey. It's early morning over there." Nora sighed. "See what I'm dealing with here, Jack? Mickey will never voluntarily leave this worrisome sport. That's just the way she is."

Nora pushed her seat back. "I don't think there's any way for you to come in tonight for a memorable visit, Jack."

"Not with Mickey on hand." He turned on the Accord's CD player. "Want to listen to something wonderful?"

Nora said, "Of course."

It was saxophonist John Coltrane with the great baritone Johnny Hartman, McCoy Tyner on piano, Hartman singing "They Say That Falling in Love is Wonderful." They listened appreciatively. Nora put her hand on his leg, turned her face to his.

"Would you say you're falling in love with me, Jack?

"I've already fallen in lust with you, my dear. Love is an entirely other matter."

She laughed. "I appreciate your candor. Your feelings are much the same as mine. I guess we're lucky to have it that way. No great expectations."

Doyle kissed her gently. "I love the looks of you."

Seconds later a gray Lexus pulled up behind Doyle's Accord, its impatient driver thumping on the horn. Doyle bristled. He prepared to get out of his car and walk back to the Lexux and set this asshole straight.

Nora said, "Not to worry about him, Jack. He lives across the hall from us. A real boring busybody. His name is Bakken. Horace Bakken, I think. The building manager told me Bakken is either unmarried, or divorced. I'd guess the latter. He's always knocking on our door to see 'How you young Irish girls are doing?' A real pain the arse. His breath smells like mothballs. Don't laugh. I'm not kidding."

She picked up her handbag. "I should go in. Mickey's probably done talking with her hometown gem."

"Listen to this first." He advanced the CD to "Lush Life."

When the song ended, Nora said, "Wonderful. Thanks. I will have to buy that CD."

He reached into his glove compartment. Extracted the CD and its case. Placed it in her hands. "Take it as a gift. I'll get myself another."

"You have many gifts, Jack."

Doyle said, "I won't disagree. I'm very good at kissing. Fondling. Clever stroking. Tenderness."

Nora laughed as she pulled his face down close to hers. He winced when her hand touched the lessening but still present bump on the back of his head. She heard him whisper, "Those are among my specialties."

Minutes later, after Nora had said good night, Doyle approached the Lexus. He saw in the driver's seat an old man so small and wrinkled he reminded Doyle of gnomes he'd read about in a long ago children's book. The man wore a black leather cap, a gray suit, and an expression of exasperation.

"What's your problem, Pops?"

"You are blocking the entrance to the front door, young man."

Doyle said, "I guess you've forgotten how to pull around? Take it easy." He stood up, tapped his palm on the driver's side window, and went to his car.

Turning out of the apartment building driveway, Doyle heard one more agitated blast from the Lexus. "That's the spirit," he said, laughing.

Chapter Forty-four

Doyle and Tenuta met for breakfast in the track kitchen just before seven the next morning. They bought coffee and donuts and sat at a window table overlooking the crowded parking lot.

"Well, Ralph, even after listening to those depressing statistics about jockey endangerment from last night, my little employer is determined to continue. What a tough little person she is. I couldn't talk Mickey out of riding racehorses no matter how much I'd like to."

Tenuta shrugged. "Look around this room, Jack. See how many jockeys are here? Exercise riders? Upbeat, jiving, laughing at each other? It's like this every morning at every racetrack I've ever been at. These people are all cut from the same bolt of cloth. Dedicated to horsebacking. God bless them, I say."

Doyle said, "You want another coffee? Fried pastry?"

"No, thanks.

"When I got home after the dinner last night, Ralph, I got on the computer and did some research."

"About what?"

"About the protective equipment riders are wearing. Very interesting."

Tenuta said, "In what way?"

"According to what I was able to unearth, the advancement in protective gear for jockeys has been ridiculously slow. Glacial. I read that it took more than twenty years in the early 1900s for jockeys' goggles to be put into use. You've seen countless times what the goggles jockeys wear now look after a race on a muddy track. They're covered with dirt. That's why riders go out there with six pair of goggles, so they can flip down a clean pair as the race goes on. Imagine what it must have been like all those years before goggles covered their eyes. Jocks must have come out of those races half-blinded and stinging."

Doyle sipped his coffee and waited for Tenuta to return with his third morning doughnut. "Go on," Tenuta said.

"Protective helmets for the riders. They didn't come into use until the mid-fifties. The jocks used to wear little leather beanies under their caps before that. That wasn't a whole lot of protection. Like wearing a yarmulke at a Klu Klux Klan rally."

Tenuta shot him a look. "I'm only kidding, Ralph. I made up the yamulka comparison. It wasn't on the Internet."

"I hope not."

"Now, Ralph, hear me out." Doyle looked down at his notebook. "The so-called flak jackets that they wear now became mandatory for riders in most US racing states in the nineties."

Tenuta said, "Yeah, I remember that. Most of the jocks that rode for me didn't want to wear the flak jackets. They complained they were too bulky. Too hot in the summertime. And, of course, they were different. Believe me, in horse racing, no matter what it is, if it's new, there's going to be resistance to it."

"All right," Doyle said. He flipped over another notebook page. "Ralph, you ever hear about this thing for jockeys called the air jacket?"

"No. What is it?"

Doyle said, "These items were developed in Japan. First, for motorcycle racers. Then some of the horse world people over there caught on and bought them for their riders."

"I don't know what you're talking about, Jack. What the hell is an air jacket?"

"It's really a vest that fastens around the rider's torso. There's a lanyard attached to it. The lanyard clips to the rider's saddle on one end and to a carbon-dioxide cartridge on the other end.

If the jockey is thrown off the saddle, the lanyard unclips from the cartridge. That triggers, I am quoting here, 'the release of the CO_2 that inflates protective pockets inside the vest."

Tenuta said, "I'm trying to picture this, Jack. Go on."

"Okay. The inflation of the vest is super fast. The air pockets in the vest help cushion impact on the ground on the base of the neck, or spine, or the chest, or the ribs. Research shows this inflatable vest can provide more than fifty percent more spinal protection than the flak jackets our riders here now use. I'm quoting again. 'The risk of rib fractures and organ damage can be significantly decreased with use of these vests.'"

Doyle closed his notebook. "If Wilfredo Gavidia had been wearing one of these things, he might not be paralyzed."

"What do these air jackets cost?"

"Right around $400," Doyle said.

"That's a helluva lot more than regular flak jackets."

Doyle said, "Listen. If they provide the increase in safety as reported, they'd be well worth it."

He got up, stretched, put his notebook in his jacket pocket. "Ralph, I've put in an order for one of these things for Mickey. They said Fed Ex would have it to me by the end of the week."

"Have you talked to Mickey about this?"

"Nope. I'm going to surprise her. And I'll pay for this air jacket myself. Nothing out of her earnings."

Tenuta said, "What if she doesn't like this thing? Doesn't feel comfortable wearing it?"

"When I think of Wilfredo Gavidia's condition today, and the dozens of other former jockeys around this country living wheelchair lives for years, I don't care if Mickey likes the thing or not. If she won't wear it, she can get herself another agent. See you later, Ralph."

Chapter Forty-five

A few mornings that summer, Eric would awaken early from an uneasy slumber. Toss and turn, finally concede that further sleep would elude him. Usually at least slightly hung over, he would exercise as a way to clear him for the day ahead. Dressed in jogging shorts, shoes, and sweat shirt, he drove his truck to one of the parking lots that ringed the Skokie Canal. Mist shrouded the ancient elms that bordered the two concrete paths running beside the turgid gray water. There was one path for cyclists and runners, the other for dog walkers, usually knobby-kneed, hand-holding senior citizens of both sexes.

He took one of these fifty-minute runs two days after his unsuccessful meeting with therapist Rita Doty, where he'd been so resentful and dismissive. As he jogged up the long path leading to a canal bridge, he saw a long-legged, pony-tailed woman ahead of him proceeding gracefully. Eric sped up and extended his stride, only to realize that the woman was not Ingrid McGuire.

That realization deflated him. He slowed to a jog, then a trot, and finally sat down on the dewy bank of the canal. Months ago, he and Ingrid had run this route almost daily. Relishing the bird songs, the faces of other earnest and healthy-looking morning athletes, some of them young women chatting away to each other as they trundled infant buggies. "Those bright mornings are long gone for me," he muttered.

He lay back down in the wet grass, unwillingly remembering. After their graduation from the University of Illinois Veterinary School, and before they moved to Chicago to launch their joint racetrack practice at Heartland Downs, Ingrid had persuaded Eric to join her for a five-day and night raft trip down the Colorado River through the Grand Canyon.

"I've always wanted to do this," she'd enthused. "We raft the river all day in these small inflatable crafts. Tent out on the sand along the water at night. It's supposed to be fantastic. We'd be able to see all the varied light and beauty of the Canyon."

They were able to do just that. The young guides in charge of the six-person rafts in their flotilla were all enthusiastic geologists, expert rafters, great meal-makers, some of them even talented musicians and singers in the evening hours.

Their final trip day, Ingrid and Eric climbed in 108-degree heat the arduous eight-mile trail from the river to the canyon rim. Both had been advised to carry a gallon of water to drink. They did. They never had to pause to urinate because all the moisture their bodies produced seeped through their pores under the powerful sun and intense heat.

Halfway up the narrow, dusty trail, Ingrid and Eric caught up with a couple of senior visitors from Scotland who had refused the mules ride upward, determined to walk the trail. Eric figured this sun-browned pair to be well into their seventies. They were taking a break together on the edge of a boulder, sharing water, both wearing large-brimmed sun hats

Ingrid said, "Are you folks okay?"

"Never better, lassie," the man said. He rose and extended his hand first to Eric, then Ingrid. "Macloid's my name. This is the missus. We're doing grand."

That night, Eric and Ingrid had dinner with the Macloids in the lodge restaurant. Dehydrated from their walk that long day, the two couples had consumed numerous pitchers of ice water, glorying in their conquest of the demanding Canyon conditions. Eric, riding the high of their strenuous achievement, had limited himself to one glass of wine. Later, as sunburned and tired as they were, he and Ingrid made love that night. He would never forget it, try as he might. Her voice. Her smile. Indelible memories of her sweet concern for him.

Eric shook his head as if to erase that memory. He jumped up off the grassy canal slope and jogged back to his truck. An empty day lay before him. He hated his life, the lonely, late afternoons that sometimes found him, a supposedly strong young man, weeping. Shamed. Embarrassed.

Eric showered quickly at his condo. Booted up his computer. Concluded, once again, that he would attempt to create a change in his now miserable life by paying back his betrayers. At ten, he checked his suddenly declining stock market balance. Another bitter blow in a percussive succession of them. The phone rang. He ignored it. Eric had heard someone once say in a university literature class that revenge was best as a dish served cold. He had something else in mind for Ralph Tenuta, who had effectively destroyed his vet practice, his livelihood.

He got up from behind the computer, stretched, walked into the kitchen and reached into the freezer of his refrigerator for his helpful weapon, his defense of choice. His best friend, now. Mister Stoly.

Chapter Forty-six

Mickey strode from the jocks' room where she shared a private area with Heartland Downs' only other female rider, Elaine Yanover. Mickey was smiling as she waved to some girls in the paddock area crowd who were hollering encouragement to her. She was a picture of confident expectation, having already won one race and finished a good third in another. As usual, she was in a great mood, especially since she was now prepared to guide Plotkin in the Futurity Prep for two-year-olds. At 4:44 on this gorgeous midsummer afternoon, the sun glinted off the fit and polished horses as their grooms walked around the paddock ring prior to the call for "Riders Up."

Ralph Tenuta smiled as he saw little Mickey approaching. "That kid sure loves this business, doesn't she?" Groom Paul Albano nodded in agreement. "We're lucky to have her," Albano said. "She's a sweet person and a helluva rider. Reminds me of the great Bill Shoemaker. Physically small but very smart. And with a great touch that makes horses respond to her."

"You should tell her that sometime, Paul. She'd appreciate it. Hi, Mickey."

"Hello, Mr. Tenuta. Hi, Paul."

Tenuta, still under suspension after attorney Englehardt had thus far failed to obtain a court stay, was prevented from saddling Plotkin. He had named veteran groom Albano his assistant trainer, and Paul would undertake that familiar task.

Plotkin was brought by groom Luis Ortega to his stall in the wooden paddock. Ortega was having a hard time leading Plotkin to where he was supposed to be. Mickey watched the colt closely as he approached. She frowned. "Jaysus, Mr. Tenuta, this little horse looks like he's on the muscle today."

Albano took over from Ortega. For the first time, Albano had trouble turning Plotkin around so he could be saddled. "Why the hell is he so jumpy?" Tenuta said. He tried to pat Plotkin's head, but Plotkin kept tossing it up. "Paul, I've never seen Plotkin like this," Tenuta frowned.

"Me, either," answered Albano, who was struggling to adjust the shifting Plotkin's girth before applying the saddle. Plotkin suddenly let out a trio of loud snorts, astounding all of his connections.

"Never heard him do that before," Tenuta muttered. He boosted Mickey up into the saddle. He said, "Plotkin's acting real different today, Mickey. Kind of strange. Watch yourself out there." He slapped Plotkin on the rump as Albano began to lead the horse out through the tunnel leading to the track. Mickey nervously tried to calm Plotkin down by whispering to him and stroking his neck. He was beginning to lather up, another first for him. Mickey used her whip to gently flick away the strands of white sweat. Her calming efforts had no apparent effect. They walked out of the dark tunnel and into the sunshine of the racetrack as the bugler played the traditional "Call to the Post." The crowd cheered.

◇◇◇

Minutes later, track announcer John Tully said, "All are in the gate except Plotkin, who is acting up. Jockey Mickey Sheehan seems to have her hands full with him. Once Plotkin's in, we'll have a start… *And they're off.*"

Plotkin was still tossing his head when the gates opened. He broke flat-footed, nearly three lengths behind the field, quite in contrast to his usual style. But once in stride, he bullied his way up between horses while running on the inner rail, almost pulling Mickey out of the saddle. Her left riding boot scraped white paint off the inner rail.

"Jaysus, what's got into him? I can't control him. Room, room, give me some room…No, no, we can't go there. No. No…"

Announcer Tully's voice rose. "Plotkin is very rank. Rider can't control him. Oh, no! He's hit the rail and dumped his rider over it into the infield. Mickey Sheehan is down."

Tenuta had his binoculars trained on the track near the five-eighths pole. Doyle gripped his arm. "What do you see, Ralph? Where is she?"

"She got tossed over the rail like a rag doll," Tenuta growled.

The riderless Plotkin had now moved to the outside, circling his rivals, obviously determined to be in his usual place, on the lead. When the field turned for home, he veered out to the grandstand fence, sped past the finish line, and kept going. It took the strenuous efforts of two outriders to finally chase him down and snatch his reins and pull him up. Plotkin fought them all the way. Doyle and Tenuta were paying no attention to that.

"Ralph, God damn it, what do you see?"

"Oh, Jack, our girl is still down."

Chapter Forty-seven

Ralph Tenuta said, "Jack, stop pacing. You're wearing a trough in the carpet. You're making me nuts."

Six-thirty in the evening. Doyle looked down at where Tenuta was perched on his plastic chair in the emergency room waiting area of Holy Family Hospital some six miles from Heartland Downs. Rose Tenuta sat next to her husband, working her worn rosary beads with her right hand. Her left hand held Nora Sheehan's hand.

This tableau had existed for the past ninety-five minutes, beginning immediately after the paramedics had wheeled the semiconscious Mickey up the hospital ramp. Since it was late afternoon, the waiting room was not nearly as populated as it would be once night developed. A skinny, pale, leather-wearing biker with a red-streaked mullet sat across the room, nervously tapping one of his booted feet, looking like he was desperate for a smoke. "My bitch fell off my bike," he had announced when Jack and his people came in. He hadn't said a word since. An elderly Hispanic man leaned forward in his chair, head buried in his hands, saying nothing. His gray "Jose Velasquez Yard Service" tee-shirt was dark with sweat stains. He gave no indication why he was there.

As Doyle paced, thinking about the little Irish girl's bruised and battered face, he recalled the depressing statistics he'd researched before agreeing to become a jockey's agent. The number of deaths of jockeys on the racetrack. The larger number of former riders now wheelchair ridden quadriplegics or paraplegics scattered about America's racing nation. The fact that at least a third of the jockey license holders in the US earn an annual income that positions them below the poverty line. But it had never previously occurred to him that anything as bad as this could actually happen to Mickey Sheehan.

At 5:49 p.m. Dr. Paul Mann entered the waiting room wearing the solemn look of an emergency-room specialist. Doyle stood still. The physician walked to where Nora sat. "Are you Nora Sheehan, the next of kin?" Doyle's heart sank. "Next of kin" had a dire ring to it.

Dr. Mann, who looked to Doyle to be about the fresh-faced age of a college senior, continued after Nora nodded yes. "I have good news," he said solemnly. "Your sister suffered a slight concussion and, obviously, severe facial bruising. That's the extent of her injuries, except for a sprained left wrist, probably damaged ligaments there. It was fortunate she was wearing that air jacket device. It probably worked to prevent severe spinal damage from the terrific impact with which she hit the ground."

The physician stopped talking to take a message on his beeper, then continued. "She should be fully recovered physically in ten days to two weeks. Amazingly enough, she didn't even incur any dental damage when her face smashed into the ground."

Nora and the Tenutas were looking up hopefully at the ultraserious physician. Doyle muttered, "If this is how the man delivers good news, I'd hate to be on hand when he brings the bad." Nora said, "Thank you, doctor. Thank you very much. When can we see Mickey?"

There was another beep on Dr. Mann's phone. He listened, then replaced it in the pocket of his green hospital top, frowning. "What? Oh, I'm sorry, I have to get back into ER. As to your question, Ms. Sheehan, you can go and see your sister now for a few minutes. I plan to keep her here under observation for at least twenty-four hours. "

Dr. Mann's smiled briefly as he offered, "She's a spunky, gutsy little person. She'll come out of this fine. Physically, I mean." He nodded at the group and turned to leave. Doyle grabbed his arm. "Doctor, what do you mean by 'fine physically?'"

The doctor said, "Well, what I've been told happened to her, Mickey Sheehan was catapulted off a horse going thirty-five miles an hour. Landed face first. Had her head bounced off the infield grass. And passed out. Only to fully awaken in our ER room. I would think that coming to grips with an experience like that would be emotionally, well, difficult." He shrugged and turned to the doorway.

Nora stood up, eyes blazing, to face Dr. Mann. "Not for a Sheehan," she barked. She took a deep breath and offered her hand to the startled physician. "I didn't mean to sharp at you," she said. "I thank you for your treatment of my sister. Believe me."

Dr. Mann nodded and left.

Doyle sat down next to Ralph. "You've been in this game for years. Have you seen accidents like what happened to Mickey?"

Tenuta sighed. "Yes, Jack. Unfortunately, yes. Not many. But the ones you do see you never forget. It's a tough, tough business. There are too many riding accidents that I've seen and can't forget."

Doyle got up and walked over to a window. Over his shoulder he said, "Why do people do this? Get into this potentially very dangerous business?" He shook his head. "I'm not sure I want to be involved in this anymore."

Tenuta got up and grabbed Doyle's shoulder, his face red. "Don't tell me you're walking out on your jockey, Jack."

Doyle, seated again, put his head in his hands. He peered through them across waiting room at the anxious-looking Latino man wearing the landscaper tee shirt. The man was sitting back in his chair, head tilted up and eyes closed, either trying to doze off as he waited, or praying.

Tenuta knelt in front of Doyle. He said, "Jack, what you've got to understand is that these people who ride race horses, men or women, young or old, do it because they love doing it.

Hell, I've seen riders come back from broken arms, legs, ankles, collarbones, crushed ribs. Bad internal injuries from getting accidentally kicked. They can't wait to start racing again. To get back into it. You just can't stop them. There was a rider on the Kentucky-Ohio circuit couple of years ago, guy named Cowboy Jones. He won a race when he was sixty-eight! They used to say Jones was way tougher than ancient leather."

Tenuta stood up. Shrugged. "It's in their blood, Jack. They're not like most of us. They can somehow wipe out the memory of what terrible thing tore them up, and still insist on wanting to return doing it. I can't explain it. These are some of the toughest human beings in the world."

Doyle said, "You think Mickey Sheehan is like that?"

Ralph smiled. "No, I don't '*think*', Jack. I *know* she's like that. If it all works out for her physically, she'll come back to race riding as soon as she can. I suspect Nora will try to talk Mickey out of it. That won't work. Mickey is committed to being a good jockey."

Tenuta said to his wife, "Let's go get some dinner." Rosa pocketed her rosary beads. Patted Nora on the hand. At the doorway, Ralph turned back and said to Doyle, "You going to stick here, Jack? Ah, I thought so. Talk to you later."

"See you tomorrow morning, Ralph. Good bye, Rosa."

Doyle sat down in the ER waiting room to wait for Nora. Nearly an hour elapsed before she returned. "She's conscious, God love her," Nora said, teary-eyed. Doyle took her in his arms. She shook there as she sobbed. "It's just so hard to see a small, sweet creature like Mickey looking like she'd fallen under a feckin' truck. Pardon my Irish."

Finally, she stepped back and wiped her face with the already sodden handful of tissues she'd been carrying. "Sorry about all that," Nora said. "Most of the Sheehans don't show much emotion. Too tough, ya know."

"We're lucky Mickey's tough enough." Doyld looked up at the wall clock. "Would you like to go and have something to eat? Or drink?"

"No, thanks, Jack. I'm going to stay here tonight in Mickey's room. She's lucky they gave her a private room. I can't bear the thought of her being in this place by herself. She seems to drift off into sleep, then suddenly awaken, looking around like 'what the hell am I doing here?' I want to be with her."

"The nurses will allow this?"

Nora said, "The head nurse I just talked to said she would bring a chair and a pillow into Mickey's room. She was kind. Very kind."

Doyle put his jacket on. "I understand. Just give me a call if you change your mind. Or if you need anything. You've got my cell number."

He intended to kiss Nora goodbye. But she pivoted and hurried back to Mickey's room before he had a chance.

Walking through the parking lot to his Accord, Doyle wondered about Mickey's future. During his amateur boxing days, he'd observed sharply varying reactions to bad beatings. His buddy Max Middleton, a promising light heavyweight, one of the toughest guys Doyle had ever known, had gone undefeated, just mowing down opponents, until he ran into a Chicago buzz saw from Cabrini Green. Middleton got the crap beat out of him. He tried to come back and fight six months later, but he was never the same. Wisely, he retired.

But then there was another stablemate of Doyle's, a featherweight named Jackie Thomsen, who had taken a brutal whipping during an AAU tournament in Waukegan. It was his first loss. He bounced back into the gym two weeks later, recovered and eager to proceed. Thomsen won the Chicago Golden Gloves championship the next year. Went on to have a very successful amateur career. Doyle thought, you just never know with people, which way it's going to go.

Chapter Forty-eight

Doyle edged into the stream of east bound traffic on Golf Road when his cell phone rang. It was Moe.

"I heard on the radio just now that Mickey got thrown. Busted up. Jack, how is she? What went on? Why didn't you call me?"

"Believe me, my friend, I was busy. Sorry."

Moe said, "Leah's driving me nuts looking for news. She loves that little jock."

"Who doesn't?"

Doyle gunned up the entrance ramp onto the Edens Expressway. "Okay, here's what happened." He described Plotkin's completely uncharacteristic behavior prior to the race. The disaster that occurred in the race. Mickey's presence in Intensive Care at Holy Family.

There was a breathless silence on Kellman's phone until he said, "God damn it, Jack. That this should happen to our leprechaun, that sweet little person. I'm afraid to ask. But what is the prognosis for Mickey?"

There was a pause in the conversation as Doyle adeptly changed lanes to avoid a red sports convertible whose driver was weaving through the traffic lanes while apparently texting with one hand. Doyle realized he had never before heard his pragmatic little friend venture so far toward the border of sentimentality.

"Moe, she'll be okay. Her physical injuries will heal. It's a question of the rest. Will she decide to get back into race riding? Ralph Tenuta thinks so. Knowing how much she loves riding, what a huge part of her life it is. But, my friend, you never know."

"What I don't understand, Jack, is that Plotkin had never done anything like that before, right? Acted so goofy? Am I right?"

"You are."

Kellman sighed. "I hope you don't think it callous of me to ask about Plotkin's condition. Did he fuck himself up after tossing Mickey over the fence?"

"No. According to what the stable help told Ralph on the phone an hour or so ago, Plotkin is unhurt. The main groom, now Ralph's assistant trainer, Paul Albano, said Plotkin looked 'healthy, but deflated. And guilty.'"

Doyle turned right off the expressway onto Lake Street and pulled into the parking lot of Mark Meyers' Tavern, a venerable watering hole and horse players' hangout, famous for its hamburgers and generously poured drinks.

"Moe, I'm stopping for a sandwich and a drink or three. Then I'm heading home to get some rest. I'll call you with an update on Mickey's situation as soon as I get one."

He found a parking slot between a battered old Nash Rambler and a panel truck advertising "Great House Painting. Inside or Out. Up or Down. Done for Almost Nothing."

Before leaving the Accord, he got a call from Ralph.

"Anything new on Mickey?"

"No, Ralph. We'll know more tomorrow. In the meantime, I'd like you to schedule Ingrid McGuire to come over to your barn in the morning to communicate with Plotkin. Are you with me?"

Tenuta said, "I'll call her right now."

He called Jack back five minutes later. "She'll be there at seven."

Chapter Forty-nine

As Doyle and Tenuta waited in Tenuta's office for Ingrid, Doyle said, "Did you watch the replay of Plotkin's race?"

"Four or five times."

Doyle said, "I couldn't bring myself to look at it more than once, seeing Mickey go down like that. But my question, Ralph, is did some other jockey have a hand in causing this disaster."

"No, Jack." Tenuta got up from behind his desk to refill his coffee cup. "Plotkin just freaked on his own. He's skimming along the rail. All of a sudden he props. Shifts his shoulders. That's when Mickey went off. Plotkin just kept charging ahead.

"I know what you're thinking, Jack, that jockey error can cause jockey disaster. Or that a jock intentionally does something to another rider. Rivalries develop among these very competitive athletes and some of them become bitter. But ninety-nine percent of the time they only amount to dirty looks and muttered threats."

Doyle said, "What about the other one percent you mention?"

Tenuta sat back in his chair, a smile on his face. "One of the great examples was back in the forties with my fellow Dago, the late Eddie Arcaro. The guy they called 'Banana Nose.' He came out of Covington, Kentucky, where his dad was a bookmaker. He was a riding natural. My old man told me this story about Arcaro.

"Eddie was riding in New York, either Aqueduct or Belmont, and one day in the feature race he got into a bumping match with a rider from Havana named Vincent Nodarse. They had some kind of bad history from a previous race where Arcaro thought Nodarse had intentionally fouled him and cost him the win. It seems these two guys hated each other. So, this afternoon I'm telling you about, Arcaro's got Nodarse pinned down on the rail. Nodarse falls off his horse after Arcaro's horse bumps into him. Fortunately, Nodarse is not badly hurt.

"The New York stewards call in Arcaro. They asked him, 'Were you trying to injure Vincent Nodarese with what you did in that race?'

"Arcaro said, 'No. I was trying to kill that Cuban bastard.'

"The stews gave Arcaro a year's suspension. It was later reduced to six months when one of the big-shot owners he rode for exerted his influence. Eddie never did anything like that again. The next year, he won the Triple Crown with Citation. He eventually was elected to the Hall of Fame. A lot of the old veterans still consider him the best American rider ever."

Ingrid McGuire rapped on the office door before entering. "Good morning, men. What's the word on Mickey?"

Doyle said, "They're pushing her out of the hospital late this morning. Amazing, our health care system. I guess if you want to stay in there for a couple of days you'd have to be spurting blood from all portals. I'll pick Mickey up and take her to her apartment with Nora. She's going to be out of action for awhile."

"She was lucky, Jack. It could have been much worse," Ingrid said.

She walked to the table with the old Mr. Coffee machine. Poured herself a cup. Sat down next to Jack after gently clearing the cat Tuxedo out of the way.

"I wasn't late getting to the track this morning," she said. "I stopped to see Plotkin before coming to meet you guys."

Tenuta sat up in his chair. "How does he look? Is he okay? When I saw him at feeding time early this morning, he looked kind of, well, downtrodden. Wouldn't touch his feed tub."

Doyle said coldly, "Did you 'communicate' with that little villain?"

"Well, Jack," she shot back, "actually I did. Plotkin is shaken up. Told me he feels terrible about throwing Mickey. He said he felt very strange going into that race. Said a man came into his stall the night before last and gave him a shot of something that drastically changed the way he felt. For the better, because he felt stronger. Faster. For the worse, because he didn't know exactly what he was doing."

Doyle said, "Plotkin said all this to you?"

"Yes, Jack."

"Jesus." He got to his feet, shaking his head. He looked to Tenuta to say something, but the trainer was as stunned as Doyle, who said, "Did Plotkin say who it was that gave him that shot?"

Ingrid laughed. "Jack, horses can't name names. No, Plotkin didn't tell me who it was. Get serious."

"I'm as serious as I can be with this scenario," Doyle barked. "Is it real horse communicating talk, or complete bullshit? That's what I'm thinking."

Ingrid's face flushed as she jumped up from the couch to almost chest-bump Doyle. "I am telling you what Plotkin told me," she spat out. "If you don't believe me, Jack Doyle, the hell with you." She turned to leave but Tenuta came around his desk and took her arm. "Ingrid, please. Take it easy. C'mon, sit back down. I'll get a coffee. Jack didn't mean what he just said." They both looked at Doyle.

Jack raised his hands in a surrender gesture. Took a deep breath. "You're right, Ralph. I was out of line. Ingrid, I apologize. I know you are doing your best."

He returned to the couch and out-stared Tuxedo before the cat reluctantly moved so Doyle could take a seat. He said, "I guess all this crap that has happened in the last twenty-four hours has thrown me, well, off what little balance I fight to maintain. I can't get the picture of little Mickey's battered face out of my head." He slid closer to Ingrid and put his arm around here. "Really, I'm sorry. I believe in you, Ingrid."

Chapter Fifty

The shot that had been secretly administered to Plotkin was identified by the Racing Commission's testing laboratory three days later. When the Heartland stewards received the report, Ralph Tenuta was again summoned to their office. State steward Henry Arroyo met Tenuta at the door. Shook his hand. They had known each other for more than twenty years. Arroyo said, "Come in, Ralph. I've got something to tell you that I can hardly believe."

When he sat in a chair before the stewards' long desk, Tenuta's puzzled look extended to the two associate stewards present who flanked Arroyo.

"What's this all about, Ed?"

"Ralph, it's about your horse Plotkin, who threw Mickey Sheehan. As the losing favorite in that race, his blood and urine were sampled and sent to the test lab." He paused to look at the printed ruling. "They reported that Plotkin was positive for Etorphine. Usually called elephant juice. The same illegal medication found in your trainee Madame Golden a few weeks back."

Arroyo shook his head. "The lab people say this drug makes horses feel livelier. Run faster. It caused a scandal in Australian racing back in the eighties."

"This is unbelievable," Tenuta shouted, jumping out of his chair. He walked over to the large window overlooking the race track. Forced himself to take a deep breath. When he sat down again, he said, "Men, I've been training for more than thirty years. As I told you when I was here last time, I have never, I mean never, given any one of my horses anything but hay, oats, water, and very legal and prescribed vitamins. Before Madame Golden, I had *never* had a ruling against me. Your lab must have made another mistake."

Arroyo sighed. "Ralph, our lab rushed a split sample to Cornell University, one of the country's major testing facilities. They confirmed the finding. Your horse Plotkin was loaded with this stuff they call elephant juice. That's probably what led to him going nuts and dumping your jockey.

"I know, I know, "Arroyo continued. "I am sure you did not give Plotkin that drug, or order anybody else to do so. But somebody sure as hell did. And, under this state's absolute insuror rule, you have to be held responsible."

"Even though I had absolutely *nothing* to do with this," Tenuta said bitterly.

Arroyo said, "The rule is the rule. In every racing state in this country. If something illegal is given to a horse you train, you are punished. It doesn't make any difference if you had been thousands of miles away last week. What happened here at Heartland Downs to Plotkin is your responsibility under the rules of racing. That's just the way it is, Ralph."

The shaken Tenuta struggled to his feet. "Henry, what's the punishment for this fiasco?"

"You are suspended for an additional sixty days on top of your thirty-day ruling from Madame Golden. Starting today, even though you got that lawyer Englehart to obtain a stay order pending appeal on the first one. And you are fined $10,000."

Tenuta had his head in his hands before looking up and saying, "I've got thirty horses in my barn. They eat every day and have to be exercised every day and have to run as often as possible so that their owners get their bills and pay me. I charge $65 per horse per day. What happens to all that if you put me on the sidelines?"

Associate steward Joe Kristufek, a sympathetic look on his old face, said, "Ralph, don't you have an assistant trainer now?"

"Yes. Paul Albano. He's worked for me for years. But he doesn't want to be my assistant. He says there's too much pressure. He wants to go back to being my head groom."

Arroyo said, "Well, Ralph, you better convince him to stay on in the interim as the stable's trainer of record while you're suspended. At least that would keep your operation going."

"Thanks, Henry. I appreciate that suggestion. I'll get right back to the barn and talk to Paul and tell him what's going on."

The four men got to their feet. Arroyo said, "You understand, Ralph, that you cannot go anywhere near your barn for the next sixty days. I'll make an exception for today so you can meet with Albano. And you're not barred from Heartland Downs or watching the races from the stands. But you are absolutely prohibited from spending any time on the backstretch during this period. Sorry, my friend." He extended his hand. Tenuta, still in mild shock, shook it.

Tenuta said, "Henry, with all the state's involvement in catching out these positives on my horses, which I know absolutely *nothing* about, are you people going to try and find out who the hell is doing is this to my horses? And to me?"

Arroyo shook his head no as he politely ushered Tenuta to the door.

"Ralph, that whole question is not up to us to answer, though we'll have track security do what they can. It's also up to you. Something's going on here that you had damned well better try to find out about as soon as you can. Good luck, my friend."

Tenuta stopped in the washroom at the end of the corridor. After he'd washed his hands, he scrubbed the wet toweling over his sweaty forehead. In the wide, polished mirror he saw a face that appeared to have aged at least five years since he had entered the stewards' office.

Doyle had driven Tenuta to the meeting but chose to wait in the car for his friend. "I don't feel like stepping into that pressure cooker again," he'd said.

They sat in Doyle's Accord in the parking lot, Doyle twitching with anger, Tenuta silent and morose. Doyle yanked his cell phone from his sport coat pocket. He quickly punched in attorney Art Engelhardt's number.

Tenuta said, "What are you doing, Jack?"

"Same thing we did after the first ruling against you, the 30-day one on Madame Golden. I'm going to have Engelhardt file for a stay order of this latest ruling pending a hearing on your appeal. He e-mailed me this morning while I was sitting here that the order on the Madame Golden case came through early this morning. I would imagine a similar stay order would cover the Plotkin case. So you'll be able to continue going to the track and properly training your horses for the time being at least. Okay?"

"Fine by me. Call Engelhardt and tell him about the Plotkin ruling. Tell him to get busy."

Doyle smiled as he saw Tenuta's expression brighten. Tenuta said, "Years ago, I read a statement made by the great trainer John Nerud. He said that 'A bad day at the racetrack is better than a good day anywhere else.' It wasn't until these last couple of weeks that I understood exactly what Nerud meant."

Chapter Fifty-one

They took Theresa's old but reliable Taurus and headed out of Berwyn. Lenny drove. Theresa slumped against the passenger door, holding an ice pack to her still swollen jaw. She was starting to nod off, the handful of Advil kicking in.

"Where are we going, Lenny?" she mumbled.

"I've got the key to a friend's cabin down near Ottawa. Take us a couple of hours. It's near Starved Rock State Park. Real nice area. We can kick back there for a couple of days. Okay?"

"Who is this guy? Where do you know him from?"

"Guy named Eddie Bostwick. We were in high school together. Until we both got booted for smoking weed." He laughed. "I went into the Army. Eddie went into his old man's landscaping business. He's been doing great."

They drove in silence for the next hour. Theresa, revived, sat up and swiveled the mirror so could examine the jaw injury Doyle had inflicted days before.

"How do you feel?" Lenny said.

"Like shit. But the swelling's gone down a lot. I guess I'm lucky that bastard Doyle didn't break it."

As they drove closer to Ottawa, the afternoon brightened. Teresa opened her window and shut off the car's air-conditioning. The road ran alongside the south side of the Illinois River. There were many people fishing and canoeing. Others hiked on the trail that paralleled the water. She spotted a bald eagle at the top of a tall spruce tree. She said, "How long you figure for us to stay down here in Hicksville?"

"C'mon, Treese. Lighten up. I'm sorry I made the mistake of trying to attack that fucker Doyle. I admit it. And I'm sorry you got hurt in the process. Really."

Lenny pulled into the left lane and passed two cars. "The hiring of the hit man idea," he said bitterly. "That was a fucking mistake. I don't know how in hell that Doyle found out about it. But it was a stupid idea from the get-go. I understand that now."

"What do you mean?"

Lenny sighed. "Cousin Ralph dead sure couldn't help me. I don't know what I was thinking, considering that action. Maybe it was just the old Italian desire for revenge. Now, Tenuta is supposedly under suspension. Unless he gets another delay."

"So, how could he give you any winners, Lenny?"

"If he wanted to, he could. I understand he had his main man, somebody named Albano, training his horses while he was suspended. But then Tenuta got some hotshot lawyer and had the suspension delayed or something. I'm sure Ralph is still calling the shots. So, how do we convince him to cooperate? To how to convince him to give me some winners?"

Teresa reached into the portable cooler on the seat between them. Yanked out a can of Pabst Blue Ribbon. Lenny grinned. "You must be feeling better," he said. "You want to stop for lunch?"

"Not hungry. For food."

She reached across the seat and put her hand on Lenny's right leg, patting it. "I know you're sorry our attack went bad, Lenny. I do."

He felt himself harden as she stroked him. "Later, babe, later. Let's try to find this cabin in the woods."

The key was where he'd been told, hanging on a hook at the back of an old porch swing. The one-story cabin was musty, dusty, cobwebbed. Teresa opened all the windows. Located a broom and went to work. Lenny lay on the lumpy bed, laptop on his chest. As usual, no e-mail for him. He'd "friended" five people on Facebook. None ever contacted him. He slammed the computer top shut.

Teresa came over to the bed and sat next to him, smiling. Took off her Lady Gaga tee-shirt. Lenny placed a hand on one of her heavy breasts. She leaned down. He leaned back on the pillow, hands behind his head, next to his pony tail. Theresa bent down and placed one of her erect large brown nipples against his tongue. "Lick," she ordered, moaning. She began to unbutton his jeans.

Twenty minutes later, they lay side to side, exhausted. Teresa said, "I've been thinking."

Lenny laughed. "Even during all that?"

"Lenny, I'm always thinking," she said sternly. She sat up and pulled her tee-shirt back on. "Obviously, revenging yourself by killing your cousin Ralph wouldn't accomplish anything. You can't make any money doing that."

"Teresa, give me some credit. I figured that out."

"So we've got to come up with a way to scare the shit out of Tenuta so that he'll cooperate with you."

She slapped his hand away as he began to stroke her right breast, got off the lumpy bed and walked to the portable cooler. Extracted another can of Pabst Blue Ribbon. Drained most of it as she looked out the window at the sun that was beginning to set above the smoothly flowing Illinois River.

Lenny said, "Teresa, you got any idea about how we could go about doing that to Tenuta?"

Theresa crumpled the beer can in her hand and tossed it out the window into the weeds. Slammed the window closed.

"Oh, yeah, Lenny. I do."

Chapter Fifty-one

Doyle picked up Nora from the apartment just after nine that morning. Mickey was due to be released from the hospital an hour later. "Or shoved out the door," as Doyle bitterly put it. "Honest to God, this must be like Third- or Fourth-World medical scheduling. Pisses me off."

"So I've noticed," Nora said. She looked drawn. "I didn't sleep much in Mickey's room last night. I finally got out of there and called a cab about four. She was resting well. I appreciate you coming to get me, Jack—I mean us—this morning."

"That's what we jockey agents do," Doyle laughed.

Mickey Sheehan arrived at the hospital entrance in a wheel chair. She looked to Doyle as if she had somehow shrunk. But the expression on her face was cheerful. Nora kissed her gently on her bruised cheek, then helped the hospital aide, a sullen young man who may have been near the end of his shift, guide the wheel chair to the curb where Doyle's Accord was parked.

Doyle had been leaning against back door. He tried to conceal his shock at Mickey's appearance as he opened the door for her, saying, "Well, here you are, Mickey. You don't look too bad. How are you feeling? Why the wheelchair?"

"Hospital rules," growled the attendant. "You spend time in ER, when you come out of there it's in a wheelchair."

"Or a hearse," Doyle shot back. The attendant spun the empty wheel chair around and walked rapidly back into the hospital. "Charming fellow," Doyle snarled.

Nora grinned. "Jack Doyle. Diplomatic marvel." He ignored her comment.

"Morning to you Jack," Mickey said from the back seat. "Can we get going now? I'm terrible hungry."

"Didn't they give you breakfast in that place?"

"Some sort of grainy, gray gruel," Mickey said. "Awful stuff."

Nora sat next to her sister in the back seat. Doyle pulled away from the curb while watching the two of them in the rear-view mirror. Despite her facial bruises, Mickey looked to be the livelier of the sisters. She said, "Ralph called early this morning to ask about me. That was nice of him. He said he and Rosa would visit me in the hospital this afternoon." She laughed. "I told him they wouldn't be finding me there."

Doyle could see Mickey smiling as she looked out the car window. "In Ireland," she said, "they teach you early on not to be scared. We all know what we do is dangerous. We just take it a day at a time. If you fall, you have to bounce back and forget about it. If you keep it the back of your mind, you won't be successful. When I went down off Plotkin and didn't break a major bone, I knew I would be good to go pretty quick."

Paused at an intersection on Rand Road, Mickey said, "There's a McDonald's up the way there Jack. Would you stop there? I'm starving.'"

Doyle shook his head. "You've still got an appetite after what you've been through?" She proved she did when Doyle pulled up to the drive-through window and she asked him to order "Two of those lovely egg McMuffin things, two sausage biscuits, and a large juice. Orange."

Dora said, "Nora, you want anything?"

"Just black coffee, please, Jack. Is this little sister of mine amazing or not?"

Mickey finished her breakfast within minutes. She noticed that day's copy of *Racing Daily* tucked between the front seats next to Jack's elbow. "Okay if I read this, Jack?"

"Help yourself."

Her eyes widened as she read Ira Kaplan's front-page article on the death of 70-year-old veterinarian Maury Burnside, described as a talented practitioner who "cared for numerous champions but who pulled off one most notorious racetrack betting coups in US racing history."

"I can hardly believe what I'm reading," Mickey gasped.

"Believe it," Doyle said.

According to Kaplan's story, Burnside in 1977 purchased two very similar looking horses in Uruguay. One was a talented speedster, the other an obscure, slow claimer. A year later, Burnside claimed the good horse had died in an accident on Burnside's farm. He collected a $150,000 insurance settlement. Burnside then came up with a certificate of foreign registration for the slow horse, providing a photo of the fast one.

"On September 14, 1978," Kaplan's story continued, "Burnside ran the fast horse under the slow horse's name in a race at Belmont Park. He reportedly bet $1,200 to win and $600 to show. The horse won easily. Burnside cashed tickets totaling more than $90,000.

"Burnside appeared to be home free with his scam until a sharp-eyed racing official in Uruguay spotted the photo of the winning Belmont horse. He knew at once this was the fast horse, not the deceased slow one. He alerted New York authorities.

"The trial lasted weeks. Burnside was eventually sentenced to a year in prison and was fined $10,000 and barred from ever holding another trainer's license."

Mickey folded up the paper and put it back between the seats. "Ballsy," she said, "what that man done."

"And costly," Doyle answered. "Sure, he made a big cheating score with his bet and screwed other horse players by subbing those horses. But this was all for what, ninety grand? And he loses his license and his livelihood."

"Couldn't have been worth it," Nora said.

Doyle drove to the entrance of their apartment house. He turned in his seat to face the sisters.

"There was a famous vet down in Kentucky years ago, involved in all kinds of supposedly nefarious, but unprovable, actions. Very smart, talented guy. The word down there on him was, 'He'd rather make $500 with a scam than $5,000 legitimately.' Go figure," Doyle shrugged.

Chapter Fifty-three

Kieran Fallon was relaxing in the den of his Dun Laoghaire seaside mansion, contentedly watching the videotaped replays of that afternoon's Curragh races, sipping champagne, which for some topflight European jockeys was the preferred vehicle of appetite depressant. Some successful journeymen riders relied on beer or vodka to alleviate hunger.

Fallon was comfortably stretched out on the on the long, beige leather couch. Next to him on a table was a small dish of caviar, some water crackers, a few slivers of low-fat cheese. Alice Dugan sat in the nearby leather chair, engrossed in Tana French's latest novel. Alice, a twenty-six-year-old employee of Kieran's accountant, had been in residence nearly three months now. She was dark-haired, smart, pretty, diminutive, quiet, and a sexual athlete of such skills as even to impress the practiced Mr. Fallon.

Kieran's cell phone rang. He hesitated before picking it up, preferring to relish the beautifully timed winning finish he'd produced in that afternoon's feature race at the Curragh. Then he picked up.

"Kieran. It's Nora. I have some news for you. Mickey went down hard here in a race at Heartland Downs. I thought you should know."

He sat straight up, heart pounding.

"How bad?"

"Not as bad as it looked. But it scared the life out of me."

"Was she conscious?

"Pretty much at first, now completely. And feisty as ever. Said she thought there was something terribly wrong with her mount. That's Plotkin. The two-year-old she's been doing so well with."

Kieran hesitated before asking, "Any spinal damage?"

"No, thank God. She landed face first on the infield turf. She was wearing this new protective jacket that her agent bought for her. I guess they work wonders in absorbing shock. So, there's nothing to be concerned about along those lines.

"Her face is a mess. She hit face first. And she evidently damaged some ligaments in her left wrist."

"Are they keeping her in hospital?"

"She was in only overnight," Nora said. "For observation. Jaysus, they shuffle the patients through hospitals here like mail through a slot. But the main thing is, she'll be okay. I don't know if you realize how tough she is. This accident is not going to keep her from getting back into the saddle. She's got a wonderful agent here, Jack Doyle, a very kind, thoughtful guy. And she works for a wonderful trainer, Ralph Tenuta. Actually," she sighed, "Ralph has got a problem now with an illegal drug finding. But I guarantee you, both Jack and Ralph have Mickey's best interests at heart."

Kieran took a sip of his champagne. Gestured an offer to replenish Alice's flute. She shook her head no.

"Nora, you think I should send Mickey some flowers?"

Nora laughed. "She'd probably grind them into the dust. You know, brother, you're not high on Mickey's list of favorite people. Not after you ignored her for so many years."

Fallon's face flushed. "I had my reasons for that, Nora. I didn't want to see the kid get into this rough business. I tried to discourage her by ignoring her. Obviously, it didn't work. Believe me, I've had my regrets."

Alice offered to refill his champagne glass, but Kieran waved her off. "Nora, give Mickey my love. I mean it. For you, too. Actually, I've been reading your Internet blog about Mickey's American experience. Brilliant stuff."

Kieran sank back on the couch." My best to you both, Nora," he said softly. Before breaking the connection, he added softly,"You'll be seeing me over there in the near future." He hung up before Nora could reply.

Alice joined him on the couch and snuggled up to him. Kieran brushed her off and leaped to his feet. "I've got to take a walk."

Chapter Fifty-four

Checking the racing news on the Internet that Friday morning, Doyle nearly dropped his coffee cup onto the keyboard. He read the item again before reaching for his cell phone. Nora Sheehan answered on the second ring. "Morning, Jack."

"Did you know your brother Kieran will be at Heartland Downs two weeks from Saturday? One of his main employers, Aiden O'Malley, is sending over a colt named Boy from Sligo to run in the Heartlands Juvenile. Against us. I mean Plotkin. Did you know anything about this?"

He could hear her groan. "I called Kieran last night to tell him about Mickey's fall. At the end of the conversation, he said something about 'seeing us soon.' That's all I know. I guess I should have called and told you. But it was late. Kieran never even said what race he was coming for. You'd think big brother would have the class to give his sisters details of his intended visit. Ah, forget that notion," she said bitterly. "Kieran goes his own way."

"This is going to be major racing news," Doyle said. "Top Irish jockey come here and faces his young sister in a million-dollar race. I've got to talk to Mickey about this."

"I'll tell her the details about the Futurity and all," Nora sighed. "Hard to believe Kieran would handle this situation this way. But that's what a cold-hearted bastard he can be.

"What about Kieran's chances?" Nora said. "Do you know anything about Mr. O'Malley's colt?"

"Not yet. But I will. I know O'Malley's reputation. He's a tremendous horseman with an eye on the chance. Ordinarily very conservative in his choice of races. 'The Prince of Parsimony' he been termed in the international racing press. O'Malley must believe he's got a big shot in the Juvenile to spend all that shipping money for him, his horse, and his jockey.

"I don't believe Kieran has ever ridden here in the States before. I'm surprised he's agreed to do this. I need to talk more with Mickey about this. I'll see you at the track this afternoon."

Chapter Fifty-five

Driving to Heartland Downs, Doyle called Moe. "You ready for some amazing news, my friend?"

"Mickey's fall was enough amazing news for me this week. But go ahead. I'll bite. Did the economy bounce back? Is the market soaring? Did the Wicked Witch of Wasilla have her lips sutured shut?" Doyle could hear the little furrier chuckling.

"You're in a fine mood. Let's see if that holds after you hear what I've got to tell you".

Doyle filled Kellman in on the very live prospect of Kieran Sheehan crossing the ocean to ride against his sister in the Heartland Downs Juvenile. Kellman responded with calm. "So what, Plotkin takes on an Irish horse and his notorious jockey? I spoke with Ralph Tenuta yesterday. He called me to correct an error he'd made in the month's training bill he sent to us in care of me. The error was in our favor, as our honest trainer pointed out. Anyway, he said Plotkin had never been doing better. He's training up a storm. Worked five furlongs this morning in :58 flat. Best work of the day. So I say, hell, let the chips fall. I just hope Mickey doesn't get thrown off stride going against her big brother. You'd better talk her through that."

"I plan to. Jockey agent/counselor Jack Doyle at your service."

"How are *you* doing, Jack? I know you've been under a lot of stress and strain. Plotkin's being doped. Mickey's fall."

Doyle waved at the security guard and drove through the Heartlands gate toward Tenuta's barn. "I'm all right, Moe. Maybe not tip-top. The impending appearance of Kieran Sheehan worries me somewhat. I went on the Web last night and did a little research on him. I printed out one passage from a book about him. Let me read it to you."

He pulled into his parking space and reached for the paper on the seat next to him. "This says, 'Tomorrow never comes for Kieran Fallon. It's probably the child in him. He was a country lad who played endlessly in the woods instead of being in school, who hurled and boxed against lads twice his size without thinking, who believed authority would never quite catch up to him.'

"Kieran in Gaelic," Doyle added, means "little dark one. I hope he doesn't bring any darkness to his sisters from whom he's been estranged."

Kellman said, "Jack, I think you need a little break from all your worries and concerns. How about me taking you to an event tonight that you might like? I can have Pete Dunleavy pick you up at your condo at seven."

Doyle didn't hesitate. "You're on."

Chapter Fifty-six

Dunleavy valet-parked the Lincoln and walked with Doyle and Kellman into the St. Regis school gym which had been converted, for the night, into a boxing arena. The ring was at midcourt of the basketball floor. Rows of portable seats surrounded it, most of them filled for this fund raiser for this financially struggling school on Chicago's west side.

Kellman handed an usher their tickets. He led them to seats in the second row, directly behind the judges and other state boxing officials. Above the ring was a large banner whose inscription defined the night's event: "Celtic Thunder."

"All right, Moe," Doyle said, "what are we about to see? What the hell is Celtic Thunder?"

Kellman ordered and paid for beers from a vendor for the three of them before answering. "This is a charity card. All proceeds go to St. Regis. It matches Irish-American boxers against Scottish-American fighters. Four bouts are scheduled, three rounds each. This could be entertaining."

Doyle waved down a program seller. The opening match pitted Sean Daley against Angus Morton, 124 pounds. Then followed Eoin Purcell—Robert Bennet, 135 pounds; Brian Callahan—James Robertson, 160 pounds; and Rory O'Rouke—George MacDonald, heavyweights.

"These guys are all amateurs, right, Moe?"

"Right." Moe turned back to Dunleavy and resumed their long running debate over who was the better fighter, the retired Julio Cesar Chavez, as Pete claimed, or the current best pound-for-pound professional in the world Manny Pacquiao, as Moe contended.

As the national anthem was being dragged along for what seemed to Doyle to be for minutes by an overweight, attention-seeking Irish tenor, Doyle's thoughts turned to his current pressing issues. Mickey Sheehan's health, physical and mental. The effect her brother Kieran's arrival would have on her. And the mystery of who was doping Ralph Tenuta's horses. He was relieved when the fighters for the opening bout were introduced and quickly proceeded to go to work on each other. The raucous crowd seemed to be evenly divided as to which fighter they were rooting for.

It was a decently fought bout, Sean Daley taking a narrow decision after a trio of busy rounds. "Those guys were pretty good," Doyle said as the referee raised the grinning Daley's hand

Moe said, "Daley was the Chicago Golden Gloves champ at that weight two years ago. I don't know where the wee bonnie lad came from. But he pretty much held his own I would say."

During the intermission between bouts, six burly bagpipers climbed through the ropes into the ring. All wore kilts, thus exposing their knobby knees, which the Irish backers in the crowd made loud fun of. The musicians responded with a lengthy and loud version of "Scotland the Brave."

Tom Donovan, chairman of the state boxing commission, was on his way to a lavatory when he spotted Moe. He came over, the men shook hands, then huddled for a minute or two of quiet conversation. Doyle shook his head. He said to Dunleavy, "Honest to God, Pete, it seems that everywhere I go with our little friend he knows somebody or somebody knows him."

"Been that way ever since I've known Moe," Dunleavy smiled.

The second bout was over quickly. Midway of the first round, Purcell unleashed a powerful right hand that dropped Bennett to the canvas. He could not make it up by the count of ten. The

Irish backers were on their feet, whistling and shouting at their side's lead of two-to-nothing.

Doyle watched as a black-suited man hustled into the ring carrying a portable microphone. He announced that there would now be "a ten minute interlude prior to Bout Number Three."

"Interlude?" Doyle said. "I thought it was an intermission. Who the hell is that guy, Moe?"

"That's Packy Sheridan. Alderman from Rogers Park and a Democratic Party gadfly. He went to an Ivy League school. Maybe that's where he got 'interlude' instead of intermission."

Moe and Pete left for the wash room. Doyle sat back in his seat. Mention of the word *interlude* brought back vivid memories of the Rush Street tavern of that name. Doyle had frequented it during his first couple of years in Chicago.

The Interlude had not lacked for colorful characters. Hugo, the one-armed karate champ. Effie Manna, who late at night would stand up in a booth and pluck the Venetian blinds, making what he considered to be harp-like sounds. Little Ralphie, a dwarf who ran a nearby Chicago Avenue news stand and could outdrink anyone in the place. And, the bulk of the clientele, students at the nearby Loyola law school. It was the latter group that frequently drew the ire of the Interlude's owner-operator, George Small. He allowed the students to run tabs and often had a difficult time getting those tabs paid. He was dismissive of these young men's abilities. As he frequently stated in a loud voice, "If I were in trouble, I'd rather have a Jewish bailbondsman rep me than a Loyola lawyer."

Action, such as it was, resumed with the middleweight match. Brian Callahan was a red-headed, generously freckled young man who bounced impatiently in his corner awaiting the opening bell. Across the ring, James Robertson waited stoically. He appeared to be very confident.

Robertson's confidence was justified in the ensuing nine minutes. There was nothing artful about his performance, but the eager Callahan was worse, swinging wildly and so hard he several times almost lost his footing. "I don't think the Irish kid has hit Robertson once," Doyle said to Moe. "Robertson has a great defense, all right. But he's only thrown about a dozen punches. What a boring fight this is." Robertson was declared the winner. The cascade of crowd boos was not aimed at the decision but as comment on the bout's lack of meaningful action.

The card concluded with heavyweights Rory O'Rourke and George MacDonald, Rafferty having weighed in at an announced 221 pounds, MacDonald at 245. As the referee gave his instructions at mid-ring, these two did more glowering at each other than principals in an average divorce court hearing.

"MacDonald looks more like 265," Moe said. "Look at that blubber gut."

"Hey," Doyle said, "O'Rourke isn't exactly a svelte-like figure. His belly wobbles like my Aunt Florence's Christmas jello mold."

All this excess avoirdupois contributed to what was easily the most boring bout of the night. The two men spent all three minutes of each of the rounds clinching, grunting, only occasionally flailing to no effect. The fight was declared a draw. High volume booing from a critical crowd almost drowned out the announcement of the decision.

Walking to the exit, Doyle said "Celtic Thunder? They should have billed this fiasco as Celtic Twilight."

"Yeah, Jack, most of those guys are probably better at driving and unloading beer trucks. But, what the hell," Moe continued. "There's always going to be young men fighting. Better this than shooting each other in the streets. And remember, it was for a good cause."

Settled into the backseat of the Lincoln as Dunleavy headed for the northeast side of the city, Doyle flinched when he heard his cell phone ring in his pocket.

"Jack, it's Nora."

"What's going on?"

"Can you make an early morning stop here at the apartment before you go to the track tomorrow?"

"Sure. But why, Nora?"

"Mickey is not in good shape. I mean mentally, emotionally. I've never seen her so down as she is now. I'm worried about her. Maybe you could help to get her back to her real self. I know she respects you greatly."

Doyle said, "Well, I'll do what I can. I can be there by 6:30. Will Mickey be up by then?"

"Oh, yes. The girl barely sleeps at all these days. Thank you, Jack."

Chapter Fifty-seven

Outbound traffic was light on the Kennedy and Edens at this early hour Thursday, and Doyle made good time. He passed it by listening to a summary of world and national news on NPR—too depressing—then a CD by jazz pianist Jacky Terrason that improved his spirits.

Nora opened the apartment door, greeted Doyle with a light kiss on the cheek, and led him into the kitchen. "Coffee?"

"Yes. Thanks," Doyle said.

The tension she felt was evident in Nora's posture as she ground the beans and activated the coffee making machine. She said, "I'm a bit of a mess, Jack. I've never seen my sister depressed." She paused and looked out the east window at the elm trees shaking in a prestorm breeze. "Mickey has always been just a super 'up' kind of person, no matter what. After our parents' deaths. After being ignored for years by brother Kieran. Day in and day out. Until yesterday and this morning. She is sadly different. Shall I take you in to see her?"

"First, let me ask you something. Is there anything else bothering Mickey? Besides the fall? And her injuries? "

"Well, Jack, there is the homesick factor. Mickey and I both miss our parents, especially Mickey. She still lives with them when she's in Ireland, you know. And she definitely misses Jaimie Donovan, her boyfriend. More and more, it seems to me, in recent weeks.

"As for me, I must admit that I am, as the auld ones say back there, feeling 'the tug of the Emerald Isle.' Not that I have not enjoyed my time here with you, of course."

Jack paused before saying, "Of course."

Nora opened Mickey's bedroom door. Doyle followed her into the darkened room with its window blinds closed and no lamp light. Mickey sat on the floor, her back against the foot of her bed. She wore a short-sleeved Heartland Downs tee-shirt, jeans, white sweat sox on her small feet. It was obvious her facial bruises had burgeoned. She looked up and smiled weakly. "Hello, Jack."

"Hey, my girl. How goes it?"

"Please sit down. You, too, Nora. I'm not in a great mood, Jack. But I could not turn you away, could I?"

Doyle gestured at the floor near where Mickey sat. There was a scattering of poker chips and paper clips. "What are you doing with that stuff?" She reached down with her injured hand and wrist. Her fingers trembled. She managed to extract one clip and one chip. She looked up, smiling. "Hey, that's the best I've been able to do with this. So far."

Nora said, "That's an exercise her physical therapist at the hospital recommended. It's supposed to help repair the damaged ligaments she suffered."

Doyle leaned down and kissed his employer's freckled forehead as she grinned up at him.

"Don't worry, Jack, I'll be back. Soon. Count on me."

"I would never count you out, kid. But I don't like seeing you at a possible disadvantage with that injured hand and wrist."

"No, no," Mickey said. "The hand and wrist aren't everything." She rose quickly from the floor and sat down on the bed next to Doyle. "Can I tell you something I've come to learn about riding racehorses? Sometimes you can goad a horse to run faster by striking him with the whip. Or shouting at him. I mean just 'sometimes.' Most horses don't like being whipped or yelled at. Who could blame them?"

She walked over to the bedside table and picked up the rubber ball she squeezed several times an hour in an effort to build up her hand strength. "The valuable thing I've discovered," she said, "came from watching brother Kieran's races on television and on tape. He's not a smooth rider by any means. But he surely gets the job done. And one of the methods he uses, although he's never been inclined to inform me of it, is thrusting his weight down on the hind legs of the horse where the traction is. You have to have strong legs, especially thigh muscles, to do this. He has. So do I, I've found. When he actually gets that weight of purchase through the back legs, a rider can make his mount go faster. Jack, you look stunned."

"Incredulous, I would call it. When did you figure this out, Mickey?"

"About a year ago. Especially when I saw Kieran win the Irish Derby on Old Croft. It was evident what Kieran was doing with his weight on that horse. And it worked brilliantly. After that, I began going to a physical trainer to help me build up my leg strength. Nora used to drive me to the trainer three times a week. The stronger I got, the more races I won."

Nora said, "Mickey is a very determined girl."

"Comes from a very determined family," Doyle said. He glanced at his watch. "Got to get going. I told Ralph I'd do the entering of his horses today."

Mickey said, "Thanks for coming, Jack. And don't worry. I'll be back in shape to ride Plotkin in the Futurity. Did Nora tell you that I ran four miles earlier this morning? I can't ride now. But I've got to stay in shape so that I can ride."

Just two weeks to go till the Futurity, Doyle thought as he walked to his car. I hope to God Mickey can do it.

He started the Accord. Turned on the windshield wipers. The thunderstorm that an hour ago had been a threat was now a reality.

But the sun shone brightly seven days later when Doyle collected Mickey from her apartment shortly after dawn. She bounced down the stairs and hurried to the car. "Morning, Jack. I can't wait to get back to riding."

"How's the hand and wrist?"

"Nearly as good as new. And the bruises on my face are almost all faded away. I'm feeling great."

Mickey's buoyant mood was obviously contagious once she and Doyle reached Tenuta's barn. "*Hola*, Mickey," shouted one of the grooms when he spotted her. He was grinning widely. So were others of Tenuta's work crew. "*Un gusto veria,*" the groom added. Several of the female hot walkers rushed up to give her hugs as Mickey said to Jack, "What was that Pablo said?"

"I've forgotten most the high school Spanish I learned. But I think Pablo was welcoming you back."

"They love that little jock," Tenuta said. "Great to have her here again."

In the next ninety minutes, Mickey worked four of Tenuta's horses, displaying her usual professionalism on each. "Looks like her old self," Tenuta commented. Many of the jockeys and exercise riders on the track were also warm in their welcomes as Mickey galloped by.

Doyle was both relieved and heartened as he walked toward the racing secretary's office to enter three of Tenuta's trainees for the next race day. *One* week until the Futurity, he thought.

Chapter Fifty-eight

Eric had left a pass for Rudy at the entrance to the Player's Lounge at Heartland Downs. This was a private area for subscribed members that overlooked the track from the third floor. It was large room with desks and individual HD television screens for watching races as well as a sizeable dining area and small bar. Three pari-mutuel clerks waited to take bets. Numerous self-help mutuel machines far outnumbered these clerks, members of a union that track management was attempting to drive to its knees.

This was where the "whales" congregated, the biggest bettors, the men and some women who bet in the five figures each day they were present. Among them was Lou Liebman, a whale so valued by Heartland management that they sent a limo to transport him to and fro each day.

Eric waved to his brother from a table near the window. He was working on his second Bloody Mary of the morning, looking pleased with himself. His face was nearly the color of the table's crimson placemat. More and more, Rudy thought, *Eric is starting to remind me of our old man.* Eric signaled the waitress, ordering another Bloody Mary and an Old Style for Rudy.

The brothers bumped fists before Rudy sat down at the table. "You hungry, Rudy? They make a good breakfast here if you're interested in that. The lunch menu is a standout, too."

"Maybe a little later, Eric. I don't have much of an appetite right now." He ordered coffee from Cindy, the attentive waitress. "What I am is kind of worried."

Surprise was evident on Eric's face. "Worried? What's bugging you, brother? For Chrissakes, worried what about? You're riding high, man. Thanks to me and EPO. What's to worry about?"

The month just passed had seen Rudy Allgauer's stable come to life with a bang. From being near the bottom of the Heartland Downs trainers' standings, Rudy had rocketed up into the top five with nine winners from his last twenty starters. He was batting nearly fifty percent during that span, a remarkable percentage for anyone, much less him. And most of his winners had been scoring at long odds, to the delight of their betting owners.

"Look, Eric, don't get me wrong. This recent run of mine has probably salvaged my career. And I have you to thank for it."

"So, what's the problem?"

Rudy sighed and slumped back in his chair. "You know how the racetrack rumor mill works. Some people are wondering openly about this great improvement in my runners. They were a rag-tag, unproductive bunch before. Now, they're running like rats in a barrel. Rumor has it I've put them on some magic juice. Even though none of your EPO has ever shown up in a post-race test.

"Remember that trainer in New York a few winters back? Went from the bottom of the pile to the top of the heap overnight? He was claiming horses for $20,000, winning stakes races with them the next week. Everybody figured he was using some new drug that couldn't be detected. He probably was. They never publicly said they caught him, but something happened. Suddenly, his streak ended. He went back to being a little less than mediocre. Guys around here are suggesting that could all happen to me."

Rudy leaned forward, talking softly. "I'm worried, Eric. I'm tossing and turning at night. Michelle knows there's something bad bothering me, but I haven't told her what it is."

"Well, what the hell is it?" Eric said.

"I'm convinced now that using your magic juice is no way for me to win races. If I can't win legitimately, I should find something else to do with my life. And I'm scared as hell the test lab is going to find me out. Word is they're on the verge of a new test for EPO. They get that going, I'll be toast."

"Fuck 'em," Eric snarled. "If they'd perfected a new test, I would have heard about it. I've started to date that cute technician, Sandy Hartung, who works in the on-site lab here. She can't keep her mouth shut about anything. She's a nice, convenient fuck, though."

He drained his cocktail glass and signaled the waitress for another. His face was flushed from the liquor and his anger as Rudy's comments sunk in. "I hope you're not going to wimp out on me with this EPO campaign. I've cashed some very nice bets on your suddenly fast horses. Without a job, I need the dough. A couple of more scores will set me up for a year. So, let's not tuck and run at this point. Besides, this burst of success has served to revive your dismal career. Didn't you tell me the other day that you'd had calls from several owners wanting you to train for them?"

"That's true, Eric. And I think if I can get my hands on better stock, I can continue to win races. Without the help of EPO."

Eric leaned across the table and spoke softly. "Two more EPO specials. Maybe next week. I'll bet, collect, and be done. You'll improve your position in the trainer standing with a couple of more wins. How does that sound?"

Rudy reluctantly agreed. How could he refuse Eric after all his brother had done for him? "What are you going to do then, Eric?"

"After the Futurity has been run here, I'm going to be in the wind. I'm thinking the California tracks. I've still got my license. And nobody out there will know about my situation here. Maybe I'll even cut back on the drinking. We'll see."

They ordered food, a half-pound cheeseburger for Eric, a chicken burrito for Rudy. The burrito was so large it wouldn't have fit in Shaquille O'Neal's hand. Rudy attacked it appreciatively. Minutes later, Rudy checked his watch. "I've got to go saddle Friar Tuckie for the fourth race."

"He's primed and ready," Eric grinned. "I bet him a thousand to win, $500 to place." He looked out at the odds board. "He's five-to-one. That's cool. Wait. I'll come down to your box and watch the race with you."

It was just the two of them on the downward bound elevator, so Rudy felt free to pose a question. "Why did you say you would stay here for the Futurity?"

"I didn't say. But I'll tell you now. I've got one more surprise in store for that fuckin' Tenuta and his fuckin' horse Plotkin."

Chapter Fifty-nine

Lenny carried the cooler with its beer and sandwiches, Teresa a manila folder stuffed with papers. They walked from the sparsely populated Forest Preserve parking lot to one of the numerous vacant, wooden tables. This popular recreation area would be packed with picnickers on the weekend. But on this warm and humid Thursday afternoon, the only other person present was a Cook County maintenance crew supervisor sleeping comfortably beneath an elm tree fifty yards away from where they set up.

Without being asked, Lenny took a Pabst from the cooler and handed it to Teresa. Next out was an Italian beef sandwich. He repeated the process for himself and sat down across from her, forearms on the worn and scarred table top. "So, Treece, what have you got there for me?"

"For us, Lenny," she corrected. "For us."

She bit off a chunk of sandwich and washed it down with a swig of PBR before continuing. "I've got some good info about pipe bombs."

His jaw dropped. "Pipe bombs? What the hell do I care about pipe bombs?"

"Lenny, you should hear me out. You can use a pipe bomb to scare the shit out of Ralph Tenuta. Convince him to go along with you. Give you tips on his horses. In other words, make you some fucking money."

He shook his head. "I don't know how to make a fucking pipe bomb. I think you're losing it."

"No, no, no. And you don't have to make one. There's a guy I know comes in the store to buy lottery tickets and smokes. Eddie Scaravilli. He works as a pipe fitter. He kind of likes me. And he would know all about making one of these things. Here, let me tell you some stuff I got off the Internet."

She opened the manila folder. "Keep in mind that these are quote extremely dangerous devices unquote."

"Terrific," Lenny said.

She ignored his look of concern. "I've gotta read this to you from what I downloaded. I can't remember it all myself. Here goes. 'Pipe bombs are used as an alternative to conventional explosives. The components are very easily available and assembled.'"

Lenny said, "Sure as hell not by me, Treece."

She grinned. "That's where helpful Eddie Scaravilli comes into it. He can choose the explosive stuff that's used as filler. Filler goes into a closed metal pipe. You set it off by a fuse running into the pipe. Once it's lit, the pipe pretty quickly quote ruptures with great force unquote. All Eddie has to come up with are the fuse, the explosive stuff, TNT I guess, and the pipe that they go into. And put them all together."

"Your Eddie isn't going to know what this thing is going to be used for, right? What are you telling him?"

Teresa said, "I gave him a bullshit story about my imaginary nephew wanting to use a pipe bomb for a science project."

"That must be some high school your nephew goes to," Lenny snorted.

"Hey, that's just a detail. Main thing is that Eddie will make one of these things for me. For us, I mean."

Lenny swiveled on his bench and looked toward the thick forest that bordered the picnic grounds. "Jeez, Treece, I don't know. And where is Eddie going to get TNT?"

"No problem. Eddie says you can find and buy anything you need for a pipe bomb on the Internet." She reached into the cooler and pulled out another beer to hand him. "So, Lenny, what do you think?"

"What does this Eddie want for his work?"

Teresa grinned. "What he wants is a night out with me. Which I told him he wasn't going to get. That I was going with a guy. I didn't say who that was, don't worry. Anyway, I said I'd give him 100 bucks if he'd make the bomb. Eddie was cool with that."

Chapter Sixty

HEARTLAND DOWNS, IL—A sparkling field of eleven two-year-old colts and geldings was entered here Thursday morning for Saturday's $1 million Heartland Downs Futurity. The one-mile race, one of the richest in the nation for juveniles, is carded as the eighth event on the card. Post time is 4:45 p.m.

Entries were taken at a special press breakfast in the track clubhouse. Heartland odds-maker Donald Terry made the Irish invader Boy from Sligo the favorite at 5-2. He was closely followed by Go Yale Blue from the barn of so-called Super Trainer Rodney Fletcher at 7-2 and Rosa Tenuta's locally-owned Plotkin, 9-2. Go Yale Blue is one of some 250 horses conditioned by Fletcher. His huge, widely spread stable leads the U. S. in purse earnings with more than $11 million accumulated to date this year.

Boy from Sligo's trainer, Aiden O'Malley, has given a return call to leading Irish jockey Kieran Sheehan. In a racing rarity, Plotkin will be ridden by Sheehan's younger sister, apprentice sensation Mickey Sheehan, thus making for a sibling matchup. Angel Velasquez Jr. again has the assignment on Go Yale Blue.

The Irish invader boasts a record of four wins in five starts, all Group 1 contests. The lone blemish on his record came in the Healy Handicap when Kieran Sheehan tumbled off him shortly after the start.

Plotkin, a winner of five of seven outings, all his victories coming over the Heartland strip, and Go Yale Blue previously met in Saratoga's Sanford Stakes. Plotkin finished a good second, Go Yale Blue four lengths behind him in seventh .

Boy from Sligo is a bay son of Ireland's leading sire Giant's Dream. Go Yale Blue was a $1.2 million yearling purchase. The modestly bred Plotkin was reportedly purchased for $50,000.

On the phone to Kellman, Doyle quickly scanned Kaplan's *Racing Daily* story. "Plotkin drew the three hole, which Ralph says is fine. He's listed at nine to two in the morning line. Ralph was in a grand mood this morning after Art Engelhardt called to say he'd gotten a stay order of the Plotkin ruling. So Ralph can saddle Plotkin Saturday."

Kellman walked to east window of his office overlooking that morning's gently rippling, blue-green Lake Michigan. "Who would of thought," he said, "you and I would have a $50,000 horse in a million-dollar race?"

"And with a good chance," Doyle enthused. "We already outran Go Yale Blue at Saratoga when Plotkin finished second and he finished seventh. So, I'm not worried about him. Ralph thinks Plotkin as gotten a lot better since then. He believes it's the Irish horse that's the danger. His trainer, O'Malley, rarely ships to the States. But when he does, he does awfully well."

Kellman said, "How does Mickey feel about riding against her brother in the biggest race of life?"

Doyle laughed. "This kid doesn't have ice water in her veins, she's got ice. She says she can't wait to compete against Kieran and then pose in the winner's circle with Plotkin. I wish I had her confidence."

◇◇◇

Some 3,600 miles away Niall Hanratty sat in front of a computer in the Kinsale, Ireland office of his bookmaking firm, Shamrock Off-Course Wagering. He scrolled down to the end of Ira Kaplan's Heartland Downs Juvenile story, which appeared on the

Internet as part of that day's Paulick Report from the US. "That's going to be very interesting come Saturday," Hanratty said.

Office manager Tony Rourke said, "What's going to be interesting, Niall?"

Hanratty swiveled in his chair next to the window that over-looked the long Kinsale waterfront. "The clash of the Sheehans, that's what I mean, Tony. Mickey versus big brother Kieran for the first time in their riding careers. And in one of the biggest races of the year. Why, this scenario is positively drippin' with drama."

"That's not all it's doing," Rourke replied. "Ever since we started taking wagers on American races last year, this Futurity promises to be one of the biggest betting attractions we've had."

"Because of the Sheehans."

"Yes, because of the Sheehans," Rourke said.

"In what direction is the early betting going?"

"The slight majority is on Plotkin so far."

Hanratty's surprise was evident. "You mean the team of Kieran Sheehan and Aiden O'Malley isn't leading the way in the betting like it usually does here?"

"That's right, Niall. Our clerks report that there's been a lot of support from women bettors for little Mickey Sheehan. We've knocked Plotkin down to five to two favoritism as a result."

"I'll be damned," Hanratty said.

Rourke picked up the printouts from Hanratty's desk, preparing to return to his adjacent office. "I must say that your man Doyle has done a brilliant job with Mickey. She's come a long way in a short time. The American racing press is crazy about her. So are the fans."

Hanratty smiled. "Ah, Jack Doyle. A sometimes difficult but always resourceful sort of fella. I should give him a call one of these days."

"What do you think about our Kieran in this Futurity?" Rourke said. "He wouldn't be up to any of his suspicious capers now, would he?"

Hanratty said, "There's no chance of that. As far as I can tell, most of his shenanigans come in the lesser races. I don't think he'd contemplate doing anything funny while on the international stage like he'll be on Saturday.

"Besides," Hanratty added, "Kieran'll be roaring to beat his little sister with Boy from Sligo. He'll ride the hair off his horse, Tony."

Chapter Sixty-one

For Doyle, Futurity Week dragged on like a scoreless soccer match. He'd attended one of them on Sunday night, the Chicago Torches versus the Minneapolis Northerners, at the invitation of the Sheehan sisters, enthusiastic fans of what Nora described as "this beautiful game." Each sister had a favorite team back home in Ireland. Doyle thought he'd never been so bored at any other sporting event he'd ever attended. But he didn't say so, not wanting to spoil Mickey and Nora's fun. He occupied himself by drinking beer and reading the paperback version of Michael Connelly's latest Harry Bosch novel.

Monday and Tuesday were both "dark days" at Heartland Downs that week, but that didn't mean Doyle was idle. He spent his mornings watching the workouts with Tenuta, paying particular attention to Mickey, who rode with grace and assurance, so much so that Doyle was confident enough to put her on three mounts Friday. If all went well, on Futurity Day, she'd have assignments on another three of Tenuta's trainees in addition to Plotkin.

Doyle called Nora Tuesday afternoon. "How about dinner tonight? We could go to that new Mandarin restaurant near your neighborhood."

Nora laughed. She was well aware of Doyle's pronounced aversion to any cuisine that had its origins in the East: Far East, Near East, Middle East. He'd tried them all at various times and each had failed his taste test. "You're a great kidder, Jack. But, seriously, I've got to turn you down. I'm spending most of my time with Mickey these nights. She keeps busy doing her the therapy exercises for her wrist and hand plus watching tapes of some of Kieran's races. She ordered them over the Internet."

"What's her purpose in that?"

Nora said, "Mickey wants to be sure she knows as much as she can about Kieran's riding style, tendencies, whatever. Occasionally, she'll marvel at his ability and start to worry a bit about her chances against him in the Futurity. That's when I step in and pick up her spirits."

"Has she seen something useful to her on those Kieran tapes?"

"Yes. She says Kieran, like most Irish and English and French jockeys who come over here, lose lengths at the start of their races. They're used to rather slow beginnings, with their horses' speed reserved for the latter part of the race, as it is where they come from. She says if Kieran persists in that practice, she'll be able to get the jump on him Saturday."

"Getting the jump is one thing. Getting to the finish first is another. I know Kieran is famous for being a powerful finisher."

"Jack, she's not underestimating her brother. She's estimating him."

Doyle sighed. "So, you're going to be busy with Mickey every night this week?"

"Yes. I'll make it up to you next week, Jack."

Chapter Sixty-two

It was what happened when he walked into the State Street Off-Track Betting parlor that Wednesday noon that set him off. First thing he heard was loudmouth Terry Schneider holler, "Hey, here's Lenny the Loser. Back for another day of money burning." The three young guys sitting at the table with Schneider laughed loudly. Lenny tried to ignore them. Schneider, who Lenny first knew as a schoolyard bully in Berwyn, had been on his case for weeks. The fact that they'd wind up years later betting races in the same place was amazing to Lenny, who walked over to his regular little cubicle at the far end of the large room. Spread his *Racing Daily* on the small table in front of him, also the notes and speed figures he'd compiled.

During weeks like this, Lenny just could not figure out where he'd gone wrong with his wagering. He knew as much, if not more, about racing as any of those buffoons at Schneider's table. They drank beer and bet every weekend day from noon on. Never seemed to run out of cash. Frequently signified their successes with raucous hand-slapping and high-fiving.

Lenny, meanwhile, had recently been plagued by a terrible streak of bad luck. He'd lost eleven straight photo finishes. Unbelievable! These disappointments had been spread out all over the racing's simulcast nation of events from the US. To be *so* close all those times was killing him. His bankroll had diminished disastrously, so much so that he'd been forced to limit his purchases of crystal meth from the Latino kid on the corner of his Berwyn block.

He couldn't sleep nights. He couldn't do justice to Teresa in their love-making. He'd never suffered through a streak as bad as this.

It continued through the afternoon. Lenny's pick won the first race at Belmont Park, so he was alive in the daily double and encouraged. But his horse in the second race stumbled on the soggy turf course and lost decisive lengths right out of the gate. Lenny slammed his newspaper down on the table. He ordered a double shot of Captain Morgan and Coke at the bar. Downed it and hustled into the men's room where he took a hit of meth.

Riding the El train to downtown Chicago that morning, Lenny had decided to make his major move of the week on two races at Heartland Downs that afternoon. Each had a horse in its field trained by cousin Ralph Tenuta. Lenny had four times tried to call Ralph—he'd gotten his home number from his mother Elvira—but failed to reach him on the first three tries. Then Ralph finally called him back to say, "Look, Lenny, I'm not giving you racing advice. I'll give you some other advice. Stop betting on horses, get a real job, and move out of your mother's basement. That's all you're going to get from me."

Lenny was about to slam the phone down when he heard Tenuta say,

"Wait. Listen. I know you're interested in horses. You want to come work for me? On a trial basis? At Heartland Downs? You'd have to start at the bottom, walking horses, cleaning stalls, cleaning feed buckets, that kind of stuff. But I'm willing to give you a try as a favor to your mother, who's a great person. What do you say?"

Lenny spat out, "That's all you've got to say to me? You want I should get up in the middle of the night to work for your measly pay at the racetrack? Shoveling horse shit? No fuckin' way, cousin."

He was still steaming after he'd ordered and drained another CM and Coke. "To think that bastard wouldn't even tell me anything about the horses he's running today," Lenny muttered. "Well, I'm going to beat them with my picks. Fuck cousin Ralph."

Terry Schneider hollered across the room, "Hey, Lenny, Tenuta's got a horse in the next race at Heartland. You heard anything about it?"

"Like I'd tell you if I did, you loud mouth?"

Lenny walked to the mutual window and put 20 dollars to win, 20 dollars to place on the favorite in the Heartland race. The horse got soundly bumped after coming out of the gate and didn't run a lick after that. Tenuta's trainee won and paid $18.60.

"Have that winner, Lenny?" Schneider chortled. "We sure as hell did."

Lenny snatched up his newspaper and notes and headed to the door. "Hey, Loser, you giving up already?" he heard Schneider say. Lenny ignored him.

Back home in Berwyn, Lenny called the racing results telephone line. Ralph Tenuta's second runner that day also won. "Payoffs of 22 dollars to win, 11 dollars to place, 6 dollars to show" said the recorded voice.

Lenny hurled his cell phone against the wall. He was shaking as he sat back in his Barcalounger, sweat popping out on his forehead. "Does that fuckin' Tenuta think he's gonna get away with shittin' on me like this?"

His mother opened the door at the top of the basement stairs. "Lenny, I didn't know you were home already. I'm going to the five o'clock mass. So, we can eat about six-thirty. I made mushroom and chicken risotto. Okay?"

He struggled to control himself. "Yeah, Ma, that's great. See you later."

Elvira closed the door. Lenny waited a minute before reaching into the slit right arm of the brown Barcalounger for his plastic baggie of meth. Minutes later he felt himself come really alive, restored. He retrieved his cell phone and dialed. "Teresa, I'm ready to go with our plan for Tenuta. Did your pal Eddie deliver that thing?"

"He dropped it off last night. What time you think we should go to Tenuta's house?"

"I'll pick you up around eleven."

"Remember, Lenny, wear dark clothes. You got Tenuta's address?"

"You bet your big, beautiful ass, Treece."

Chapter Sixty-three

That evening, as Lenny Ruffalo was resting up in preparation for his pipe bomb foray, Doyle walked out of the Heartland Downs racing secretary's office carrying a half-dozen condition books and two *Racing Dailys* in one hand. With the other, he fumbled his sunglasses as he took them off to place in one of his sport jacket's inner pockets.

"Hey, agent Doyle, you need a little help there?" Doyle turned and saw the smiling face of Ingrid McGuire. The tall, tanned veterinarian had stopped on her way toward the building's entrance.

"Hi, Ingrid. Yes, I frequently need help. But not this time. You're looking well," he said admiringly. "What brings you over here? I thought you never left the backstretch."

"Usually, I don't. But I'm about to meet Brad Molitor for dinner as soon as he's off work."

Molitor was one of the bright young assistants in the secretary's office. Doyle nodded approvingly. "Brad's a good guy. You been going out with him?"

"For about a couple of weeks," Ingrid said. "We enjoy each other's company. And, very much in his favor, Brad doesn't drink."

That unveiled reference to Ingrid's former partner and lover caused Doyle to shake his head. "I saw Eric Allgauer the other morning. He looked like hell."

"I can't worry about him anymore, Jack. Nice to see you." She turned and walked quickly toward the nearby door.

Doyle headed down the red-brick path to the parking lot but had to stop at the bottom when a long, black limousine stopped at the curb in front of him. The driver got out and opened the rear door of the ostentatious vehicle. A small, bare-headed man wearing a brown suit and white open-collared shirt emerged. He reached back into the limo and took out a small suitcase and a duffel bag to which a whip was attached.

"Well," Doyle said, "could that be Kieran Sheehan?" He stepped forward to introduce himself and find out. After Sheehan had tipped the limo driver, Doyle said, "Kieran, I'm the agent for your sister Mickey. Name's Jack Doyle." He extended his hand. Sheehan ignored it.

"Evenin' to you, Doyle. Will you tell me now how to get to the riders' room at this fine racetrack? I've had a long flight and I want to get settled in there before I go to the hotel. By the way, how are my lovely sisters? I assume you know Nora as well as Mickey."

The jockey was some eight inches shorter than Doyle, but Doyle felt as if he were being looked straight in the eye by this self-assured little man. "Your sisters? What the hell do you care? I understand you have as little to do with them as possible. If you're hoping to get any information from me about Mickey and her injury, forget it."

Sheehan took off his sun glasses, tucked them in his coat pocket, and gave Doyle an appraising look. "You sound quite protective of my siblings. I understand you've made a very good living getting mounts for Mickey. And the lovely Nora…Have you gotten along well with her then, Doyle?"

He picked up his luggage before adding, "And who are you, mister, to be commenting on my family relations?"

"An interested observer. Welcome to the States, Kieran. May your visit be a fruitless one."

◇◇◇

The Chicago area's blanket of August heat and humidity was still draped over the uncomfortable citizenry late that night.

The air conditioning in Lenny's car hadn't worked all summer. In-rushing air from their open windows did little to relieve the discomfort he and Teresa suffered on their west-bound drive.

During the drive, Lenny and Teresa agreed again that they would not bomb Tenuta's house. Such an action would involve getting too close to the home, risking discovery. Instead, their target would be the garage. "We blow a big hole in that fucker," Lenny said, "and get the hell out of there, and cousin Ralph will get the message that he's gone too long pissing somebody off. Me."

They reached Arlington Heights shortly before midnight. Lenny took nearly twenty minutes to locate Tenuta's home. It was midway of a block of ranch houses on a dimly lit street on the south side of town. He drove past the house twice, checking to make sure he had the right address and that no lights were on. A circle of the block showed them that Tenuta's back yard had a dark, wide alley behind it. Lenny parked in it, close to the adjacent wire fence, figuring this position would allow for a rapid escape. He and Teresa sat for a couple of minutes listening to the ticking noises coming from the car's engine. He took a hit of meth. He offered Teresa one but, as usual, she refused. Finally, courage up, they quietly exited the car and Teresa followed him through the squeaky back gate and onto the gravel path leading to the garage.

The house remained dark. "Tenuta's probably asleep," Lenny whispered. "These trainers, they got to get up around four in the morning. They go to sleep early." Teresa muffled a laugh. "Tenuta's going to get an early wakeup call in a few minutes."

Lenny tripped slightly as they crept to the north side of the garage, almost dropping the duffel bag containing the bomb. Teresa said, "Watch your step, Lenny. That thing is fuckin' dangerous."

"I know, I know." He could feel sweat trickling down his spine. He tried to stop his hands from shaking.

Chapter Sixty-four

"We heard this lound *thump*. I thought maybe it was a blown electrical transformer. It was enough to wake me up. And Rosa, too."

"What time was this?" Doyle said.

Tenuta looked up at Doyle. He was sitting on a bench outside his track office this dreary, rain-dripping Thursday morning. Unshaven, face drawn, he looked, Doyle thought, like hell. "Right after midnight," Tenuta said.

"After the thumping noise, there's this terrible loud scream. Then a whole lot more of them," the trainer continued. "I went into the kitchen and opened the back door. Next to my garage, there's a body on the ground. I can see the legs and feet. They're not moving. The top part is covered up by this sizeable young woman who keeps on screaming. By now, lights are going on all over the neighborhood and dogs are barking like crazy. Before I go out the door, I tell Rosa, 'Call 911.'

"In between her shrieks, I hear the young woman say something over and over. I go up to her and tap her on the shoulder. She turns and looks up at me, still crying hard. 'Oh, Lenny,' she keeps repeating.

"I can see the rest of the body now." Tenuta paused. Took a deep breath. He was trembling. "The body had no head, Jack."

Several minutes later, after Doyle had gotten Tenuta a cup of coffee, the trainer continued his account of that early morning's horrible proceedings.

"The woman's name is Teresa Genacro. She's, she was, Lenny Ruffalo's girlfriend. Once the police got there, right before the Fire Department, she told them she and Lenny came to my house intending to set off a pipe bomb to damage my garage."

Doyle said, "A pipe bomb! What the hell for?"

"This girl was pretty incoherent. What the sergeant in charge eventually got out of her was that Lenny wanted to throw a scare into me. So that I'd change my mind and give him information about my horses. The dumb bastard had been pestering me, and I told him to get the hell away from me. That's what he came up with this goddam bomb idea."

Once she had been somewhat calmed down and placed in their ambulance, Fire Department members elicited details from Teresa, Tenuta said.

"She told them Lenny had used some of that crystal meth stuff both when they were on their way to my house from Berwyn, and once they'd gotten there. Said it made him jumpy as hell. When he tried to light the pipe bomb fuse at first, he dropped the match. Did that twice. Finally got it started and he waved her to back away. She could see him bending toward the bomb, peering into where the fuse went. Then all of a sudden it went off. So did his head."

"Christ," Doyle said.

"There was blood and pieces of the poor bastard's head splattered all over the side of my garage. I was so shook up I couldn't bring myself to call Lenny's mother. Rosa did that, she's the one that broke the news to Elvira. I'll tell you, Jack, it was a night neither Rosa or I will ever forget."

Unforgettable is how Doyle termed the pipe bomb fiasco when he phoned Moe later that morning. Kellman asked, "How is Ralph taking all this? It's the damnedest thing I've ever heard of. Or at least one of them."

"Ralph has, as they say around racetracks of a horse who is tough and resilient, a 'lot of bottom.' Naturally, he's shook up."

"The good news is that Ralph is already starting to think about tomorrow's races and Mickey's rides. And about Saturday's Futurity."

Chapter Sixty-five

Friday proved to be a dismal day for Doyle. Mickey went winless. And Moe left town.

Mickey lost on all three of her Friday mounts on her comeback day. Exiting the track late that afternoon, Tenuta said, "Jack, don't be so gloomy. Mickey looked fine on those horses. She just didn't win on her first day back from the injury. Not unexpected."

"So zero for three should make me happy?"

"I didn't say that. I'll just point out that none of those three had much of a chance today. I didn't want to put a lot of pressure on Mickey by giving her favorites to come back on." He patted Doyle on the back. "Cheer up. Tomorrow's going to be a much better day. Plotkin will see to that."

There was a phone message from Moe to call him. Moe picked up in his Chicago office. "Jack, I wanted you to know I'm leaving town."

"Under a cloud?"

"Very funny. No, through the clouds. I've got to fly to Florida tonight. I hate to miss the Futurity, but I have to do it. One of my good friends from the old neighborhood passed away. Solly Brockstein. Keeled over on the golf course at his retirement community. Funeral's Saturday."

Doyle said, "I'm sorry to hear that. About your friend, I mean, and that you won't be with me for the Futurity."

"So it goes, Jack. The ironic thing is that Solly loved golf, but he was a terrible golfer. I used to kid him with what Mark Twain said about golf: 'It's a good walk spoiled.' His son said Solly had birdied the previous hole and was in a great mood. So, I guess he died happy.

"Anyway, Jack, call me after the Futurity. I'll be too busy with the after-funeral reception to watch it on television. Tell Mickey and Ralph good luck."

"Will do."

Also wishing Mickey good luck was Wilfredo Gavidia. The injured rider, now home and engaged in extensive physical and mental therapy, telephoned her to advise, "Listen, *chica*, don't worry just about your brother Saturday. You've got to think about all of them. Okay?"

"Okay, Wilfredo," Mickey said. "Thanks for the call."

Gavidia said, "I'll give you another call tomorrow before the races."

Chapter Sixty-six

Rudy Allgauer helped his brother carry the heavy steamer trunk to Eric's pickup. They hoisted it onto the flatbed, placing it among several boxes of Eric's possessions, then pulled a tarpaulin over the lot. Arriving at their homes this early Friday night, a couple of neighbors glanced incuriously at the Allgauer brothers. There was always a lot of coming and going in this Arlington Heights neighborhood inhabited by many racetrack transients.

Back in Eric's rented condo, Rudy sighed and sat down heavily at the kitchen table. Eric said, "If you want this table and chairs you're welcome to them Rudy. Same with the couch in the living room, the bed. I've got possession of this place for another week. I'll leave the key with you."

"Damn, Eric, I wish you weren't doing this. I still can't see why you need to move to California."

"I've got to move someplace, bro, in order to make a living. I'm dead meat here, thanks to Ingrid and Tenuta. Nobody hires me. But I've still got my license and I'll be able to work in California. I've decided to start up out there in the north, Bay Meadows, then Golden Gate Fields. Move down to the southern tracks later on, once I've gotten established."

He walked around the table and put his hand on Rudy's shoulder. "I'll miss you, bro," he said affectionately, "and Michelle, too. But this is what I've got to do."

Rudy hesitated before saying, "Does Ingrid know you're leaving?"

Eric's face flushed. "Why would I tell that bitch? *She* left me."

"Where are you going tonight?"

"I've got to make a final visit to Heartland. After that I'll be heading West. I'll make it to Des Moines by early morning, catch a few hours of sleep at an Interstate rest stop, then head for Omaha. There's a casino there where I can watch the Futurity Saturday afternoon."

Rudy left just before 10. Eric closed the front door behind him and returned to the kitchen. He picked up his black leather jacket and put it on.

Before turning out the light, he filled his silver flask with icy vodka from the refrigerator.

At the door, he checked his pockets. They were there, the Nembutol-filled syringe on the right side, the syringe loaded with elephant juice on the left. He smiled, thinking *I've got enough juice in there to put Plotkin over the moon.*

A final look at his soon to be vacated living space briefly reminded him of the happy days he had spent there with Ingrid soon after their move from Urbana. Good times, indeed. How lovely and accepting she was. Then it all fell apart. He knew he bore some responsibility for their breakup. But not as much as "that damned horse communicator herself," he said to himself.

Eric slammed shut the condo door. Took a deep breath of the cool night air, then a long pull on the flask of vodka. He was glad to note that heavy cloud cover in the night sky obscured the moon. He had a couple of hours to waste before going to Heartland Downs.

◇◇◇

That afternoon, Doyle had invited the Sheehan sisters to have dinner with him. Mickey declined, saying she wanted to spend the evening concentrating on reading *Racing Daily* past performances of the Futurity field and again reviewing videotapes of brother Kieran's races. Nora said she needed the time to catch up on her blog about Mickey. "I've fallen a bit behind, Jack. My editor back home said the website is being inundated with queries about Mickey and Plotkin's chances tomorrow."

Doyle laughed. "I didn't know you were going into the prognostication business, Nora. I'm not going to ask you who you're picking to win. I already know. See you at the track tomorrow."

Chapter Sixty-seven

Pre-race tension was starting to get to Doyle, to whom tension was usually a stranger. He puttered around the kitchen in his condo after pouring two ounces of Jameson's into an ice-filled glass. He didn't feel like going out to eat. Finally, he decided to utilize the bachelor's major weapon against hunger, his George Foreman grill. The resulting hamburger turned out fine, but he didn't have much appetite. Another Jameson's did little to calm his nerves.

The more he thought about it, the less confidence he had in Tenuta's security plans for that night. Tenuta's old friend Harry Schwartz, a nice guy but a poster person for ineptitude in Doyle's view, was to be joined by Delmar Schwartz, Harry's middle-aged son. From what Doyle had observed of Delmar, the apple hadn't taken a lengthy tumble from the tree.

As Doyle pointed out to Tenuta, Harry Schwartz had not prevented previous drugging attacks on Tenuta's stock. Tenuta was defensive. "Harry may not be what he used to be, but he's a friend of mine, and he needs the job. It's good his son will help him. I'm going to keep both of them on the night payroll for the rest of the season here."

Doyle's tension level escalated when he fielded a phone call from Ingrid McGuire shortly after nine-thirty. "Sorry to bother you, Jack, but there's something you *should* know. Plotkin is worried."

"*Plotkin* is worried! Like *I'm* not on the eve of that horse's biggest race. Mickey's biggest race?"

Phone to his ear, Doyle went into the kitchen and turned on his coffee pot. "When did this happen?"

Ingrid said, "Just minutes ago. I was taking a bath, thinking about tomorrow's Futurity. All of a sudden, Plotkin sent some thoughts to me. What he was communicating was a sense of foreboding he felt. He's concerned about whoever doped him before showing up again tonight."

"Any new ideas as to who would pose that threat? From either you, or Plotkin?"

"Don't be facetious, Jack. The two 'possibles' I had in mind I've now eliminated. That angry groom Ralph fired? Hector Martinez? He was scooped up in an immigration raid for illegal aliens late yesterday afternoon. He's in jail awaiting deportation.

"Old Ambrose Pennyfeather, the vet Ralph let go? He's been living in an extended care facility for the last two weeks. I found that out from Buck Norman when I was having breakfast in the track kitchen this morning. Poor old guy has galloping Altzheimer's. I understand he was diagnosed a month ago and his family just recently got him placed."

"Maybe Plotkin isn't up on current news," Doyle kidded. "If he was, he might not be so concerned tonight."

Ingrid snapped, "That's not funny, Jack. Plotkin couldn't possibly know what happened with Martinez and Pennyfeather. He just knows what's going on his mind. And that is troubling him." There was a pause before she said, "I hate to think this, but the threat might well be Eric. He's been so bitter about Ralph's dismissing him, and so screwed up by his drinking, he might be capable of drugging Plotkin. God, I hope not."

Chapter Sixty-eight

Immediately following the WGN ten o'clock news, Doyle said to himself, "The hell with it. I'm going out there." He pulled on his windbreaker and hustled down the two flights of stairs to the garage and his Accord. Traffic was light, so Doyle's drive toward Heartland Downs took only forty-four minutes. But then it came to an abrupt halt at the Wilke Avenue railroad crossing where Doyle briefly pounded the wheel of his Accord in frustration as he watched an interminable freight train move slowly past. He stopped counting the cars after the first eighty. At last, the caboose went past and the wooden barriers were raised. Doyle gunned his Accord over the tracks.

Shortly after eleven, Delmar Schwartz said, "Pop, I've got to get me some coffee from the track kitchen. I'm startin' to fade here. You want any?"

"No thanks, Delmy. Hurry on back." Harry sat back in his camp chair in front of Plotkin's stall and returned his attention to his *Racing Daily.*

Heartland's backstretch gate guard glanced up from the little television on his desk that was showing a rerun of *American Idol* and absent-mindedly waved Eric's black pickup truck through. Eric drove slowly on the main backstretch road and turned off his lights before parking in the shadows at the far edge of Tenuta's barn. Closed the truck door gently. He pulled on a black ski mask. Pulled the Nembutol hypodermic out of his right hand pocket. Walked softly to the end of the barn and started up the shedrow. Some of the horses noticed his approach, but not Harry Schwartz, who was engrossed in his newspaper.

Plotkin nickered loudly and Harry looked up from his paper just as Eric quickly covered the last couple of yards of his approach. Seeing the masked intruder, Harry started to rise from his chair. "What the hell?" he said loudly. Eric pushed Harry back down and held him firmly in his seat with one hand. With the other, he plunged the needle into Harry's neck. The Nembutol acted quickly and the old man slumped forward. Eric thrust that empty needle back into his pocket and replaced it with the elephant juice needle. He moved toward Plotkin's stall. The horse backed away from him. "Goddam," Eric muttered, "I'll have to go in there to do him."

Fifty yards away on the other side of the barn, Doyle spotted a familiar-looking pickup truck parked in the shadows. He hit the brakes of the Accord and slid to a gravel-spewing stop, threw open his car door, and sprinted toward the other side of Tenuta's barn.

At the corner, Doyle stopped to take in the scene. He saw the apparently unconscious Harry Schwartz. The masked figure outside of Plotkin's stall who was beginning to run straight at him. Eric lowered his shoulder and bowled over the crouching, startled Doyle. He sprinted to his truck.

"Son of a bitch," Doyle said as he scrambled to his feet and started chasing after the man. Approaching his truck, Eric ripped off his mask. He wanted no distractions in his rapid retreat from the racetrack. Doyle clearly saw Eric's face as the veterinarian's truck sped past him. Doyle dashed to his Accord.

The stable gate was closed but had not been padlocked by the television-watching guard. Eric busted through it. Doyle saw that, but he stopped to address the guard, now standing open-mouthed in the doorway of the gate house. "That truck that just left here, that's Eric Allgauer driving. Call the track medical department and security and 911," Doyle said loudly. "There's a security guard who's been attacked. At Ralph Tenuta's barn. Get them over there right away." He rolled up his window as he tromped on the Accord's accelerator.

Eric was several blocks ahead of Doyle, speeding north on Wilke. Not trusting the startled Heartland guard to quickly make all three calls, Doyle dialed 911 on his cell phone. "There's a dangerous man driving very fast north on Wilke Road maybe a half-mile south of the Addison intersection. In a black pickup. He attacked a man at Heartland. His license plate is VET639. He's probably flying on booze. He's weaving all over the road."

"Sir, who are you?" the dispatcher said. Doyle clicked off the connection to concentrate on catching the black pickup. He knew he was gaining as Allgauer's truck careened around a slow-moving sedan where Grove Street crossed Addison. Doyle whisked past that car and its startled driver, missing it by a yard. He pressed down harder on the Accord's accelerator.

Doyle heard the wail of a police siren. In his rear view mirror, he saw a squad car coming rapidly, its lights flashing. "C'mon, men, let's get this bastard," he muttered.

Three blocks south of the Wilke-Addison intersection with its Metra railroad crossing, Doyle roared up to within a block of Allgauer's truck. He could see the white crossing barriers ahead beginning to descend and hear the *ding-ding* warning signal and the blare of the train engineer's horn. He hit his brakes hard and his Accord slid to a halt at the Wilke curb.

Allgauer's truck seemed to slow briefly before shooting forward again toward the crossing and its now lowered white barriers. The truck smashed its way through onto the tracks. "The crazy son of a bitch is trying to beat the train!" Doyle said.

The hurtling black pickup and the speeding train engine arrived at the middle of the Metra tracks simultaneously. Allgauer's truck was propelled through the air with a wrenching noise. It landed in pieces a half-mile up the track, its cab crumpled like a discarded tin can. Doyle shuddered and laid his forehead on his steering wheel. "Crazy son of a bitch…"

An Arlington Heights squad car pulled up next to Doyle's car. Two officers jumped out. One ran to the rail crossing and peered down the tracks toward the wreckage. The other one asked Doyle to step out of his Accord.

"Sir, are you the person who made the 911 call about this?"

"Yes."

"Do you know who was driving that truck?"

"Yes. His name was Eric Allgauer."

"Can I see some identification please?"

Doyle gave the officer his driver's license, which was carefully perused and returned, also his jockey agent's license. The young officer looked at it before saying, "So, you're a racetrack guy. What did you have to do with this accident, or catastrophe, this mess, whatever we call it?"

"It's a long story," Doyle said.

After his making his statement to detectives in the Arlington Heights police station, Doyle got back to his condo shortly after two o'clock. He downed a Jameson's before attempting to sleep. Images of the horrendous collision at the rail crossing kept popping into his memory. It was Futurity Day for Plotkin and all his connections. Concern over the colt's chances was another pressing issue.

He gave up trying to sleep just before six o'clock and was completing his second set of 100 sit ups when his cell phone rang. Moe said, "Jack, I just heard on CNN about some 'fatality involving a Heartland Downs veterinarian, name withheld at this time.' Who was it? What happened? You know anything about this?"

"Unfortunately, yes." He recounted the previous night's happenings, the attack on Harry Schwartz, Doyle's discovery of Eric Allgauer outside of Plotkin's stall, the subsequent chase. "I was on Allgauer's tail, the cops were coming up fast from behind." He paused to drink from a water bottle.

"Then what?"

"Allgauer was either drunk, or desperate, or both. He tried to beat the train across the tracks in order to leave me and the police behind."

Doyle got to his feet, cradling the phone as he opened another bottle of water. "It was a photo finish, Moe. Allgauer lost."

Chapter Sixty-nine

The eastern sky was just hinting at morning illumination when Doyle parked his Accord behind Tenuta's barn. For a couple of minutes he sipped from the coffee cup he'd brought with him while listening to the familiar sounds of water buckets banging, horses whinnying for their breakfasts, rapid exchanges in Spanish by their caretakers before he walked to the trainer's office. Tenuta put his phone down when Doyle entered.

"Jack, how are you? Word is you were involved with what happened to Eric Allgauer last night. Am I right?"

Doyle pushed the resentful cat Tuxedo to the side and sat down on the couch. "I continue to be amazed at the efficiency of the racetrack grape vine. Unbelievable. Yeah, Ralph, I was involved."

When Doyle had finished his recounting, Tenuta said, "My God, how lucky we are you arrived in time to protect Plotkin. And that Harry Schwartz came out of it okay. Delmar called me this morning. Said his old man had been kept in the hospital overnight but was out and about. Said Harry gave him money to bet on Plotkin.

"I had another call," Tenuta continued. "Ingrid McGuire cancelled her appointments here for this morning. She was pretty broken up about Allgauer. She also said she was thinking about Plotkin and had been communicating with him. I guess she was trying to get her mind off the Allgauer disaster. According to her, the colt feels he's going to run big this afternoon."

Doyle raised his cup in a toast. "As my Aunt Florence used to say, 'May it be so.'"

◇◇◇

The afternoon got off to an unpromising start. Mickey finished out of the money on her first mount, then third aboard Tenuta's Madame Golden. She was furious with herself as she unsaddled, telling Tenuta, "I moved too late. Madame Golden wasn't to blame. I was." Before the trainer could respond, Mickey turned and strode to the jocks' room.

"She's too hard on herself," Tenuta said when he rejoined Doyle in the box. "So many things can go wrong in a race that a jockey can't foresee. Maybe the horse isn't feeling tip-top. Maybe he doesn't like the track because it's too hard. Or too soft. Maybe he gets bumped by another horse. With Mickey in that last race, Madame Golden really had nowhere to go until it was too late. Not Mickey's fault, although she thinks so. Just the way the race unfolded."

Doyle said, "She looks mighty tense today. I've never seen her like this before."

"She's never had a day like this before, Jack. Biggest race of her life. Facing her brother. She's got a right to be uptight. I know *I* am."

◇◇◇

In the small room she shared with Elaine Yonover, Mickey changed into Rosa Tenuta's red and white silks that she would wear in the Futurity. That race was an hour away. She thought about what Wilfredo Garcia had said to her on the phone the night before.

So Plotkin drew the one hole. With his speed away from the gate, you should be fine, Mickey. When I rode a speed horse like Plotkin, I always felt more comfortable being on the outside, where I'd have more options. It's easier to get a horse to relax when he's on the outside. He doesn't feel closed in. But Plotkin has such great acceleration from the gate, you should make the lead without any trouble, without being pressured. Then you can dictate the pace.

"Just remember to stay relaxed, stay loose, in the post parade, in the gate. A horse can sense tension and react badly. The more relaxed you are, the better chance he'll break good. But you know all that, Mickey. Any questions? No? Well, have a safe trip. God bless you.

Elaine Yonover came into the room carrying her helmet and whip, hair plastered against her forehead, having completed one of her rare riding assignments.

"How'd you do, Elaine?"

"Got fourth money. Mickey, the rail is fast, it's golden. There's a nice path there for you and Plotkin. Speed is holding today."

Mickey nodded, saying "That's what I thought, too, after Madame Golden's race. Hope the rail stays that way."

"Not to worry, girl. You gotta lighten up," Elaine patted Mickey on the shoulder before heading for the shower.

In the adjacent jockey's room, the large one housing the male riders, Kieran Sheehan relaxed in a lounge chair in the recreation section watching a ferocious game of table tennis being played to his right, a jibe-filled game of nine-ball progressing on the pool table to his left. He'd already donned the silks he would wear aboard Boy from Sligo.

Some of the riders had attempted to engage Kieran in conversation. But, as was his habit before a race, he politely rebuffed them, preferring to consider and concentrate on the upcoming Futurity. He'd often thought of the irony involved in his silent solitude in rooms like this contrasted to the vocal exchanges that often took place during races. He knew that most fans would be surprised to learn that riders talked back and forth during their races, especially the experienced ones. If they were good friends, they might joke with each other about their chances. Or they might angrily plead to be let through a hole that was closing in front of them.

The valet assigned to him for the day, Larry Hejna, approached with Kieran's recently polished boots. "Thanks," Sheehan said. "Nice job."

"You want a cup of coffee or something, Kieran?"

"No, but thanks. But you can crack the champagne in about a half-hour or so, Larry."

Hejna had been around the racetrack most of his adult life and heard countless expressions of confidence from jockeys, most of them unjustified. "So you say you like your Futurity chances?"

"Bet your money, Larry. Boy from Sligo is a runnin' rascal."

Chapter Seventy

As the eleven two-year-olds began to assemble behind the starting gate for the sixty-eighth running of the Heartland Downs Futurity, Doyle leaned forward in his seat, binoculars trained on Plotkin. He could see that Mickey had the colt moving easily toward stall number one. Kieran Sheehan on Boy from Sligo waited to be placed in stall eight. His colt was fractious and sweating heavily. Kieran reached down with his right hand and rubbed Boy from Sligo's neck, attempting to settle him.

To Doyle's right in the Tenuta box, Rosa was working her set of rosary beads. Doyle smiled as he felt in his sport jacket pocket the set of black worry beads Moe had given him months before. "I bought these in Tel Aviv when Leah and I were there two years ago," Moe had said. "I reach for them on special occasions. Use them when you need them. They help."

Rosa paused in her praying to wave at her husband. Ralph had chosen to watch the race from the rail. He interrupted his nervous pacing to wave back up at Rosa and Jack.

In one of the visiting owners' boxes in front of them, Doyle noticed Teddy Moseley, the loud mouth from Saratoga, owner of number six, Go Yale Blue. Moseley put down an empty Bloody Mary glass and snatched a full one from the tray of the young waiter standing in the aisle adjacent to the box.

Doyle's cell phone rang. It was Moe, checking in from Florida.

"Moe, it's almost post time. I'm looking down a couple of boxes from us and who do you think is there but your Ivy

League buddy Teddy Moseley. Should I ask him if he brought the $2,500 he still owes you from Saratoga?"

"Fat chance of that, Jack. Don't concern yourself with that blowhard. How many minutes to post time?"

"Two."

"What's Mickey's strategy?"

"Same as always. Use our horse's speed. Like Ralph always says, 'Give me a natural front runner every time. He'll be gone from where the others haven't gotten yet.'"

Doyle looked across the track at the gate. One-mile races such as the Futurity began in a chute at the far right of the oval. "They're all in, Moe." He resumed fingering his worry beads. "I'll call you when it's over."

Plotkin broke from the gate like a shot. Doyle felt his heart leap. He heard Heartland Downs announcer John Tully say:

> *And that's Plotkin away in stride to take the early lead. He has two lengths on Harlan Dee. Doctor Chuck goes third on the outside, followed by Don Terry, Go Yale Blue, Market Slump, Date of Play, Catcall Cal, the Irish invader Boy from Sligo under a tight rein in ninth. Then comes Roisterer Roy, In the Dark, and Quicker Time can see them all.*
>
> *Plotkin continues to lead, his first quarter in a brisk :22 1-5, the half in :46 flat. As they approach the far turn, Doctor Chuck moves into second while Harlan Dee drops back. Go Yale Blue takes over fourth. And Boy from Sligo is starting to pick up horses while racing on the outside...*

Kieran was stuck behind a wall of horses. He knew he didn't want to go six horses wide with Boy from Sligo, losing all that ground. Not with Mickey's horse going so well on the lead. He needed an opening. Exhibiting the patience that had made him one of the world's best reinsmen, Kieran waited. And waited. And waited. Then, just inside the sixteeth-pole, Doctor Chuck drifted slightly inward and the weary-legged Go Yale Blue drifted out. Boy from Sligo shot through the resultant narrow hole into second place.

Doyle could hear the rattle of Rosa's rosary beads, hear her imploring "C'mon Plotkin. C'mon Plotkin." Doyle put the worry beads in his pocket and stood with his fists clenched. The roar of the crowd was escalating rapidly.

Plotkin had curved around the stretch turn tight to the rail, Mickey still sitting chilly on him. Straightened out for the long run to the finish line, she briefly peered back under her right arm to see Doctor Chuck starting to flatten out, Harlan Dee and Go Yale Blue shortening stride. But gaining ground in the middle of the track was Boy from Sligo. The finish line momentarily seemed to be receding in front of Mickey. But she still hadn't asked Plotkin for his best. As Wilfredo Garcia often advised her, "Jesus saves. You should remember to save something with your horse."

Inside the sixteenth pole, Mickey felt pressure from her right. Kieran Sheehan had steered Boy from Sligo from the crown of the racing strip to a path just outside Plotkin and had pulled to within a half-length of Mickey's mount. The rest of the field was far back. It was a two-horse race from here on in.

A hundred yards to go. Kieran steered Boy from Sligo over even closer to Plotkin. Kieran, frantically striving to gain the lead, had begun rapidly whipping Boy from Sligo in the upper stretch. He never missed a beat, switching hands from left to right and back. "He's like a damned machine," Doyle said to Rosa.

Fifty yards to go for the embattled pair when Kieran's stick, now in his left hand, came across and cracked Plotkin on the nose. The startled colt threw his head up and momentarily slowed slightly. Boy from Sligo thrust his neck in front. "That bastard," Doyle shouted to Rosa. "Did you see what Kieran did?" He knew that any review would find Kieran contending that his whip action was "inadvertent."

If Kieran's intention was intimidation, it didn't work. Plotkin's resentment over being struck on the nose transferred into resolve. Mickey could feel him power ahead. She urged him on with her hands pressing forward on his neck. They flashed across the wire nose to nose with Boy from Sligo as the crowd noise reached crescendo level.

Doyle kept his binoculars on the riders of Plotkin and Boy from Sligo as they galloped out past the finish line. They appeared to be talking to each other.

Around him, he heard other box holders debating the order of finish. "Boy from Sligo got it" from a man to his left. "No, no," argued the woman beside him. "It was Plotkin." Doyle hardly noticed when a red-face and obviously disheartened Teddy Moseley led his party up the stairs and toward the exits, brushing past Doyle without saying a word.

Doyle and the other 32,456 fans on hand waited anxiously for the result of the sixty-eighth Heartland Downs Futurity to be posted.

◇◇◇

It was 5:55 p.m. in Miami when Moe Kellman heard his cell phone ring. He moved out of the crowded living room of the late Solly Brockstein's ranch house, a room filled with the post-burial crowd, and onto the adjacent patio.

"Jack, I figured the race to be over ten, fifteen minutes ago. What happened in the Futurity?"

"Photo finish, Moe. We won."

Chapter Seventy-one

Twelve hours after his narrow loss in the Futurity, Kieran deplaned at Dublin Airport. Walking toward the exit, he passed a line of newspaper vending machines. A headline on that day's *Irish Times* stopped him in his tracks. It was atop an article describing the previous day's sudden death of "prominent Irish businessman Paddy Hanrahan," who had succumbed at his Connemara estate of "a massive stroke."

Kieran was still stunned when he heard his cell phone ring as he neared the airport parking lot. It was Martin McCluskey. "Welcome back, Kieran. We need to talk. If you're not jet-lagged, or too depressed at losing that big race to your sister, we should meet. How about our usual place. Tomorrow morning."

As usual, McCluskey was there first at the end of the long Dun Laoghaire pier. Dawn's arrival had failed to force any sunlight through the thick layer of fog that carried with it a fine layer of mist. McCluskey's tweed cap was pulled low over his broad forehead. Kieran grimaced as he saw the dog Behan at his tall, bulky master's side. He remembered how much he despised that huge brute.

"Can't say I'm sorry about your man Paddy," Kieran said.

"I didn't expect you would be. And you'll not be sorry about what I'm about to tell you, either."

McCluskey paused for the length of a foghorn blare. "With Paddy Hanrahan gone to his rest, I'll be delivering no more demands on you to fix horse races. You'll hear no more from the Hanrahan clan. Or from me. I'm retiring from that sort of business."

A look of surprise preceded one of relief on Kieran's face. "That's a grand bit of welcome news."

McCluskey bent down to adjust Behan's collar before saying, "I never much liked making you do what you did. We're now finished. You'll have to find another way to finance your poor son's maintenance."

"I will. I'll ride more winners and spend less money on my lifestyle. Sure, there's a lot I can cut back on there."

McCluskey nodded to Sheehan and turned to walk away down the long pier. "It's goodbye to you then," Kieran called after him. "By the way, that dog of yours is looking grand."

Chapter Seventy-two

Doyle turned into the O'Hare International Terminal parking lot just before four p.m. Five minutes of searching the crowded aisles produced an open slot at the far end. He got out, opened the trunk of the Accord, and pulled out their suitcases and carry-on bags.

Nora reached to help him, but he said he'd grab a cart to convey all the baggage to the Aer Lingus check-in counter. This cloudy September afternoon, filled with blustery winds and the smell of early autumn, was a far cry from the day several months ago when he had first met the Sheehan sisters here. This was an airport trip he had not expected to make, at least not at this time.

The sisters were quiet as they followed him to the elevator. So was he. The previous morning, Doyle was sitting in Tenuta's office, working on the week's scheduled stable entries on the computer, when Mickey rapped softly on the screen door and entered. "Good morning, Mr. Tenuta. Jack, I need to talk to you."

The usual brightly cheerful little jockey's face was drawn, her expression serious, if not doleful, as she slumped down on the couch.

"What's up, Mickey?"

"Jack, best you take me off those horses you lined up." She hesitated. "I'm going home. So is Nora. We made the decision a few days back. She's already bought the airline tickets."

"Well, I'll be damned," Doyle said. "You girls have raised the element of surprise to a new level." He shook his head. "I don't get it. I was just with Nora two nights ago. She didn't say a word about this to me."

"Nora was reluctant to tell you, to hurt your feelings. She left it to me," Mickey said sadly.

"I miss home. So does Nora. I miss my folks, and my boyfriend. And Nora has been offered a position with the *Irish Times.* The people there were impressed by her blogging about me and what I did here. It's a great opportunity for her."

Doyle said, "Mickey, have you thought about the opportunities you'll be throwing away here? You've just won a million dollar race. Trainers are falling all over themselves to retain your services. Trainers here and around the country. The racing press loves you. You've been written up in the papers and the weekly magazines, you've been interviewed on TV. You're in a position to have a memorable career. Plus make a lot of money. How can you walk away from all that?"

"By putting one feckin' foot in front of the other," she said. "You think we haven't thought this through? You're not the only one who thinks they know best, Jack." She blinked away tears. "Oh, don't pay attention to me, Jack. I'm sad that we're leaving you, but I'm not showing that in a very nice way. I shouldn't be lashing out at you."

She rose from the couch and came around behind the desk where Doyle was now standing. "Oh, I'm sorry," she said. He could see tears starting to accumulate. She hugged him tightly, her forehead pressed against his breast bone. "You've been marvelous to me, Jack. I feel terrible about the way this is ending. Nora feels the same. But we've decided that going home is what's best for us."

Doyle's cell phone rang just as Mickey walked out of Tenuta's office. It was Nora. "Has she told you?"

"Yeah, she has. I would have appreciated hearing it from you, Nora. We had a wonderful time just two nights ago. You gave me no hint of your decision to go back home. That kind of pisses me off."

There was a brief silence. Nora said, "Understandable, Jack. I didn't handle this well. I thought you'd be disappointed, and

I just couldn't bring myself to do that to you myself. Mickey volunteered. I don't mean to hurt you, Jack. Nor does Mickey. Although I believe you're a hard man to hurt."

"You're not quite right on that, darlin'," Doyle said softly.

He heard a riffling of papers on the other end of the phone. "I'm going over my pre-trip notes," Nora explained. "We have a lot to wrap up, what with the apartment deposit, bank accounts, so on. Here's a note I made about you. Does Mickey have to sign anything to end her business relationship with you?"

"No, Nora. Mickey and I have never had a written contract. Jockeys and their agents here in the States don't have such things. It's always a verbal agreement. When a rider and his or her agent end their association, for whatever reason, the racing press always describes it as 'an amicable parting.' I certainly have heard of some that had absolutely nothing amicable about them. But that's not the case here. I'll make sure Mickey is forwarded all of her final earnings from Heartland races."

Nora said, "Perhaps some day you'll come to us in Ireland."

"Perhaps." He hesitated as he waved a hello to Tenuta who had come into the office. "How about if I take you two to the airport tomorrow?"

"Are you serious," she said with a laugh. "You would?"

"Serious as ever," Doyle said. "I'll pick you up at two." He turned off the phone and took the Heartland Downs condition book out of his jacket pocket. He ripped it in half and threw the torn pieces into the waste basket. "Won't need that anymore," Doyle said bitterly. "Mickey'll be my one and only jockey client."

Tenuta said, "What's going on here Jack?"

"Ralph, I'm out of business. The Irish are leaving us to go back home."

The car was mostly silent on their ride to O'Hare. Doyle answered a few questions from Nora about Eric Allgauer's horrific demise, adding that "in the remnants of his clothing, the coroner found traces of both Nembutol and EPO."

"What a terrible man," Nora said, "drugging that old guard and trying to drug Mickey's horse again, even after all the damage he did to her the first time."

"He was nobody's idea of virtue exemplified," Doyle said.

Doyle paid the toll and turned into the airport lanes. He said, "Mickey, I've meant to ask you. What did you and Kieran say to each other when you were galloping back after the Futurity?"

He could see her grin in the rear view mirror. "First was what you would call an exchange of unpleasantries. I screamed at him for hitting Plotkin with his whip. He swore at me for beating him. It was lovely. Then, as we pulled up our horses, Kieran suddenly grinned at me. Said, 'Sister, you should come back home. You'd be a sensation, the best female rider in Irish history.'"

The two women passed through airport security as Doyle watched from the cordoned-off area. Mickey carried her travel-on bag, whip attached, that he had first seen her with months ago. She turned to wave a final goodbye. Nora, head down, preceded Mickey down the long corridor to their gate. He waited a few minutes, hoping there might be a miraculous re-emergence of the Sheehans.

Doyle turned and walked rapidly to the exit escalator. His cell phone buzzed. He heard Moe Kellman say, "So, the Irishers are off?"

"How the hell do you know that?" Doyle snapped.

"Because Nora called me three nights ago to say what their departure plans were. And to ask me, as your friend, how best she should break the news to you. She was very concerned. I gave her my best advice about dealing with you.

"I'm sorry it wound up this way," Moe continued. "I know this is a hurtful development for you. The Sheehan girls are great people. And you had a helluva good summer with them, am I right?"

"You usually are. That doesn't make me feel any better right now."

He keyed open the Accord, sat down and back, exhaled, heard Moe say, "How about dinner tonight at Dino's with Leah and me?"

"Naw. But thanks. Give Leah my best." He paid the exit fee and gunned the Accord toward Mannheim Road. He realized Kellman was still on the phone.

"I'll miss Mickey and Nora, too, Jack. But remember one thing."

"Yeah?"

"We'll always have Plotkin."

Doyle's black mood lightened. Grinning, he pounded the steering wheel for emphasis as he said, "Yes, by God, Moe, we will."

To receive a free catalog of Poisoned Pen Press titles, please contact us in one of the following ways:

Phone: 1-800-421-3976
Facsimile: 1-480-949-1707
Email: info@poisonedpenpress.com
Website: www.poisonedpenpress.com

Poisoned Pen Press
6962 E. First Ave. Ste 103
Scottsdale, AZ 85251